RYAN
DUNK
DISTURBED BY ANYTHING."

It was as though something seriously scared the great dragon, a notion that was preposterous to Ryan. *What could he possibly be afraid of?* Whatever it was must be extremely powerful.

"The device as you describe it," Dunkelzahn said over the com link, "is not fully active, but it may soon be so." Ryan heard the dragon take a slow breath. "Here's what you will do," Dunkelzahn continued. "Return immediately and talk with Black Angel. Instructions from me will await you. I will not have time to meet with you personally, but this next assignment will be the most important of your life."

Another voice cut in. "Excuse me, Mr. President, but I've detected a delay glitch in the transmission." It was Jane-in-the-box, the decker who was monitoring the connection to ensure confidentiality. "We are no longer secure. Repeat, we are *not* secure."

"The fate of our world rides on this next mission of yours, Ryan. Be careful and do not fail me," Dunkelzahn said, and he disconnected.

Ryan was stunned. *The fate of the world . . . ?*

SHADOWRUN

STRANGER SOULS

**Book 1 of the
Dragon Heart Saga**

Jak Koke

A ROC BOOK

ROC
Published by the Penguin Group
Penguin Books USA Inc., 375 Hudson Street,
New York, New York 10014, U.S.A.
Penguin Books Ltd, 27 Wrights Lane,
London W8 5TZ, England
Penguin Books Australia Ltd,
Ringwood, Victoria, Australia
Penguin Books Canada Ltd, 10 Alcorn Avenue,
Toronto, Ontario, Canada M4V 3B2
Penguin Books (N.Z.) Ltd, 182–190 Wairau Road,
Auckland 10, New Zealand

Penguin Books Ltd, Registered Offices:
Harmondsworth, Middlesex, England

First published by Roc, an imprint of Dutton Signet,
a division of Penguin Books USA Inc.

First Printing, July, 1997
10 9 8 7 6 5 4 3 2 1

Copyright © FASA Corporation, 1997
All rights reserved

Series Editor: Donna Ippolito
Cover: Doug Anderson
Legend of Thayla: Tom Dowd

 REGISTERED TRADEMARK—MARCA REGISTRADA

SHADOWRUN, FASA, and the distinctive SHADOWRUN and FASA logos
are registered trademarks of the FASA Corporation, 1100 W. Cermak, Suite B305,
Chicago, IL 60608.

Printed in the United States of America

For Mom and Dad . . .
who taught me how to learn,
showed me how to live,
and instilled in me the drive to realize my dreams.

ACKNOWLEDGMENTS

Many thanks to my wife, Seana Davidson, who is not only my constant support and companion, but also my collaborator in the generation of ideas, the first reader of my early drafts, and a sensitive critic. Every writer needs a critic who is sympathetic to his or her moods and emotions; Seana is perceptive and resolute without being excessively harsh or overly lenient.

Credit should also go to Mike Mulvihill for his expert development of the Shadowrun universe, and especially for his help on the plots and characters in this trilogy. I'd also like to thank Jonathan Bond, Marsh Cassady, Jim Kitchen, Nicole Brown, and Tom Lindell for their insightful critiques of the manuscript. And finally, my appreciation goes to Donna Ippolito at FASA and to Jenni Smith at ROC for producing an excellent line of Shadowrun novels.

NORTH

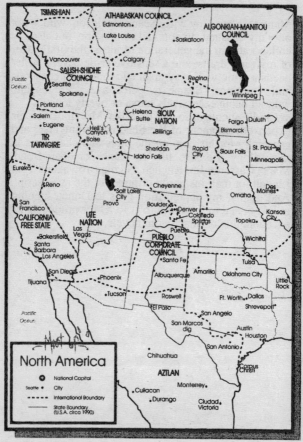

TSIMSHIAN

ATHABASKAN COUNCIL
Edmonton
Lake Louise

ALGONKIAN-MANITOU COUNCIL

Vancouver
SALISH-SHIDHE COUNCIL
Seattle
Spokane
Portland
Salem
Eugene

Calgary
Saskatoon

Regina
Winnipeg

Pacific Ocean

TIR TAIRNGIRE

Hell's Canyon
Boise

Helena
Butte
Billings

SIOUX NATION

Fargo   Duluth
Bismarck

Eureka

Sheridan
Idaho Falls

Rapid City

St. Paul
Sioux Falls
Minneapolis

Reno

Salt Lake City
Provo

Cheyenne

Des Moines
Omaha

San Francisco
CALIFORNIA FREE STATE

UTE NATION
Las Vegas

Boulder

Denver
Colorado Springs

Kansas City
Topeka

Bakersfield
Santa Barbara
Los Angeles

PUEBLO CORPORATE COUNCIL

Pueblo

Wichita

San Diego
Tijuana

Phoenix

Santa Fe
Albuquerque

Amarillo
Oklahoma City

Tulsa

Little Rock

Tucson

Roswell

Ft. Worth   Dallas
Shreveport

Pacific Ocean

El Paso
San Marcos dig

San Angelo

San Antonio

Austin
Houston

Chihuahua

AZTLAN
Monterrey

Corpus Christi

Culiacan
Durango

Ciudad Victoria

North America

- ⊕ National Capital
- Seattle • City
- – – – International Boundary
- ········· State Boundary (U.S.A. circa 1990)

AMERICA

Hudson Bay
Ft. Albany • Waskaganish
Sept Iles
Gulf of St. Lawrence
QUÉBEC
Charlottetown
Thunder Bay
Quebec •
Fredericton
Lake Superior
Halifax
Sault Ste. Marie
Ottawa
Montreal
Sudbury
Montpelier • Augusta
Lake Huron
Kingston
Toronto Ontario
Albany • Concord Boston
Milwaukee
Lake Michigan
Lansing
Buffalo
Hartford
Atlantic Ocean
Detroit
L. Erie
Newark
Cleveland
Chicago Gary
Philadelphia
Manhattan
Cincinnati
Indianapolis
UNITED CANADIAN AND AMERICAN STATES (U.C.A.S.)
Springfield
Charleston
FDC
East St. Louis
Louisville
Richmond
Roanoke • Norfolk
Durham
Nashville
Knoxville
Raleigh
Memphis
Charlotte
Columbia Wilmington
Birmingham ⊙ Atlanta
Jackson Montgomery
Charleston
Savannah
CONFEDERATE AMERICAN STATES (U.C.A.S.)
Baton Rouge
Mobile
Albany
Jacksonville
Orlando
Gulf of Mexico
Tampa West Palm Beach
Miami
Delta Clinic
Key West
CARIBBEAN LEAGUE
PANAMA

Prologue

The year is 2057.

Magic has returned to the earth after an absence of many thousands of years. What the Mayan calendar called the Fifth World has given way to the Sixth, a new cycle of magic, marked by the waking of the great dragon Ryumyo in the year 2011. The Sixth World is an age of magic and technology. An Awakened age.

The rising magic has caused the archaic races to re-emerge. Metahumanity. First came the elves, tall and slender with pointed ears and almond eyes. They were born to human parents just as were dwarfs shortly thereafter. Then later came the orks and the trolls, some born changed, like elves and dwarfs, but others goblinized—transformed from human form into their true nature as the rising magic activated their DNA. Manifesting as larger bodies, heavily muscled with tusked mouths and warty skin.

Even the most ancient and intelligent of beings, the great dragons, have come out of their long hiding. Only a few of these creatures are known to exist, and most of them have chosen a life of isolation and secrecy. But some, able to assume human form, have integrated themselves into the affairs of metahumanity. They have used their ancient intellect, their powerful magic, and their innate cunning to ascend to positions of power. One is known to own and run Saeder-Krupp—the largest megacorporation in the world. Another—Dunkelzahn—claims to seek the improvement of the metahuman condition and has just been elected to the presidency of the United Canadian and American States.

The Sixth World is a far cry from the mundane

environment of the Fifth. It is exotic and strange, a para-doxical blend of the scientific and the arcane. The advance of technology has reached a feverish pace. The distinction between man and machine is becoming blurred by the advent of direct neural interfacing. Cyberware. Machine and com-puter implants are commonplace, making metal of flesh, pulsing electrons into neurons at the speed of thought. People of the Sixth World are a new breed—stronger, smarter, faster. Less human.

The Matrix has grown like a phoenix out of the ashes of the old global computer network. A virtual world of com-puter-generated reality has emerged, a universe of electrons and CPU cycles controlled and manipulated by those with the fastest cyberdecks, with the hottest new code.

It is an era where information is power, where data and money are one and the same. Multinational megacorporations have replaced superpower governments as the true forces on the planet. In a world where cities have grown into huge sprawls of concrete and steel, walled-off corporate enclaves and massive arcologies have superseded two-car garages, vegetable gardens, and white picket fences. The megacorps exploit masses of wageslaves for the profit of a lucky and ruth-less few.

But in the shadows of the mammoth corporate arcologies, live the SINless. Those without System Identification Num-bers are not recognized by the machinery of society, by the bureaucracy that has grown so massive and complex that nobody understands it completely. Among the SINless are the shadowrunners, traffickers in stolen data and hot infor-mation, mercenaries of the street—discreet, effective, and untraceable.

The Sixth World is full of surprises, not the least of which is the recent election of the great, gregarious dragon, Dunkelzahn, to the presidency of the United Canadian and American States. Never before has a great dragon been elected to run a country. Never before have so many been so polarized about the results. Many people are ecstatic, enthu-siastic, and optimistic about Dunkelzahn's ability to bring hope and faith back into their lives. But just as many are envious and resentful, full of hatred toward the wyrm.

As the magic level continues its inexorable rise, Dunkelzahn has attracted a great many enemies with his high-profile campaign. Some think he has gained too much power. Some are afraid of what he might do next.

9 August 2057

9 August 2057

1

The ancient amusement park tower stuck into the Texas sky like a rusty needle, its tip piercing the sliver of the low-hanging moon. A presence climbed the scarred metal ladder of the long-dead tower in silence and darkness, a droplet of black ink moving against gravity. A shadow, unnoticed in the night.

A hundred meters up, Ryan Mercury clipped his safety harness to a metal rung and took several deep breaths to center himself. Ryan was large for a human, just over two meters tall and weighing in at a dense 130 kilos, all of it well-conditioned muscle, magically enhanced and accelerated flesh. No cyber, no bio. Not so much as a datajack for this chummer.

Ryan's coppery red hair was tucked into the skin-tight black hood of his plycra nightsuit. He was deep undercover behind the Aztlan border, and if discovered would be tortured and killed. His olive skin was painted in monochromatic black and white to hide the shadows of his face—the recognizable shape of his sharp nose, the hewn angle of his jawbone, the glint of his silver-flecked blue eyes. He leaned slightly against his harness, testing its strength.

The heat of the night air baked around him, bringing a prickle of sweat to his brow. Trying to ignore it, he studied the scene down below through his night binoculars.

Far beneath him, down the hill from the tower he had climbed, work crews excavated the bottom of the lake. Underwater lights glowed below the crystal clear water, twenty meters down. Crews in wetsuits and submarines dug and cleared away the limestone, vacuuming out the silt as it was stirred up by the trenchers.

Where is it? he thought. *Did they really find one?*

Then Ryan saw it, a smooth black surface, unmarred and
perfect. The submarines cleaned the river dirt and blasted
rock from the obsidian glass as he watched. The rock seemed
to absorb the light from the flood lamps, leaving nothing to
reflect. And, as the crews continued, Ryan saw the rock take
shape. Its edge was perfectly flat, cut like a gemstone, and
obviously created by man or some other sentience, before
being buried here long ago. This was no naturally occurring
rock. And it was huge, at least ten meters on a side, and
seemed to be diamond-shaped, though Ryan had no idea
what it would look like once they'd finished the excavation.

Ryan's gut sank as he watched. *I'd better tell Dunkelzahn,*
he thought. *The dragon will want to know right away. Even if
this is inauguration night.*

Dunkelzahn had sent Ryan here on the suspicion that
Aztechnology—the corporation that owned the Aztlan government—was searching for a Locus. A Locus, as far as
Ryan understood it, was an ancient and extremely powerful magical lens that channeled arcane energies through
manalines.

Ryan was Dunkelzahn's most trusted undercover operative. The dragon himself had orchestrated Ryan's instruction
into the magic of body motion and the senses, teaching him
the powers of a physical adept. Dunkelzahn had shown Ryan
the Silent Way—the path of stealth and disguise. Of crucial
action behind the scenes.

Ryan's current mission was explicit, not subject to inter-
pretation. *"If you discover that Darke has found a Locus,"*
Dunkelzahn had said, *"you must contact me immediately.
Understand, Ryanthusar? Immediately."*

Ryan wasn't absolutely certain that this black stone was
really a Locus, but it matched the description Dunkelzahn
had given him. Close enough to give him the chills when he
looked at it. And Ryan never questioned Dunkelzahn's
instructions. Never.

Which means I make contact now, he thought. *Regardless
of the fact that it puts me at great risk.*

Ryan put his binoculars back into his belt case, then he
tipped his wrist toward him and punched up the private LTG
number for Black Angel, also known as Carla Brooks—

Dunkelzahn's head of security. She would know how to connect him with Dunkelzahn.

After a moment Brooks answered, her voice hushed and urgent. "Quicksilver, is that you?"

His wristphone would have transmitted his identity. "Yes."

"Verify."

Ryan punched an encryption code into his wristphone.

"Thank you. Our decker reports this line is clean."

"Good, Black Angel. Connect me with Dark Tooth, I must speak with him immediately."

"This is a bad time. Dark Tooth is otherwise occupied."

"It's urgent."

"It better be."

Ryan looked back down to the excavation site, to the encampment of security forces and military armament next to the river. "I'm in a vulnerable position, Black Angel," he said. His gaze tracked from the encampment up to the step-pyramid *teocalli* that overlooked the water. "I wouldn't have called if it wasn't extremely important."

Brooks sighed. "Frag," she said. "All right, I'll connect you."

Ryan understood her reluctance. Nobody wanted the task of interrupting a great dragon—regardless of what he was doing, regardless of the importance.

The background hiss grew louder as Brooks patched him through. He could hear the white noise of loud conversation, music, and celebration. "Ryanthusar?" came the voice of a human male with a nondescript accent, but the overlay indicated that this human was speaking through Dunkelzahn's phone. For security purposes, the video was blanked.

The dragon must be in human form for the inauguration ceremonies. "Master, I have to report. I think Darke has unearthed a Locus."

The noise of conversation dulled, then subsided into the background as Ryan heard the click of a closing door. Dunkelzahn's voice was clearer now, "Where are you?"

"San Marcos, forty klicks south of the CAS border in Austin."

"That is a likely junction," Dunkelzahn said. "Describe the item to me."

Ryan told him of the lake, emerging crystal clear from springs, water like liquid glass. He told the dragon of the work crews and the heavy security that surrounded the site, and he described what he could see of the huge rock. Its smooth surface like a geometric black hole, sucking in light.

"Quickly look at its aura, Ryanthusar. Tell me what you see."

Ryan stared down at the scene below. He focused for a second, concentrating on the shift of perception into the astral plane. Physical objects blurred, the black and gray of the night images giving way to the brilliantly colored landscape of the astral. Life force gave off light in the astral plane—auras that were unique to each creature and object. Magical creatures and items were the brightest, but everything had an aura of some sort.

The aura of the Locus was distorted slightly by the living matter in the water above it, but still it was unmistakable. The rock glowed dully, a deep violet, and across its surface shone a tracery of gold lines. That was orichalcum, a massive quantity if those veins passed through the whole stone. The gold veins pulsed, glowing brightly before subsiding again. A moment later they pulsed once more, a very slow beat, like the heart of a sleeping giant. And as Ryan described the rock to Dunkelzahn, the dragon's questions grew more and more urgent.

Ryan had never heard Dunkelzahn so obviously disturbed by anything. The dragon had always been inquisitive and calm, a concerned observer without being reactionary. Only lately had he shown genuine urgency. It was as though something seriously scared him, a notion that was preposterous to Ryan. *What could he possibly be afraid of?* Whatever it was must be extremely powerful.

"The device as you describe it," Dunkelzahn said, "is not fully active, but it may soon be so." Ryan heard the dragon take a slow breath. "Here's what you will do," Dunkelzahn continued. "Return immediately and talk with Black Angel. Instructions from me will await you. I will not have time to meet with you personally, but this next assignment will be the most important of your life."

Another voice cut in. "Excuse me, sir, but I've detected a delay glitch in the transmission." It was Jane-in-the-box, the decker who was monitoring the connection to ensure confidentiality. "We are no longer secure. Repeat, we are *not* secure."

Dunkelzahn finished, "The fate of our world rides on this next mission of yours, Ryanthusar. Be careful and do not fail me."

"Of course."

"Faith and luck go with you, my child," Dunkelzahn said, and he disconnected.

Ryan was stunned. *The fate of the world? Frag me, Dunkelzahn, what does* that *mean?*

Ryan might've chalked up what Dunkelzahn had said to the melodrama of the moment—the dragon was known to be melodramatic. But he had never been so with Ryan; Dunkelzahn had always been genuine with him.

In the distance, Ryan heard the rhythmic beat of an approaching helicopter. He sucked in a breath and glanced around. There it was, off to his left, an insectlike machine sweeping the area with its floodlight feeler brushing the ground. Back and forth. Approaching rapidly.

Time to fly.

Ryan unclipped his tether from the metal rung and placed his soft-booted feet on the outside of the ladder, holding himself in place with his hands. He slowly eased himself down, beginning a semi-controlled slide, using his feet to guide his fall. Using his magic to maintain perfect balance. He watched the ladder through his feet as his speed increased, growing and growing until the rungs sped past. His hands and feet grew hot from the friction as he plummeted, a controlled free fall. It was a hundred meters down and the wooded hillside below was pitch-black.

Ryan dropped, sliding like a droplet of black oil down the side of the old rusty needle as the rhythmic thunder of the helo's blades grew louder and louder. The sweat on his neck grew chill as he fell, sending prickles over his skin. There was something pure about movement and magically enhanced physics. Something primal and ultimately satisfying, like sex.

The thrill within Ryan stepped up a notch as the column of light from the helo's searchlight grazed the tower just above him. The helo's engines roared in his ears, its wind cool and

fresh over his falling body. Ryan concentrated. Only a few
more seconds and he would be down, amid the cover of trees
and undergrowth. The world flashed bright around him for
an instant as the helo's searchlight caught him. A freeze-
frame microsecond. Then it went black again as he fell
through the circle into the growing darkness.

They're close, he thought. *Too close.*

His ears caught shouts from the helo, and the light scanned
along the tower above him as the insect-machine pivoted
back around to his side. They would pin him down in
seconds.

Ryan concentrated as the concrete platform loomed up
beneath him. He was going too fast to stop. Still, he
increased the pressure of his feet and hands against the
ladder to slow his descent. It wouldn't be enough, but it
might prevent him from breaking his legs. His heart resonated through him like a palpable drumbeat. *One,* gloved
fingers gripping flaking metal. *Two,* hot dry wind slapping
him in the face as he looked down and knew he was going
too fast.

Three, they had him. Centered in the column of light.

Gunshots sputtered, the sound sharp as bullets ricocheted
off the tower. Luckily, none hit home.

Got to get out of their slotting light.

Ryan kicked off from the ladder, pushing himself away as
hard as he could. He jumped away from the tower, trying to
get enough outward momentum to clear the raised concrete
platform and land in the trees. Lurching out of the helo's
light, pivoting in the air in a desperate attempt, a last-ditch
maneuver to escape. But he was falling too fast.

Like a droplet of black rain against the dark sky. Waiting
for the impact, but not knowing how far he had to fall. Not
knowing whether or not he was about to splatter against the
unyielding earth.

Counting the beats of his heart before the end.

2

She stood tall and beautiful, a goddess of alabaster and emerald. An elegant evening dress clung to her slender form like a sequined glove. Its color was deep green, almost black, and it shimmered as she moved. Her raven hair hung straight and full to her waist, and her eyes glinted green like deep-set emeralds. She smiled demurely, her seductive lips a pale burgundy. The sculpted shadows of her face highlighted her elven features—high cheekbones, a narrow nose, and ears that rose to a delicate point. All of it one hundred percent natural, no cosmetic or technological enhancements.

No artificial flavors or colors.

Her name was Nadja Daviar, and she was the voice of the great dragon Dunkelzahn. When she spoke, the mostly male crowd around her became entranced. Her voice was deep and resonant, smooth and silky, utterly accentless. Her speech was mesmerizing and musical, befitting a great dragon who was ancient beyond reckoning, supremely intelligent and wise. Charisma radiated from her, casting a spell over the gathering of politicians and megacorporate executives around her.

Nadja found herself feeling alone for the first time since before the inauguration. She wasn't truly alone, of course, considering the press of metahumanity in the Watergate Hotel's Grand Ballroom around her, most of whom wanted to get close to her and Dunkelzahn. No, Nadja felt alone because Dunkelzahn had excused himself a few minutes earlier, in the middle of a tango with her. They had moved so well together on the dance floor, the dragon superbly in command of his human form. The crowd had watched at first, awestruck. Then they had joined in.

It was Carla Brooks, Dunkelzahn's chief of security, who

had interrupted the dance so that Dunkelzahn could take a
private telecom call. It must have been extremely important.
Dunkelzahn graciously excused himself to find a private
chamber, leaving Nadja alone in the midst of the many
dancing couples. Feeling naked without the dragon's
thoughts in her head.

Normally, she spoke for him because he disliked assuming
human form unless absolutely necessary. Like tonight. Now,
she stood in the small crowd listening to Damien Knight
speak. "Is that it for our new president then?" he asked. "I
suppose he *is* getting on in years." Knight paused for
laughter from the other suits. Then he looked directly at
Nadja, his hazel eyes boring into her. "How old is the president anyhow, Miss Daviar?"

Nadja gave Knight a smile, making a conscious effort to
maintain the illusion of confidence. She suspected that he
knew how much she disliked him, but this was a social occa-
sion and the press was present. All the proper graces must
hold true. "That's confidential," she said. "Dunkelzahn is a
little sensitive about it, really. He keeps telling me he's not a
day over twenty-nine . . . thousand."

All the men laughed, including Knight, but Nadja knew it
was more political than genuine. Everyone around her was
highly adept at the art of kissing hoop. And there certainly
was no end of powerful targets in the ballroom tonight,
huddled in tight groups amid the masses of the voting public
who had shown up to celebrate Dunkelzahn's victory and eat
the free food.

The group around her was a Who's Who of Ares
Macrotechnology, all here because Ares had been a major
contributor to Dunkelzahn's election bid. Knight, who had
helped Dunkelzahn choose Kyle Haeffner as his running
mate, was the CEO of the megacorp, one of the six most
powerful transnationals in the world. He stood just shorter
than her two meters, and was broadly built, with salt and
pepper hair and a rugged face that was quite attractive. A
platinum-plated datajack gleamed discreetly on his temple,
almost hidden under his perfectly coifed hair.

Next to Knight was his aide, a balding human of about
forty-five, with blue eyes and a winning smile that seemed
almost genuine. His name was Gerrold Watkins, and he paid

close attention to everything Knight did, probably recording it via an internal video link.

Also present was Roger Soaring Owl, CEO of Knight Errant, a short man with a modest paunch and a slight rusty brown tint to his skin, indicating some Amerind blood. Soaring Owl had an excellent sense of humor, but he seemed inhibited by Knight's presence as though he were playing lackey to the Ares president. Knight Errant was an Ares subsidiary, and Knight involved himself in its operations on a regular basis. Nadja had heard stories of friction between the two, and perhaps that knowledge, if true, could be of use to her at a later time, but she hadn't seen any hint of it tonight.

On her other side and slightly behind her stood her own aide, Gordon Wu, carefully recording everything on his headware so that it could be analyzed later if need be. Promises made could not be accidentally forgotten, and even though Nadja's memory was photographic, she didn't take chances.

Nadja looked around the ballroom, secretly trying to catch sight of Dunkelzahn's human form. She hoped he wouldn't leave her stranded for too long; she hated having to make small talk with these corporate sharks. The Watergate Hotel's ballroom was spacious and elegantly appointed. Thick curtains of purple velvet hung along the walls, and chandeliers of smoky crystal illuminated the chamber. At one end, a dais had been erected, and upon it stood a massive trideo display showing a recording of Dunkelzahn in his true form, giving his victory speech on election night.

Even the huge display couldn't capture the dragon's size as he crouched on the platform. His blue and silver scales shone under the spotlight, tendons and muscles sending a rainbow of colors across the screen as he adjusted his position and his scales rippled.

Nadja saw herself on the screens, standing in front of him, a tiny figure next to Dunkelzahn's bulk. A necessary and crucial element of the show as she spoke the dragon's words. She was his voice as he perched behind her and grinned as wide and full as Lewis Carroll's Cheshire cat.

In the trideo, her voice rang out. "This is not my victory. It belongs to everyone who voted for what I represent—hope, progress, a brighter future for all of us. A new golden age."

The words were Dunkelzahn's, but Nadja believed them as though they were her own. The dragon was the most noble creature she had ever met. Dunkelzahn wanted to make the world a better place, wanted to give hope to the downtrodden and cynical metahumans of this age. And he had a plan to make it happen. Nadja was totally committed to him, and she had grown to love the dragon. He was her closest friend.

Now, Nadja looked away from the trid screens and continued her discreet scan of the ballroom. She wasn't used to being out of Dunkelzahn's presence for very long and had grown quite attached to having his thoughts in her mind. Then she saw him emerging from one of the private anterooms. His presence was diminished somewhat in human form, but he radiated power nonetheless. It was almost a joke that secret servicemen swarmed around him, accompanied by the dragon's own private security. Carla Brooks walked alongside, a tall, black-skinned elf who was in charge of the security arrangements.

His personal power far exceeds the combined strength of those forces, thought Nadja. *But I suppose it just wouldn't look right without the show of security.* She smiled at the execs around her. "Please excuse me," she said. "The president has returned."

Dunkelzahn's human form was striking without ostentation; he stood shorter than Nadja, and he had a broader build. He looked very young, perfectly proportioned, like Michaelangelo's David, with olive skin and curly brown hair. Only his eyes betrayed his supernatural origin—metallic blue and silver with pupils that were unnaturally black, like pinpoint windows into a deep void. Nadja noticed that nobody would meet his gaze for long.

She felt his thoughts touch her as he stepped into the crowd and faced Damien Knight. *I must take my leave of you, Nadjaruska.* The dragon's thoughts passed over her like a static charge, and she understood them, not as words, but as an extension of her conscious mind. She did not draw herself up and enter the trace-like state that allowed her to translate, but she had been with Dunkelzahn for many, many years; her mind and his had become connected.

Dunkelzahn spoke, his voice smooth and young, "I extend

my thanks and gratitude to you, Damien. You are to be commended for such an exquisite celebration."

Knight extended his hand. "You're leaving so early?"

Dunkelzahn shook Knight's hand, "I'm afraid something urgent has come up, and I must return to Prince Edward Island at once."

"Goodbye then," Knight said. "Congratulations once again."

Dunkelzahn nodded, then took a brief moment to take his leave of the others. The secret servicemen cleared a path through the crowd in front of him as he made for the double doors.

Nadja followed on his heels, out of the noisy ballroom, down the escalators and into the lobby of the hotel. Beyond the crowd of trideo cameras and reporters, a limousine awaited on the curb, but Dunkelzahn stopped just outside the door.

He turned then and touched her on the shoulders. When he looked into her eyes, she saw sadness in the depths of his ancient ones. His thoughts entered her mind. *I have received distressing news, Nadjaruska. News that I must act upon before our enemies destroy us. I will send for you in a few days.*

Nadja simply nodded.

Until then, you will be my voice, Nadjaruska. Goodbye.

Dunkelzahn gave a photogenic smile to the crowd, then slid into the open door of the waiting limo. A secret serviceman closed it behind him, and the procession got underway. Two motorcycles in front, followed by a security limo, followed by Dunkelzahn's limo. More police and secret service came behind.

Nadja stood stunned, the humid Washington air closing down on her. *What was so urgent?* Even though Dunkelzahn was given to sudden, unannounced departures, Nadja had grown accustomed to participating in his decisions, especially in the recent months as she had managed his presidential campaign.

Carla Brooks stepped up beside Nadja as the trid cameras swiveled to follow Dunkelzahn's limousine. The security chief was taller than Nadja by a good ten centimeters, and significantly stronger despite her willowy stature. Brooks looked slightly uncomfortable in the midnight blue dress she wore, her muscular arms and legs seeming to strain against the confining fabric. Brooks was enhanced with the latest cyber and bioware, and she was quite striking; snow-white hair, deep brown skin, blue eyes. Almost the antithesis of Nadja's porcelain skin and black hair.

Nadja saw that Brooks moved her mouth slightly, though no sound came out; she was subvocalizing instructions to her security teams through her internal headware. Nadja also noticed the micro-thin fiberoptic wire that connected Brooks' datajack to a tactical computer hidden inside her dress. Mimetic tape made the wiring nearly impossible to see, but Nadja was trained for such observations. She always had to look perfect for the cameras. Perfect meant no augmentation, no blemishes. No cyber. Dunkelzahn himself had been adamant about that, and since he was paying the bills, she obliged.

Brooks leaned close to Nadja. "That call," she said, her voice pitched low, barely audible. "It was Quicksilver." She looked at Nadja questioningly.

Nadja shrugged. She didn't know anything about Ryan's current mission. He never told her and she'd learned not to ask. She did miss him, though. More than she cared to admit. A sudden surge of loneliness passed over her. Their last parting had not been on the best of terms.

She sighed, deciding to put it out of her mind and get on with the business of extracting herself elegantly from the party so that she could get a little sleep before beginning the White House conversion. Dunkelzahn actually planned to do much of his work there, and he wouldn't want to stay in human form unless it was absolutely crucial.

"Only Dark Tooth knows what Quicksilver was doing," Brooks said, her gaze tracking Dunkelzahn's procession as it crossed Virginia Avenue. "I was just hoping—"

An explosion ripped the night in front of them. Dunkelzahn's limo vaporizing in an instantaneous fiery blast. A spiked sphere of plasma and searing orange heat, flashing for a second.

Then the fire was gone and only its effects remained.

What the frag?

In the moments before the blast wave hit her, Nadja saw the security limo in front of Dunkelzahn's car lift into the air and fly forward, riding an invisible swell of heat and shrapnel. The maple trees along the median were bowed from the blast, branches and limbs stripped off, leaves turning instantly to charcoal though no fire touched them. They atomized in the burning wind.

Nadja felt a single beat of her own heart, and she knew she was going to die. The explosion was too close, the bomb too powerful. No time to move. No place to go if she could move.

Time slowed in those final instants. She saw Dunkelzahn in dragon form, his body a ghostly white behind the flash spot on her retina. He was a see-through specter, without substance. The detailed scalloped ridge of each scale glimmered with white fire, but there was no solidity to him. Nothing left, only the outline, writhing in desperate agony as his ancient flesh disintegrated.

The white glow dimmed as Dunkelzahn bellowed in pain, a thunderclap of telepathic agony exploding in her head before the physical sound of his scream reached her. A blood-red shimmer tinged his vaporized flesh in the final moment.

Then he was gone and the blast wave hit her, a wall of heat and sound, lifting her off her feet and hurling her backward through the hotel's genuine glass facade. The windows crashed into shards around her, cutting her in a thousand places as she landed inside on the plush carpeting. Still alive. Still in one piece.

How?

Brooks jumped to her feet next to Nadja, brushing glass from her body while she subvocalized commands to her security forces. She bent down over Nadja, indicating for her not to move. Brooks scanned Nadja for injuries, and when she had determined that there were no broken bones, she helped Nadja to her feet.

What happened to Dunkelzahn?

Nadja tried to see through the crowd and shattered front doors to get a glimpse of the aftermath, but her line of sight was blocked by an ork security guard who came rushing up to her. He was tall and bulky with cyber and augmented muscles, a first-aid bag in his hands.

"Jeremy," Brooks told the ork, "get Ms. Daviar cleaned up and out of here fast. She's got some cuts, but nothing serious."

"What about you?" Nadja asked.

"I'm fine," Brooks said. "I don't know how or why, but I have sustained no serious injuries." Brooks narrowed her blue eyes on Daviar. "That explosion should've killed us," she said. "Should've taken the whole front of the hotel with it."

"Why didn't it?"

"Not sure yet. I'd suspect a magic shield, but it'd have to be more powerful than anything I've ever seen. And some of our security say they saw the blast reverse itself. Like there was some sort of implosion."

"What about Dunkelzahn?"

Brooks shook her head. "That's what I'm going to find out." With that she turned and picked her way through the crowd, joining a team of her security people.

"Ms. Daviar?" It was the ork, Jeremy.

"Yes?"

"I'd like to bandage this cut on your shoulder," he said. "Then I think we should get you away from here. There's a car waiting."

"Sure."

Four other guards joined Jeremy, and they all escorted Nadja through the shattered remains of the front doors. Jeremy held her arm as she stumbled onto the glass-littered walkway and stared at the destruction. Evidence of the explosion radiated from the center of the avenue—a massive crater in the road, at least five meters in diameter and three deep. The trees around the crater's perimeter were uprooted and bent over, all leaves stripped off, the grass around their burned trunks turned black from the heat. Taxis and limos lay strewn like flipped turtles, and the nearest hotel windows were shattered, blown in.

Was there any way Dunkelzahn could have survived? Nadja didn't think so, and the shock of that realization made her knees weak.

The damage stopped after a point, however. Windows two

stories up were completely intact, and the trees past an imaginary radius were healthy and green. The grass lush and verdant. *It's as though the blast just stopped.*

Nadja followed the arc that traced the edge of the destruction and noticed that she and Brooks had been standing on the very rim. *Lucky,* she thought. *Yet again.*

An image of Ryan came to her mind, his copper brown hair blowing in the ocean breeze as they walked hand in hand. Maui. He had told her then that they were connected in some way and that luck was part of it. It had something to do with their luck. Both of them seemed to have exceptional luck.

Oh, Ryan, what did you say to Dunkelzahn? Do you know anything about this?

Jeremy rushed Nadja into a limousine and then climbed in next to her. Her world came crashing down around her as she sat, the blood from her cuts sticking against the leather seat. She put her head in her hands, and blackness crept into her vision. She didn't know if it was shock or loss of blood, but she nearly blacked out.

What would she do if Dunkelzahn were gone? It felt like he was. That telepathic scream. How could anything, even a great dragon, survive that blast? Dunkelzahn was all she knew, all she cared about. The dragon had been her life. Her whole existence had been devoted to him.

Now, all that had changed.

3

Ryan tumbled through the black sky. Plummeting. Ground rushing up, invisible in the darkness.

He heard the dragon's voice in his memory as he fell, pivoting in the air, executing a perfect layout double somersault. Trying to slow himself. Dunkelzahn's voice was crisp and urgent in Ryan's mind, ". . . this next assignment will be the most important of your life . . . The fate of the world rides on this mission . . .

"Do not fail me."

Blackness loomed in the heat around Ryan.

I can't die, he thought. *Because then there will be no one to carry out Dunkelzahn's plan.*

He braced himself, anticipating imminent impact.

I refuse to fail you, Dunkelzahn. I will not die here.

Any moment now . . .

He covered his head and face with his arms when he hit the branches. Live oak and pecan trees snagged his back and legs. He crashed through the smaller twigs first, then a large limb smashed into his shoulder. And another caught his thigh.

Then he was through the trees, and the ground rushed up like a maglev train. Black and unyielding.

Ryan tucked into a ball as he hit. Pain exploded in his shoulder and back as he rolled. The trees must have slowed him a little because he rolled downslope somewhat effectively, sliding and careening. And when he finally rustled to a halt, he focused on his pain and used magic to channel it away. Then he stood carefully and examined himself. His shoulder was the worst, dislocated from the impact. But he'd otherwise sustained only bruises and scrapes. No internal injures that he could determine. No major flesh wounds.

It's that luck thing again, he thought.

Ryan concentrated on his shoulder for a minute as he lifted his bad arm into the fork of a tree branch. Then he probed the socket with his good arm, and with a jerk popped the ball of his bone back into place. Be good as new in a few hours; he healed exceptionally fast.

Ryan checked his equipment to make sure none of it had jarred loose. The chest holster of his Walther PB 120 jutted a little from the webbing that held the gear around his midsection, but the minigrenades and his belt of throwing darts were still in place. He tucked his pistol back into position and slowly pulled the leaves and twigs from his clothing; they would make silent movement difficult.

The helo overhead scanned the tower and the trees with its bright white feeler as Ryan crouched in the undergrowth. He took in the hillside around him, using his magically enhanced eyesight to see infrared and heat signatures, but he came up dry. Nothing. Then he looked into the astral plane.

The trees glimmered around him, and he could see no movement. No spirits or people. Then he caught a glimpse of a figure floating above the trees, hovering against the blue-black sky. The figure looked like a human, with glowing red robes that sparkled all over as though he was surrounded by a galaxy of silver stars.

Drek, Ryan thought. *A mage.*

The astral image was a projection of a magician's spirit into astral space. Shamans and mages could do it, plus certain adepts. Ryan knew he couldn't outrun the astral form; movement in astral space was much faster than normal physical motion. *But I might be able to hide from him,* he thought.

Ryan flattened himself against the tree and stood perfectly still for the moment, trying to use his aura masking to blend his astral presence with the trees around him. He needed a few seconds to weigh his options. His vehicle was up the hill, over the perimeter fence, and a half-kilometer hike away.

He'd driven up from the Aztechnology pyramid in San Antonio in a company Mitsubishi Runabout, trying to get out of the city without breaking his cover. He'd been operating under the assumed identity of Travis W. Saint John for

several months. Now, his cover was as good as blown. There
was almost no way T.W. Saint John would return to his labo-
ratory tomorrow. Ryan's best chance was to try to make it
across the border near Austin and into the Confederate
American States.

Ryan knew it was unlikely he would reach his Runabout
without the mage spotting him or the helo closing down, but
what other choice did he have? Steal another vehicle?

I could take the helo, he thought. *They would never expect* that.

As if on cue, the insect-machine descended to land on the
concrete platform next to the old tower. Ryan took it as a
sign and went to work, moving in silence and stealth back up
the hill. He used his magic to pass through the undergrowth
without disturbing the leaves, blending his aura so that the
mage above the trees would have a harder time seeing him.

He reached the edge of the concrete slab with no incidents.
The mage was off scanning the trees downhill as Ryan
watched the helo land. Ryan crouched in the dark hollow of
the trees, and scanned the opposition.

Through the helo's tinted macroglass foreshield, Ryan
caught the shape of the rigger pilot, a woman with dark hair
pulled tightly into a neat ponytail. She was straight-wired
into the console via a fiber-optic cable that plugged into the
datajack at her temple.

The copilot sat next to her, less visible, though his heat
signature indicated an ork or perhaps a troll. Ryan guessed
ork by the size, and he was packing a big weapon that Ryan
recognized as an Ares Alpha Combatgun from its distinctive
silhouette. The side door opened as the helo's runners
touched down, and one person jumped out—a hulking
shadow of a man moving fast and smooth. Like a simsense
suspense hero on double speed.

Ryan quickly scanned the inside of the vehicle while the
door was open, rapidly cataloguing his adversaries. There
were only two people in the back, both human. One was a
standard-looking corporate security guard; the other was
slumped in his seat, most likely the mage who was astral
projecting. His spirit was out of his body, cruising around
astral space in a search for Ryan, but it could return to his
body at any moment.

Ryan kept mental track; two in front, one heavily armed; two in back. *Null sheen,* he thought. *If it doesn't get ugly, I can take them without bloodshed.* Ryan wouldn't shy away from killing them if it was necessary to complete Dunkelzahn's instructions, and he was very adept at the taking of life. But more often than not, killing wasn't necessary to accomplish his goals.

Then Ryan's gaze was drawn to the . . . thing that had disembarked.

He looked human for the most part, but there was an aura of inhumanity around him that Ryan felt like a cold radiance. In the physical world, the man was very big, at least a half-meter taller than Ryan, with a density to him that spoke of cybernetic limbs and torso. *Pure chrome under that vat-grown skin.*

Ryan never missed a detail like that, even through the dark, loose-fitting combat fatigues the man wore. His bald head was eerily symmetrical and too small for his massive shoulders and chest. And his legs were oddly proportioned—too long in the shin for his height.

This chummer's mostly machine. A cyberzombie.

Ryan had heard of such creatures, but this was the first he had encountered in flesh-and-chrome reality. Most of their spirit was gone, and they were supremely dangerous. Robots with a tenuous grip on the distinction between dead and alive.

In one hand, the man held a netgun poised and ready. The other was empty for the present, but a veritable arsenal hung from his belts and harnesses. In the astral, the man was a fireworks display, aglow with magic and quickened spells. His aura was a dark shadow amid the flares, and it made Ryan's skin crawl to look at it. His aura was somehow separated from his body. Out of phase, if that was possible.

Ryan had never seen anything like it. He noticed a slight hazing in the astral wherever the cyberzombie passed. This creature was polluting astral space by its mere existence. Rumor told that powerful spells, quickened so that they had become permanent, acted like a tether to the spirit of someone who had taken so much machinery into his flesh. Un-fragging-natural.

Then he noticed the watcher spirit, a small bloodshot eye,

hovering around the cyberzombie's aura. The watcher saw
Ryan, looked right at him, but it didn't move. It was tasked
for something else. *Probably to warn some mage or shaman
if any big astral nasties decided to take an interest in robo-
slag here.*

Ryan brought his vision back to the physical and took a
few controlled breaths to center himself. *So they plan on
capturing me,* he thought, his gaze coming back to the
netgun. *Interesting, that makes escape all that much easier.
All I have to do is get past robo-slag before the helo lifts off.
The slots inside will go down easy.*

The cyberzombie scanned the area with intense scrutiny,
and Ryan suddenly feared that his concealment magic would
fail to hide his heat signature enough from this creature's
infrared sight. But the gaze passed over him without hesitation, and the man turned to survey the whole clearing.

Ryan remained absolutely silent and still, waiting for the
perfect opportunity to make his move. He watched as the
cyberzombie drew a taser gun from one of his belts and
moved to the edge of the concrete slab. The robo-slag's
movements were superfluid and quick, decisive and precise.

He might be even faster than me, Ryan thought, which was
frightening because he had never met anyone, except
Dunkelzahn, who could match his speed in combat. *Best
to avoid a fight with this one. Can't be certain of the
outcome.*

At the same moment, the wind beneath the helo's rotors
grew to a deafening roar, and the vehicle began to lift off. As
the craft rose slightly, Ryan made a lightning-quick dash
to the still-open side door. One of them inside reached to
close the door just as Ryan fired a narcotic-coated dart into
his chest. Silent, fast, and oh-so-powerful. The dart buried
itself to the shaft, hitting with a subliminal *thunk* that was
lost in the roar of the rotors.

The man froze in two heartbeats, and crumbled to the
floor, nearly falling out the open door before Ryan caught
his body. Then Ryan was inside, laying the incapacitated
guard on the floor as he glided over the body, moving as fast
as his magically accelerated muscles would carry him. He
jabbed a second dart into the prone body of the mage—a

human in tan Aztechnology armor with a Jaguar Guard shoulder patch.

Best that he not wake up and frag me with a spell.

Ryan drew his pistol, and, in a smooth practiced motion, placed the barrel to the side of the copilot's head. *"¡Cállete!"* Ryan whispered. "No sound, *pendejo.* Or your brains will paint the foreshield."

The copilot was an ork with obviously jacked-up or wired reflexes, but he didn't try anything with the cold metal of Ryan's gun against his warty skin. The ork slowly raised his hands, allowing Ryan to grab his Ares Alpha Combatgun.

Ryan didn't have time to keep track of the copilot so he jabbed him in the neck with a dart. It took a few seconds longer for the big body to sink into the molded seat, but soon the ork was safely out.

It had all happened so fast that the rigger pilot, jacked into the helo's external sensors, never even noticed. *But she will soon,* Ryan thought. *When she checks the internal cameras.* Ryan took position behind the rigger's seat and brought his pistol to bear on her temple. He hoped she feared death because he needed her to fly the helo, and so it was necessary *not* to kill. He always preferred to incapacitate his opponents unless it was necessary for them to die, but now he couldn't even afford to drug the pilot. Though he might have been able to figure out the controls, he'd never flown one of these before, and he didn't relish the idea of learning under these circumstances.

The helo was about three meters up, just starting its forward bank that would take it around the *teocalli,* when the floor tilted abruptly. The helicopter canted right, then straightened. *This rigger obviously needs a lesson in pain,* Ryan thought. He knew just the nerve cluster to hit.

But it wasn't the rigger at all. Out the corner of his eye, Ryan caught the immense shape of the cyberzombie pulling himself into the open door of the 'copter. He had jumped straight up from the ground, and it had been his weight landing suddenly on the helo's frame that had caused the floor to tilt.

What the—?

Ryan spun to meet him, squeezing off two rounds that

should have hit him in the head. But the cyberzombie was fast and had already dodged slightly. One of the bullets caught his shoulder, ricocheting off with a metallic ping. The other missed.

The netgun fired just as Ryan dove into the front, the net's polycarbonate weave expanding as the explosive force threw it toward Ryan. But the interior was too small and there wasn't enough room for the net to open. It hit the plastic-lined metal wall just over the prone body of the Jaguar Guard mage. The hard plastic buckled with a loud crack under the force. But it missed Ryan.

Ryan pulled a mini flash grenade from his webbing and tossed it toward robo-slag. The cyborg watched it arc toward him as if in slow motion, seeming to be fascinated by the intricate rotating designs on the mini grenade. The absurd moment stretched forever, like watching a meteor rotate in zero G, and it was then that Ryan noticed the name etched in the man's flesh-toned forearm. Modular, exact letters spelled "BURNOUT" in dull gray.

Then the flash went off like a thousand suns in the darkness. At that exact moment, Ryan leapt at the cyberzombie, Burnout. Ryan lowered his shoulder to crash into the killer and threw him out the side door. Burnout snapped out of his brief reverie when the grenade went off, and Ryan could almost see the instantaneous contraction of his cybernetic pupils.

Ryan knew that electronic flash compensation replaced the overloaded image with an exact duplicate of the image in memory for a mere microsecond until the new image could be perceived. It was in that microsecond when Ryan's shoulder connected with the cyberzombie's torso. But the man's body was heavy, an easy two hundred kilos, and it was hard metal and banded, synthetic musculature. Like hitting a marble statue. And up close the smell of synthetic lubricant filled Ryan's nostrils, nearly making him gag.

Ryan dug in and pushed, bringing all his strength to bear. The cyberzombie staggered back in that instant of lost senses. Back and out the side door. Into the scream of wind beneath the helo's rotors, the acrid smell of gunpowder sharp in the air. Ryan let go at the last second, and Burnout teetered on the edge, his one free arm swinging wildly, looking for something to hold.

Ryan concentrated on a magical attack—a psychokinetic strike that didn't involve actual physical contact. He made a motion with his hand, as if to push the cyberzombie over the edge. And even though Ryan stayed well inside the helo, his attack landed home, hitting Burnout square in the upper torso.

The cyberzombie grunted as the force of Ryan's blow struck him. And he rocked back; another second and he would be gone. The helo was ten meters above the dark and mottled mat of trees. A fall would mean serious injury. Then Ryan heard the sound of oiled metal as the fingers of Burnout's free hand cocked back to reveal telescoping chrome fingers. Blood dripped around the severed skin where the fingers bent. The extendible fingers shot out like tiny prehensile tails and coiled around the safety handle like blood-tinged chrome snakes. Burnout held on.

Ryan fired his pistol at the cyberzombie's exposed form, and bullets hit home several times, but the Walther's ammo didn't have the power to penetrate Burnout's armor. Then Ryan remembered the copilot's Ares Alpha Combatgun. He bent and scooped it up in his hand as Burnout regained his footing. Ryan aimed the heavy machine gun and pressed the trigger.

But the cyberzombie had regained his balance, and he swung the netgun in a blinding-quick motion, its butt connecting with the barrel of the Ares gun. The burst of bullets sputtered before the jarring shock of the impact vibrated through Ryan's hands as the weapon was knocked loose. *This slot is strong.* A few rounds must have landed home because Burnout flinched. Then the gun clanged on the ribbed steel flooring and ricocheted under the seating.

Ryan tried to step away to get more room to attack, but his back pressed against the wall of the copter. There *was* no more room. *Frag,* he thought. *Now what?*

Burnout swung again, as fast as a scorpion strike, trying to hit Ryan with the butt of the netgun. Ryan ducked, and Burnout's blow smashed into the helo's interior, cracking plastic and denting the metal frame. The netgun twisted from the impact.

He's closing off the exit, Ryan thought as Burnout's huge form pressed close.

Ryan's strike was fast and elegant, a sweeping kick to the knees. Trying to knock him off balance so that he could use the split second to vault around the fallen cyberzombie and escape. But he got only one knee, and although it bent sideways from the impact of Ryan's foot, it wasn't enough to topple Burnout.

Then one of the cyberzombie's hands clenched Ryan's ankle, striking like a coiled rattlesnake before he had a chance to pull it back. Ryan felt the cybernetic fingers press through his nightsuit, tightening like a hydraulic vise. He twisted and pulled, placing a focused kick precisely to Burnout's wrist, trying to break the grip. To no avail; the cyberzombie held on with inhuman strength, his fingers nearly crushing the bones in Ryan's ankle.

Ryan used his distance strike again, an upward pummel to the throat, anything to get loose. But just as the blow hit home, making Burnout's head snap back, Ryan heard the soft sound of metal on metal. Everything contracted down in his vision as he watched Burnout's wrist. As he saw the huge needle emerge, its tip glistening with a droplet of milky liquid.

The roar of the outside wind died. The smell of gunpowder vanished. Ryan's entire existence tunneled down onto that silent, silky drop sliding down the sharp needle that poked out from the cyberzombie's wrist.

And then the slow-motion surreality of the long, icy pinprick as the needle penetrated his calf muscle. The realization that he had lost to this machine hit him just before the end. The certain knowledge that Dunkelzahn's plan would fail because he had lost. *I have failed you, Master. I am eternally sorry.*

Then the chilling numbness spread up his leg, locking up his muscles. And his sight telescoped down to the inky black of oblivion.

Ryan Mercury was no more.

12 August 2057

4

In her Lake Louise office, Nadja sat at her desk and stared out the window, contemplating. Trying to get her mind around what had happened in the past three days since . . . Since the horrible explosion outside the Watergate Hotel.

Since Dunkelzahn's death.

Three days and the vision still hung in her mind like the afterimage of a flash. The silence of the destruction, Dunkelzahn's telepathic agony frying every nerve in her body with its power. The being who had served as her mentor, idol, benefactor, and friend was gone.

The office around her was in disarray. Piles of hardcopy lay across every surface, chips and CDs scattered among the paper. The trash was full to overflowing with shredded documents, wiped datachips, and the remnants of the lunch she had barely touched. The whole thing was a sharp contrast with Nadja's immaculate appearance.

In the past two days since Dunkelzahn's death, Nadja's life had transformed completely. On the night of the explosion, Carla Brooks had sent Nadja back to Lake Louise for security purposes. The Dragon's lair was nestled on the massive flank of Mount Hector, part of the old Canadian Rocky Mountains. Lake Louise was technically in Athabaskan Council territory, but that nation treated the dragon's property as a fiefdom of his own, especially because Dunkelzahn had been there since 2014, three years before the Great Ghost Dance had liberated the Native Americans from the racist oppression of the old United States government.

Nadja didn't know whether that status would change now that Dunkelzahn was dead. She hoped not. She had learned only two days ago that she was to be executor of Dunkelzahn's will, a task that required the founding of a new corporation—the Draco Foundation. Her work load, along with the power of her position, was skyrocketing. She held the reins of a new megacorporation in her hands. She would be doling out fortunes to some five hundred people and corporations specified in both the public and private sections of Dunkelzahn's Last Will and Testament.

And only today, she learned that now President Kyle Haeffner had nominated her for Vice President of the United Canadian and American States. She would have some political influence to carry on Dunkelzahn's strategies. Her nomination was contingent upon the findings of the Scott Commission, which was actually investigating her as a suspect in Dunkelzahn's assassination.

It's been a busy week, she thought, trying to get herself to laugh at the understatement. She failed. There was just too much to think about.

She'd planned to return to the Federal District of Columbia to read Dunkelzahn's will, but riots had broken out in Washington, and the violence had spread throughout the sprawl and then across the whole continent. The riots showed no sign of abating despite serious efforts by the troops of Lone Star, Knight Errant, UCAS, and Ares military units.

Now, despite her massive and growing pile of work, Nadja forced herself to take a breath and focus. She spared a moment to admire the view from her office window. She loved Lake Louise. The scenery was spectacular—snow-covered peaks that shone beautifully in the sunshine; steep forested slopes; the glacier-covered rock face, glowing a dull blue-white. Her office was in one of the mirrored glass buildings on the edge of the dragon's lair cavern. She was glad it was isolated from the VisionQuest Theme Park, mercifully out of sight around one of the massive flanks of Mount Hector. VisionQuest was a cutting-edge virtual reality research center and a huge game park rolled into one. Dunkelzahn had purchased the whole thing from Ares Macrotechnology many years ago, and Nadja still wondered why Damien Knight had sold it. VisionQuest turned a huge profit every year.

On her immediate left, Nadja could see the huge maw that opened into the rock. This was the "public" entrance to the lair, and it was extremely well protected by the best magical and technological security that existed.

At least that's what Nadja had been led to believe. But she had also been led to believe that Dunkelzahn was invulnerable. And that assumption had been false. Dunkelzahn was dead.

There's still a chance he's alive, Nadja reminded herself, even though she didn't really believe he'd survived. She didn't want to give up hope, but everything she remembered about the blast, every detail indicated that the dragon had been assassinated. And if he was alive, where had he gone? He'd never been out of contact with her for longer than a day since she'd met him that fateful evening in Paris.

She still remembered his human form as he stood in the center of a small crowd, discussing *Shifting Vienna,* one of Aloné's paintings. His boyish face and hands, his ancient eyes. He looked up at her, into her with his mind, and a clean-lined smile touched his flawless face. Just before he excused himself from the others to come over her.

There had been an electricity between them. He touched part of her soul that she'd let no one come near; too many had tried in years gone by. Too many had been shut out since her parents had died. It was as if she'd been reserving that part of her spirit for Dunkelzahn. It wasn't sexual. It wasn't romantic. It was simple connection, friendship on such a visceral, natural level that there was no denying it.

Nadja fought off the memory. She wiped her eyes, cursing herself for weakness at a time when she needed to be strong. *If only I could talk to Ryan,* she thought. *He'll have some answers about what happened.*

But Ryan had not made contact from wherever he was, even though Nadja knew he would try as soon as he learned of Dunkelzahn's death. Ryan Mercury was perhaps the only other person who had been as close to the dragon as she was.

Nadja checked her reflection in the telecom's blank screen. She took a deep breath, pushed back a stray strand of her black hair, and put on a smile for her telecom call.

"Gordon," she said to her secretary. "Please connect me with Jane-in-the-box."

"Yes, Miss Daviar," came Gordon's reply. "A moment please."

"Thank you."

A minute later, Jane-in-the-box's icon appeared on the screen. The decker's persona was an idealized woman with billowing blond hair, impossibly long legs, huge gravity-defying breasts, and tiny feet. She wore red leather pants and a low-cut jacket stretched tight over her bosom.

The image brought a smile to Nadja's lips. She knew Jane—a thin, homely brunette with more intelligence than femininity. Her use of this persona was a statement about the ridiculousness of society's ideal female.

"Yes, Nadja," Jane said. "What can I do for you?"

"I need a favor."

"Fire away."

"First, I want to know how . . ." Nadja searched for the right word, found it. "How *loyal* are you to me, now that Drunkelzahn is gone?"

Jane's icon gave a relaxed smile. "Not to worry, Nadja," she said. "I was devoted to Dunkelzahn because of what he was striving to do. I'm no less committed to that goal now that he's gone."

Nadja almost let herself sit back in the chair. *Excellent.* But she didn't want her relief to show too much. "That's what I was hoping to hear," she said. "The favor, then, concerns Quicksilver."

"Yes?"

"I need any information you've got about what he's doing and how I can get in touch with him."

"I can give you a recording of his last communication with Dunkelzahn."

"Please do."

"I think you should come down here in person. The data is very sensitive—too sensitive even for internal fiber-optic lines."

Nadja looked hard at Jane. "You've listened to it?"

Jane's icon nodded.

"Can you draw any conclusions?"

"Yes. Quicksilver was supposed to return right away. He should have been back here by now."

"He hasn't made contact at all?"

"No."

Nadja shifted in her chair, trying to do it delicately so as not to show any of the discomfort that she felt. "I'd like you to track him down, Jane," she said. "Use whatever resources you need. Track him down and get him back here."

"I was hoping you'd say that," Jane said.

Nadja disconnected and stood up. Then she spent a few minutes stretching her muscles, using her yoga techniques to help her relax. It was important for her to stay focused on work. She needed to speak with Ryan to see what he knew about Dunkelzahn's death, not for any other reason.

Then why am I so worried about him? she thought. *Why can't I stop thinking about him, despite all this work I have?*

The answer came to her mind and she tried to ignore it. But she couldn't, and it hovered inside her, filling her. Making her body tremble. The simple, undeniable truth of it left her weak. She put her head in her hands, feeling tears well in her eyes.

I love him.

5

He rolled on a hard mattress, sheets burning rough against his wounded skin, and dreamed of his past.

A pinpoint of light pricked into existence off to his left. He floated in a current of dark silk, twisting and arching against the delicate flow of sublime fabric. The pinpoint grew as he approached it. Or it approached him. He couldn't tell which.

The light overtook him in silence and inexorable serenity. And when it did, it brought a memory with it . . .

The sensory details of the room crashed down on him. His head was on fire, the nerve endings on his scalp and neck screamed. Blood trickled from the corner of his mouth to his chin, the iron tang of it sharp on his tongue. He realized then that he couldn't move, his hands and feet were bound, tied to a wooden chair. His wrists burned from the tight restraints. His muscles ached as though he'd been beaten.

The room around him smelled musty, its ancient, blue carpeting showing a grayish-white diamond pattern. Smelled old. Or maybe that was the floor-to-ceiling curtains, same dark blue, but solid except for the black stains along the top and bottom.

What is this place? Why am I here?
Who am I?

The room was very dark, lit only by a flashlight in the hand of one of the people standing around him. He could see their heat patterns in the dark, three of them—one troll woman, huge in her red robes covered with arcane symbols; one human woman with runic scars over her white skin; and the other . . . seemingly a bearded human man, but there was something *off* about him. Something blank, like cyberware from astral space. But it wasn't cyberware.

He couldn't remember their names, though he was certain

that he should. Especially the strange one; he knew that one. In the dark, he couldn't make out the man's features; shadows seemed to darken around him. The rest of the room was filled with old tables and chairs in various stages of disuse and decay. Like an ancient restaurant or buffet. He caught the dusty reflection of a huge fish tank on his left, long since dry.

"Basta ya," said the troll, the twisted single horn on her head touching the ceiling as she stood. "I've gotten all I can from him."

"Mr. T.W. Saint John," said the other woman, "was acquired from Fuchi four months ago. We paid handsomely to get his inside knowledge. He's been working on the artificial mage project at HQ in Tenochtitlán. Three days ago, he went on a temporary transfer to San Antonio. We found his company car a kilometer from here.

"But my mind scan reveals that his name is Ryan Mercury. His DNA and retinal data must have been tweaked to the Saint John identity."

Ryan Mercury? T.W. Saint John? The names meant nothing to him.

"What else?" asked the bearded man.

"Nada. His mind is blank as though he is resisting, but that's not possible. He hasn't the strength."

"He's not resisting, Gretchen," said the human female with the runic scars on her skin. "Something else is interfering with the mind probe. There's some sophisticated masking on him that I can't break through. That might be it."

The bearded man stepped forward. "We have no more time to waste. Ryan Mercury is known to us. He's one of Dunkelzahn's spies. We don't need to know more. Try some more . . . *conventional* persuasion techniques. Then kill him."

"Yes, Señor Oscuro."

A trideo box that Ryan hadn't noticed before sparked to life. A man's torso came into view—dark brown hair, dark blue eyes, white skin. Young and quite handsome. He wore a business suit and tie. His voice resonated into the room, deep and rumbling from the trideo's speakers. "Darke?"

The bearded man who was called Oscuro turned to the trideo unit. "Ah, Mr. Roxborough, to what do I owe this interruption?"

Ryan noticed that Mr. Roxborough's image looked strange when it moved. It was a very subtle thing. The texture of his skin seemed too uniform; the symmetry of his face struck Ryan as eerie.

"I would like the body for my experiments," Roxborough said, his voice booming in English with a heavy British accent. "Is there any way you can keep him alive for me?"

Darke turned to face the trideo. "This one is extremely dangerous—"

"My people are fully competent to handle him." Roxborough smiled, self-confidence showing even through the video link. Then his eyes grazed over Ryan. "He has just the body I've been waiting for. I will gladly compensate you for your effort."

Darke considered for a minute. "Very well," he said. "Although compensation is unnecessary. I ask only that you promise me two things. One, if your biologists or mages learn anything of his past or his involvement with Dunkelzahn, you will tell me immediately."

"Of course."

"And two, kill him when you're done."

Roxborough nodded. "Certainly. I'll send a team for him immediately."

The three-dimensional image flattened and winked out, and Darke turned back toward the others. Gretchen, the troll, had pulled a heavy hose of rubber-coated metal from under one of the tables. She looked questioningly at Darke.

Darke's shadowy face nodded. "Proceed," he said. "I will be out by the lake, monitoring the excavation. Inform me of anything he says."

Gretchen smiled. "Of course, Señor."

Darke turned and walked further into the shadows. When he was out of sight, Ryan followed his retreat by the sound of his footsteps. The man walked across about six meters of carpeting before hitting hard tile. Two meters further, Ryan judged, he passed through a door. If only he could loosen his bonds, perhaps escape was possible.

"Now," Gretchen said, swinging her arm to warm it up, "you *will* talk. Tell me about who you are and why you're here."

Ryan knew what was going to happen and clenched his

teeth. The troll hit him and he said nothing. Pain flared where she hit, but it was only momentary. Each time the hose came down, Ryan felt a brief spike of pain, then it was gone, channeled away by his magic. The hose came across his back, his legs, chest, arms. He got hit in the head and groin.

Gretchen was wrong; Ryan did not talk. But as the blows continued to fall, the pain remained longer and longer until his magic gave out. All the pain came crashing down on him abruptly, and his body screamed from the sudden agony. Thankfully, Ryan lost consciousness.

He was back in the flow of silk clouds. Dreaming. Remembering. The light retreated until it was only a flicker. A pinpoint of whiteness dwindling on the rim of his awareness. Then gone.

He floated timelessly. The landscape of his existence was shadows; grays and deep, deep blues. A static black river without sound, without smell. Only touch and sight. A womb of the dead.

Other memories came to him. Sporadic and without order . . .

A beautiful elven woman straddled him, her naked porcelain skin zebra-striped by the mini-blind shadows from the window. Her raven hair falling like dark rain over her shoulders.

The ocean rumbled outside, its subsonic murmur touching a part of his primitive spirit, soothing it. He moved inside her slowly, gripping her with his strong hands. She seemed almost fragile next to his musculature, her thin frame delicate against his rock-hard strength.

He trickled his fingertips down her back, over the slim curve of her butt, then up front to her breasts—exquisite and full with red-brown nipples. She moaned when he moved up to take one in his mouth.

The smooth texture of her areola on his tongue. The rock and shift of her hips against his. The growing burn of ecstasy.

Gave way.

And she with him.

. . . then it was gone; he was swept up in the current of silken tatters. Dark swimming fabric surrounded him, buoyed him. Abruptly, another vision came, flying white-hot from somewhere off to the right. A flicker of a dream, a taste of a memory. He writhed and wriggled to escape, but it overtook him like a tsunami. A fragment of a life long dead.

The dragon crouched next to him, immense and overwhelming. Dunkelzahn, a creature with scales that glinted deep blue and silver in the dim yellow light of the chamber. Ryan stood next to the dragon, his head coming about halfway up Dunkelzahn's folded front leg. The room around them was a huge vault of hewn rock, and even though it featured modern lighting and electronics, the chamber was more reminiscent of ancient fantasy settings than of twenty-first-century technological society. It was a room fit for medieval magic, for knights and maidens. For terrifying and unstoppable evil.

For heroes. For those who instinctively recognized the difference between right and wrong, and who fought for the right despite the allure of the wrong.

Ryanthusar, came the dragon's voice in his head. *Do not succumb to the way of thinking that has trapped so many in this time. Heroism has not vanished from the universe. It is hidden, certainly, more raw in form and subtler in manifestation. But heroes do walk the cynical streets of the Sixth World.*

Dunkelzahn's head was larger than Ryan's body. Immense black horns jutted straight from the top of the wyrm's skull, and his nose hooked into a sharp beak in the front, like an eagle's, but studded with spikes. His eyes glistened an oily yellow, slit-pupiled and reptilian.

Even though Dunkelzahn could easily rip Ryan in half with one quick strike of a massive claw, Ryan did not fear him. Ryan had grown up with the dragon, and he trusted the wyrm with his life.

Are you ready to enter the Matrix, Ryanthusar?

"Yes, Dunkelzahn."

Jane?

"I'm ready for him," came the reply. She was in her midthirties, a human with an emaciated body that indicated neglect and a general distaste for the corporeal. Scraggly brown hair sprouted from the top of her head and hung down over the shaved area along the back of her skull where a clear plastic panel covered six datajacks and a softlink. She waved a skeletal hand for Ryan to join her at the decking console next to the wall.

Ryan walked over, aware of the dragon's gaze on him. He sat down next to Jane, sinking into the extremely comfortable cushions of the chair.

I will follow along, came Dunkelzahn's telepathic words. *If Jane doesn't mind. I don't want you to use my icon, however.*

Jane nodded, then looked at Ryan. "Have you ever used a 'trode rig?"

"No."

Jane picked up a skull cap made of black nylon webbing and fiber-optic lines. Then she stood up and moved around behind Ryan. "It fits over your head like so." She proceeded to stretch the cap over Ryan's skull. It fit tight and snug.

"I slot this end into the hitcher jack on my deck, and you're ready to cruise the data stream with me. You won't have any control, and the feedback filters ought to jack you out if we hit trouble, but there *is* a risk. This 'trode rig is SOTA, state of the art, chummer. It's hot out of the Vision-Quest tech labs, and its specs're as good as a cheap datajack. Which means you'll feel it if any intrusion countermeasures hit me."

Jane slotted the plug into the shiny black panel on the deck, then pulled another cord from under the panel and snugged it into one of the datajacks on her skull. "Of course, the IC seldom ever hits me, and this is an easy run. We're just going to slide into the Fuchi star, Villiers' camp, to implant the fabricated identity of T.W. Saint John. *You,* my friend."

Jane looked at the dragon. "Ready for trance," she said.

Proceed.

Jane stiffened slightly as Dunkelzahn entered her mind. He would see the Matrix through her, telepathically. It was almost like the dragon was doing the decking. Ryan felt his presence as Jane engaged the link.

Then he forgot everything as they fell through the neon sky of the Matrix. Free fall.

Falling and falling and falling . . .

Until the memory careens away in silence. Billowing

blankets of the softest silk caress him as he falls, nearing the rim. The event horizon of the blackout fringe.

Over. Gone.

He regained consciousness slowly and with great effort. Even before he opened his eyes, he felt himself to be lying on a hard mattress, a thin foam pillow under his head. Rough sheets chafed at his raw skin. The dull ache of bruised muscles throbbed from his extremities, as if from a great distance. As if through the haze of pain dampers or drugs.

He rolled over slowly, carefully. Opened his eyes a crack, letting them adjust to the harsh white of overhead fluorescents. Nothing of who he was remained. Even the memories he knew he'd just experienced were lost to him, drifting away from his consciousness like leaves in a breeze.

Who am I?

He sat up abruptly, wincing from the sudden pain. He had to see what he looked like. The light made him squint at first, but he needed to examine his body. Needed to check, for some reason he could not trace, that the sanctity of his flesh had not been violated by machines.

He threw back the white clinic sheets and looked down at his body. Human, male, with white skin, tinted slightly olive. He was solidly built and strong, but he could see that he'd been bruised recently. Purplish red splotches and webs of blood vessels floated under his skin.

He checked his face with his hands, finding himself unshaven, but generally intact. No broken bones, no permanent physical damage. Mentally, however, he was unsure. When would his memory return?

"Good morning," came a voice from above. A deep rumbling sound from the speakers, a British accent he thought he recognized. "I trust you feel better?"

He looked around the room for the first time. He was on a single bed in a small room that boasted only a small sink, the bed, and a bank of machinery along the wall next to him. In the metal facade of the electronics was a small screen, flickering to life.

The man on the screen was someone he had seen before. He knew it, but was unable to put a name to the handsome young face. The deep blue eyes, the curly dark hair, the confident smile—it all seemed familiar.

"I seem to be in one piece," he told the man on the screen.
"Excellent."

He knew the voice to be the same as the one he'd heard in his dreams, a reassuring bass in proper English. The voice comforted him, made him feel secure. He trusted the man with that voice.

"There is one thing," he told the man. "I can't remember who I am or why I'm here. I don't remember anything."

The man smiled on the screen. "Worry not, my friend. Your memory will return over time. And for a while you might be confused, but that will pass. As for who you are . . ."

"Yes?"

"Your name is Thomas Roxborough. You're *me*."

He sank back into the rough sheets of his bed. *Yes,* he thought, *that makes perfect sense.*

6

The Aztechnology cybermancy clinic was a squat, three-story block fortress, hidden in the jungle of northern Panama. Only those with connections and nuyen to burn could afford the services provided by the clinic's doctors and mages. Most of that nuyen went into research, and much of that research was aimed at solving one problem. Getting the clinic's major owner and permanent resident into a functional human body.

Today, the clinic's board room was small and cozy, its rectangular shape just large enough to accommodate the centerpiece—an oval-shaped, fake cherrywood table surrounded by high-back synthleather chairs. Thomas Roxborough saw the room from the video cameras, his rig interface sculpting the input from the three cameras and the room's microphones into a seamless composite—a 360-degree sensory perception of the board room.

Roxborough had become used to seeing the world this way. For the past six years his body had been confined to a support tank—a vat of saline and enzymes upon which his physical existence depended, controlled by computers and constantly monitored by technicians. He was barely alive; his own immune system had nearly destroyed him. It had only been his wealth and determination that had let him survive for so long. His massive funding of Universal Omnitech, and his refusal to sit idle and die without a fight.

At the board room table were Meyer and Riese, sitting opposite each other as they waited for Roxborough. Meyer was the mage—an elf man with a long brown ponytail, brown eyes, and a typically arrogant disposition. But he was the backbone of the cybermantic procedures, so Roxborough put up with his ego and insubordination.

Riese was the scientist—a short human woman of remarkable energy and intelligence. Roxborough actually liked her because she was usually pleasant, content as long as she could perform her research. Riese had a pretty, round face and brown hair that hung just below her ears.

Roxborough activated the holoprojector so that he would appear in the chair at the head of the table. The two hushed their discussion as Roxborough's holographic representation solidified. His simulacrum looked nothing like his old body, from long ago when he was a corporate raider, walking around in the real world. No, this was the image he'd been using since being locked into his vat—a human, young and handsome with blue eyes and curly brown hair. He might have looked that way in his twenties had he not been so addicted to the rich delicacies of a gourmet diet and the exquisite taste of tobacco.

"Hello," he said to the others.

"Good morning, Mr. Roxborough," they said.

Roxborough shuffled through some holographic papers. "Let's get down to business," he said. The papers were unnecessary, of course, but he found that it put others at ease. Made them more comfortable with his simulacrum. "I have spoken to the subject, and he seems to be reacting well to the treatment. Is this your prognosis as well, Riese?"

Riese brushed a hand through her mouse-brown hair. "Essentially, sir . . . yes, it is. But it's too early to tell if his memory is completely destroyed. The laés did the trick, but we'll have to wait and see whether the synaptic remapping is effective."

The elf leaned in. "I think there's a serious problem with this subject," he said in a voice that was both condescending and effete.

"And what might that be?" Roxborough asked.

"His magic is extremely strong. His aura hasn't changed since the laés was administered. I just have an odd feeling about him. Even if the biology is effective, I'm not sure the cybermantic procedure will work on this one."

Roxborough looked at Meyer, focusing down on his face. The on-line voice stress-analyzer indicated that Meyer was telling the truth as far as he knew it; he didn't seem to have any hidden agenda for telling Roxborough this. *Except perhaps to cover his hoop if the magic frags up.*

The experimental procedure that would liberate Roxborough from his prison of macroglass and saline was a two-step process. Step one was technological—the subject's mind was wiped with drugs and his brain was remapped by implanting new memories. And also, according to Riese, retroviruses and trypanosomes were used to redistribute the synaptic relationships, strengthening some while weakening others until the actual neuronal map looked like Roxborough's. This step had worked on eight or nine test subjects and was almost routine by this point.

But the second step, which involved magic, had worked on only three test subjects. Roxborough didn't understand the details, but it involved techniques similar to those used in cybermancy. Meyer had explained it to him several times, but Roxborough always had to think of it as an exchange of spirits. In cybermancy, the mages tried to tie the subject's spirit to his body even though there was too much metal in the flesh to hold the spirit. The spells acted as a tether to the subject's will.

The experimental spirit transfer was supposed to work similarly. Meyer and his mages would tether Roxborough's spirit to Ryan's body after Ryan's spirit was forced out. According to Meyer, the trick was to bring Ryan's body to the point of death, but not over, then form a bridge with blood magic such that Roxborough's spirit would cross into Ryan's body. Ryan's spirit would be released, then the body's wounds would be healed, but it would contain Roxborough's mind, memories, and spirit.

I will be physical again.

"So," Roxborough said, letting loose with his full sardonic tone, "you want me to scrap this one, an otherwise perfect specimen, because you have an 'odd feeling' about him?"

Meyer was used to these sorts of meetings, however. "I'm

just giving you my opinion as head mage. I advise caution. After the last suite of retroviruses, we should give this subject plenty of time to adjust to your brain patterns. Your memories may take longer to settle in. If his aura has changed some by then, perhaps we can proceed with the transfer."

"Your concern is noted, Mr. Meyer," said Roxborough. "But hopefully unwarranted." His simulacrum leaned in close and his voice rose slightly. "Let me make one thing perfectly, *fragging,* clear. I want this one. This man's body is perfect. Unmarred. Beautiful . . ."

They sat speechless, knowing better than to interrupt.

"You will make it work, or I will replace you with those who can. Understood?"

Riese nodded, but Meyer just stared into the glossy surface of the board room table. "I don't think you—"

"No slotting excuses!" Roxborough's voice was blaring from the speakers now. "It has worked on our test subjects, and it will work with this one. You will *make* it work, or I will get rid of you . . ." He paused to let them think about that. Nobody left the delta clinic to pursue other careers. They would be killed and they knew it.

Meyer looked up into the eyes of the simulacrum, his face a mask of controlled rage. Mouth drawn into a tight line. "I scan," he said, then abruptly stood and walked out.

Roxborough put a smart frame tracer on him to follow him with the hall cameras. There was nowhere he could go inside the complex to escape Roxborough's scrutiny. And the great thing was—the wiz thing—Meyer knew he was trapped, but couldn't do anything about it.

That's why I'm the fragging boss, thought Roxborough. *That's why I own nearly a third of Aztechnology.* Power, he was addicted to it. Power over the little people. Over the information.

Power over everything, with one exception. One *huge* exception—his own body. His corporeal form, which had decided to eat itself up from the inside.

Soon, he thought. *Soon I will have that power as well. I will be fragging unstoppable in Mercury's body. And I will have it. The man who was Ryan Mercury is gone, erased like a recycled datachip. And in his place, grows the man who will become me. First, my personality and my memories. Then, in a few weeks or a month, the ultimate hostile takeover—my will. My spirit. Me.*

7

"I call you Lethe," came the voice of the goddess, "for you have forgotten your way."

Lethe basked in the sound of the goddess' voice. He soaked in the blinding light that shone from her. The light and the sound that radiated from her, washing away shadow and fear.

Lethe had existed in that place of exquisite beauty for as long as he could remember. And only recently, in the last few moments as he measured time, had the goddess stopped her singing. A song so perfect, so painfully wonderful that he could not move. Could do nothing but bathe in the beauty of her song.

The goddess was smaller in form than Lethe, and she had a distinctive shape—a body, marked by symmetrical appendages. Legs and arms, he suddenly knew. Delicate and beautiful in their fragility. Her hair was black, the antithesis of the light that radiated from her, and it framed her face and gave it juxtaposition. Shadows to her light.

"Lethe, listen to me," she said, "I am called Thayla, and I need your help." A thrill passed through him as she spoke. He would do anything for her. "You are an extremely powerful spirit, and you can help me. You are here for a purpose, though I don't know exactly what it is. Dunkelzahn must have sent you, or Harlequin. You have an important role to play or you wouldn't be here. You aren't from Darke, that much is obvious, so you must be here to help."

Lethe had no memory of anything other than this place. Nothing other than the goddess—Thayla, with her light and song. He wanted to help her, but didn't know how to answer her. Her speech seemed to be a physical thing, and he had no physical form. He didn't think it was *necessarily* physical, however. He approached her, and projected his emotions, his love for her. And they came out as words, "What can I do?"

"Look around you," she said.

Her light waned slightly as he took in the landscape, and a stiff dry wind came up. Lethe felt it, though the air passed through him. The sky above was colorless and flatly bright without any light source. The ground below was hard and cracked, a brown rocky surface underneath him. And as Thayla's light diminished, Lethe saw that a deep chasm surrounded them on three sides. That they stood on the tip of a sharp outcropping of stone.

Thayla stood at the very tip, the chasm dropping away in front of her precipitously. Lethe had no concept of the depth of this chasm; he could not see the bottom. And as he turned, he saw the outcropping widen behind them, thickening into a broad arc. The chasm marked the edges of the arc's surface with the dark line of its abyssal depths as it stretched away behind them, widening ever so slightly as it extended. Until finally it connected with solid land in the distance.

"This outcropping is the result of unnaturally high magic," Thayla said. "The Chasm, here, is the gap between our worlds and those of the ... the ..." She faltered, pain evident in her speech.

Lethe turned to look out across the abyss. Now that Thayla had stopped singing, wind roared around them, throwing her hair across her face. The far side of the chasm was barely visible in the blowing distance, but Lethe could make out a similar cliff at the reaches of his perception. He could see a similar outcropping protruding toward them from the land on that side. Darkness clung to the land mass, and revulsion rose inside Lethe as he looked at it.

"I am here to prevent them from completing their bridge," Thayla continued. "They are evil and horrifying and more powerful than we can imagine. If they can finish the bridge, they will come in droves. And when they come, they will destroy everything they can touch. They will torture us. They will make us all do things ..." Again her voice wavered.

Lethe shivered at her distress. Her voice was powerful even in shock.

Thayla took a breath and composed herself. "As the natural cycle of mana increases, the Chasm will grow narrower. But these outcroppings are unnatural—spikes above background that result from the use of blood magic. Our worlds are not ready."

"But your singing . . ."

She smiled at him, the light beaming from her and warming him. "My song stops them. You see, they cannot stand to hear it, and my voice carries even across the Chasm."

Lethe knew it to be true; her song was the light. It was the beauty that had immobilized him for as long as he could remember. In fact, he recalled nothing of his existence before, if he had even had one. Time had had no meaning for him until she had chosen to stop her song and name him.

"There are those on our side who are working to accelerate the completion of the bridge, those who are puppets of the Enemy and who are trying to hasten their coming. Look." She pointed back down the outcropping.

At first Lethe didn't see it because it was so small, a shadow among shadows. But when Thayla began to sing again, filling the world with light and beauty, a tiny blemish of darkness remained. It was almost insignificant, and it lasted only briefly, but Lethe had seen it—a flaw in her song.

"They have found one who can withstand the song," she said. "She is not strong enough to stay long, but I fear her strength will grow. And when it does, others will come. They will kill me or make me leave."

Lethe's spirit sank as Thayla's song died away.

"Unless you stop them," she said.

"How?"

"You must find the great dragon called Dunkelzahn. He came to me a while ago to see how I was. It seems that Harlequin, the elf who helped restore my voice and put me here, never told anyone about Mr. Darke. Never warned his companions about the efforts of Aztechnology to use blood magic to bring on an early Scourge. That elf has such hubris!

"When Dunkelzahn learned that Harlequin had entrusted the fate of our worlds to the strength of my song, he came to see me. Dunkelzahn knew that my song had failed once before, and he was furious at Harlequin for his over-confidence. For leaving me with only the protection of mortals.

"Dunkelzahn told me that I would not be able to hold off the Enemy's forces for longer than a few hundred years. He said they would find a weakness in my song. He said he needed more time.

"Dunkelzahn promised to create an item that would ensure that the Enemy would not cross over prematurely. The Dragon Heart."

Thayla bowed her head. "But that was some time ago, and the dark spot is growing. I fear something has happened. Will you go and find Dunkelzahn? Will you bring the Dragon Heart to me?"

"I will."

"Thank you," she said. "Go now, so I can continue my song. You will not be able to leave after I start singing."

It filled Lethe with sadness to leave the goddess, Thayla, but he did as he had promised. He moved at the speed of thought, traveling along the spine of the arc to the main landscape. In search of the great dragon Dunkelzahn and the Dragon Heart. He hoped his quest would be quick because he already yearned to hear Thayla's song again, to bask in her light.

8

He woke from a nightmare, gripped by chills. His body slick with sweat, his chest heaving as he gulped air. The drenched sheets clinging to his body in the heat. He opened his eyes to a dark clinic room, trying to focus on the dim lights of the electronics on his right and the soft sounds of distant voices.

The images from his nightmare flickered too strong in his mind, the terrible sounds and smells overpowering him. They were more like memories than dreams. Like forgotten trauma that he had shoved from his mind because the act of remembering was too painful. Crashing back on him now, shivering through him like cold wind.

Sensation of drowning. Locked into a plexan vat filled with saline and enzymes. He had no lungs, and his next breath never came. He panicked, thrashing and struggling. Aching just to inhale once more. Just to take one more breath.

But he knew he never would. That he would never escape the vat.

Now, sitting up in his clinic bed, he breathed deeply. Relishing the clean air. Filling his lungs long and slow.

More visions of his dream rushed through him. Sensations of his disembodied heart thudding inside his liquid tomb, sending subsonic ripples through the vat. Thud. Thud. Thud. Until his ears resonated with the endless ticking, like Chinese water torture. Driving him slowly, inexorably, insane.

He shook his head and took another breath. The clinic room was dark around him as he swung his legs out of the bed and stood for the first time since he'd awakened. *How long had it been? A day? A week?* He didn't know; there were no windows in his room.

He walked to the sink, three steps across the hard tile

floor. The only light came from the wall of electronics and
through the small window in the door. He turned on the
water and cupped his hands under the flow, bending to get a
drink. The water was cold and clean against the back of his
dry throat.

There was a mirror above the sink, and suddenly he
wanted to see himself. To know that he was whole and
human. The disparate images from his nightmare had faded,
but a solid memory was forming in his mind. A cohesive
pattern.

His body was very different in the memory, fat and weak.
A body that broke into a sweat just standing up. One that was
addicted to rich food, ate constantly, and smoked cigars that
were very expensive and strong-smelling.

The memory snapped into place. An experimental
chamber. Bright and smelling of blood. Dark and forbidding
liquid swirled and bubbled in a cylindrical vat next to him.
He stood on a scaffold, about three meters up, level with the
top of the tank. Attached to the ceiling above were heavy
fiber-optic cables looping down like thick arteries.

A technician in a Universal Omnitech labcoat sat at the
monitoring console at the base of the vat. And another bent
down to attach the wide canvas harness through his legs and
around the huge girth of that body. Two more tested the dark
saline in the tank.

His heart labored in that flabby chest as he waited to be
lowered into the huge cylinder that would be his life-support
for the next few weeks as he underwent an experimental
treatment. Gengineering to repair the SLE, systemic *lupus
erythematosus*, an autoimmune disease that was eating up his
tissues.

The cable grew taut on the harness, lifting his weight from
the scaffolding like a cow to be processed. He felt like a
brain trapped inside defective meat. Meat that had been
going steadily bad for six months. Ever since a slight pain
had blossomed in his right knee, then had grown into unbearable agony over the next three days.

The pain had spread quickly to his other joints until he
couldn't move. His doctor had told him that he had severe
systemic lupus, that his connective tissue was disintegrating.

His immune system was destroying his own body tissues. He would be lucky to walk again.

He had fired that doctor.

The disease had worsened, spreading from his cartilage to his bones and from there to his muscles and organs. Until finally, his new doctors gave him six months to live. The pain was unbearable, and the doctors said they had never seen anything like it. It was the worst case of SLE in history. They said there was no cure.

He had fired them all.

Then he had decided to try an experimental treatment by Universal Omnitech. The doctors said the germline therapy was experimental and might not work at all, but it was a chance for life. No one else had even given him that. *A fragging chance.* He shelled out the nuyen and flew to Houston. The whole process was supposed to take no more than three weeks. And if it worked, he would be completely healed. Better than the original.

That was his only comfort as he watched his naked legs disappear into the dark liquid. A pretty technician double-checked the connection of his datajacks and his blood-exchange systems for the last time. Then he took his last breath before the saline flowed up over his head and filled his lungs.

The Matrix appeared around him, the virtual space he was used to by then. A rendered home laid out like his mansion in London, very high-resolution. He couldn't feel his physical body at all.

He didn't realize until much later he would never feel it again. That he was stuck in the vat forever. Stuck in the lonely virtual halls of his mansion.

The therapy was supposed to repair his immune system and regenerate the damaged tissues. And it had worked brilliantly. But the side effects nearly killed him. When three weeks were up, he learned that an unforeseen synergistic reaction between the regeneration therapy and his disease had caused his tissues to dedifferentiate, becoming cancerous for a while before they took on new forms. Becoming something else.

Muscle cells differentiated into bone and skin. Intestine cells became fat and kidney and muscle. The doctors were

able to slow the process, but it was too late to fix it. *Too late.*
They told him he would never leave the vat. He would never
breathe in the real world again.

All the doctors could do was improve his Matrix connection. He continued with his life. He wasn't going to let anything slow him down. He still owned a hefty portion of
Aztechnology, not to mention various holdings in many
smaller corporations, including a significant chunk of Universal Omnitech. He would be damned if he'd give up
on life.

Now, standing over the sink in the clinic's bed chamber,
he touched the button that turned on the light over the
mirror. *Am I finally out of the vat? Perhaps.*

The face looking at him from the mirror was handsome
despite the bruises. His eyes were silver-gray and flecked
with blue, and there was a line of stitches through the red-
dish-brown eyebrow that arced above his left eye. There
were blackened purple patches on his jaw and neck, some of
the bruises disappearing under his copper-colored hair.

He stepped back from the mirror to look over the whole
body. *Quite nice,* he thought. A substantial improvement
over the fat and flabby form he remembered. *I'll have to take
better care of this one.*

He heard footsteps out in the hall, two people approaching
his door at a rapid pace. Urgent. And as the door opened, he
crouched down and pressed himself against the wall. Quick
and silent, without thinking.

What am I doing? he thought.

Two people entered. One was a human who wore a form-
fitting white suit, and carried weapons. *A stun baton and
netgun,* he knew suddenly, though he could not remember
how. The other was dressed in loose pants and a jacket made
of purple silk, embroidered with gold thread. He was an elf,
tall and slender with a brown ponytail and arrogant eyes.

A mage? Again the thought just came into his head,
though he didn't know how. But he knew it to be true.

"Hello?" said the elf. "Mr. Roxborough?"

He stood up.

"There you are," said the elf. "Is something wrong? Night-
mares again?"

He thought of the vat. "Yes."

"Please come and lie down," the elf said. "My name is Meyer. Are you hungry? Thirsty?"

"No."

"What was your dream about?"

He felt compelled to tell this one. Maybe it would help to get it out of his head. Maybe they could help him. "I dreamt I was drowning. I was put into a vat of some sort, and I couldn't breathe." He looked right at the elf, giving him a hard stare. "Is this something that happened to me?"

Meyer nodded solemnly.

"Tell me about it."

"Why don't I show you?"

The elf put a reassuring hand on his arm, wrapped him in a thin cotton robe to cover his naked body, and escorted him from the room. The hallway outside was brightly lit by overhead fluorescents. White and black tiled floor, white walls. There was an almost antiseptic air about the whole place.

They passed what the elf described as recovery rooms, where the people who came here for surgery were allowed to rest while they healed. It seemed that every one of the patients was here to get some sort of metal implanted. The feelings he got from that discovery were mixed. Part of him was proud of the clinic as though he had some stake in its performance, but underlying that pride was a sense that there was something deeply wrong with whatever went on here.

The hall was segmented every twenty paces by a fire wall and double doors made of reinforced steel. Security cameras scanned the hall at these checkpoints, and autofire turrets tracked along.

High security for a hospital, he thought. *Cameras everywhere.*

Nobody else walked the halls except for a few others who wore the same form-fitting white suit and weaponry as his human escort. The other patients were either asleep or behind closed doors. He could hear some faint conversations, though he couldn't make out the words.

Meyer and the human guided him to an elevator. Upon entering, Meyer looked into a small glass port on the steel control panel as the machine scanned his retina. A second later a few previously hidden buttons lit up on the panel.

Meyer pressed the one marked B5-Roxborough, and the elevator began to descend.

"Where are we going?" he asked.

"You must realize that you aren't complete," Meyer told him. "Part of you is still inside the tank. We're taking you to see that part."

A chill took him as the doors slid open, revealing a dark corridor. Security cameras and autofire drones scanned them. He pulled the thin robe tighter around him, but the chills did not abate.

The hallway was raw duracrete and very thick, probably enough to withstand a small tactical nuke. Fluorescent lighting hung on metal posts embedded into the duracrete ceiling. There was a short open section that ended in a door. Again, Meyer had to submit to a retinal scan to get them through, and on the other side were two guards standing alert, ready to draw weapons.

The guards wore tan uniforms over body armor with black and red jaguar-shaped patches at their shoulders. Their heads were completely shaved and they had no visible ears, just tiny chrome dots on the sides of their heads. Their eyes were covered with dark violet glasses that were jacked into their skull through a microthin wire. The wide area behind the guards was blocked by floor-to-ceiling fencing, through which the only access was the door between the two guards.

Behind the fencing stood another guard, a dark-haired Hispanic woman without any visible cyberware. Another mage.

The guards took a drop of blood from each of the three of them, pricked from the tip of their fingers. The blood soaked into a strip of paper and into a scanner mounted next to the door. While the scanner checked their DNA with the files on record, the guards searched each of them for weapons. The search was a formality only because they had already been scanned by the SQUID that Ryan had noticed in the hallway. The SQUID was a quantum interference device, and it would have picked up any weapons and any cyberware.

How do I know all this? he wondered. *More memories?*

After a few minutes of unpleasantness, they were through. The elf turned to him and explained. "We can't be too careful," he said. "You're one of the major shareholders of Aztechnology. You're responsible for making decisions that affect millions of people. Your life must be protected at all cost."

As he took in the details of the room, the door clicked closed behind them. A series of large plexan tanks lined the semicircular wall. There were twelve in all, black tanks about five meters high and cylindrical, about half as wide as they were tall. Machinery hummed and pumped near the base of each vat, and a veritable spider web of fiber-optic cables spread across the surface of the tanks, connecting to sensors and probes. Two catwalks provided access, one about halfway up, and the other at the top where more cables, thicker this time, plunged into the apex. *Matrix connections,* he knew suddenly.

Lights illuminated only four of the tanks, those in the middle. The machinery and electronics on the others remained off. A bored-looking human technician in a white lab coat unjacked from a terminal as they approached. Another tech watched them from the topmost catwalk.

"Can you depolarize the tank?" the elf asked.

"As you wish," the tech said, turning back to the control panel and tapping a few keys.

This must be what I was, he thought, watching in horror as a broad window appeared in the side of the vat. The black plexan changing color to become clear.

Lights came on inside, showing him the results of his disease. Organs and differentiated tissue floated in a soup of saline and connective tissue. Bits of blood and bone, clumps of liver and intestine all jiggling inside the vat like a cellular chili.

His heart rose to his throat as he watched. His breath caught, his chest pinned. *I'm drowning.*

He turned to look at Meyer. Concentrated on his lungs, and managed to take a shallow breath. "Part of me is still in there?" he asked.

"Yes," the elf said. "This tank, and the one next to it. The scientists don't want to restrict any of your growth."

Then through the viscera, a large solid mass floated close to the window. Wires and tubes permeated it, and some of the shape was recognizable. The brain, mostly intact, but larger than normal and most of the skull and face dissolved away. Thick tendrils of brain matter floated like wet dreadlocks behind it. The thing turned then, rotating until he could see an eye, large and vein-riddled, peering back out the window at him.

Bile rose in his throat. His stomach lurched, and he could no longer stand. He fell to his knees and heaved. Vomiting until there was nothing but a dry acidic taste in the back of his throat, purging until his abdominal muscles were sore from the exertion.

Meyer knelt next to him. "We should get you back, sir," he said. "You're still recovering."

He tried to stand. The elf and the human supported his arms as he rose to his feet. The technician had polarized the tank's plexan surface, but the image still floated in his mind. *The injustice of such a disease. How could I have survived like that for so long?*

He didn't remember much yet, and now he didn't want to. "I want the procedure completed as soon as possible," he said. "I want to be out of that tank."

The elf smiled, broad and genuine. "We're moving as fast as we can, sir. The progress has been quite good for the first three days, and we just passed a major hurdle. It should only be another week or so."

9

Lucero dreamed.

She was the dark spot in the blinding light. The tiny shell of silence amid a sea of song. Beautiful music on a cracked plane of rock.

She thought perhaps that it was the voice of Quetzalcóatl singing, trying to cleanse her innate evil. But she doubted that even his power could rid her of the taint, the curse of her blood desire. Her yearning for its power.

Her addiction.

That dark stain on her soul refused to be washed away. Uncleansable like blood on Lady Macbeth's hands.

For several moments of exquisite beauty and terrible pain, she basked in the flow of light and the wash of music. Then, abruptly, her dream gave way to a nightmare. The glorious rush of light plowed over her, shredding her skin like a hard shower of needles. Too much to stand. Overwhelming her in its painful beauty, its agonizing perfection.

It was gone and she rolled over, consciousness hitting her like a sledge. The cold granite of the altar pressed against her back and neck as she rolled into a fetal position. The air baked around her even though it was well past sundown, and sweat slicked her scarred body.

Lucero's head was shaved and smooth, the only skin that was free of the runic scars that marked up the remainder of her petite body. She tucked her face into her arms and tried to hold back the tears. *The exquisite beauty of that place,* she thought. *Gone.*

"Excellent," came a deep male voice.

She felt a soft cloth fall over her, and magical warmth filled her. "You have the gift, Lucero," the man said. "You

are the paradox that can love both the darkness and the light.
Now get some rest. You will not be sacrificed."

Lucero looked up at the face of Señor Oscuro. He grinned
down at her and clasped his hands together in chilling glee, a
maniacal glint in his black eyes.

She had passed the test, a trial that so many before her had
failed. She would not be sacrificed.

Hands supported her, urging her to stand. Servants in drab
robes helped her down and led her from the sanctuary
chamber at the center of the San Marcos *teocalli,* out toward
the priests' residences. How long had it been since she had
last seen the interior of a sanctuary?

Since the last Blood Mage Gestalt ritual, when her magic
was still strong. At least several months ago. Now the power
was all but drained out of her, swallowed up suddenly when
she extended herself too far. When the backlash of the
Gestalt's ritual had crashed down on them, and she was too
weak to withstand it.

She had collapsed from the loss of blood and the ritual's
drain. She had felt her magic slip away then. Not all of
it, just a little. But that little was too much. It weakened
her so that she could no longer cast the high-force spells,
could no longer provide enough power to the Blood Mage
Gestalt. There were many initiates awaiting their own
chance.

She had expected to be sacrificed like the other burned-out
Blood Mages before her. Now it didn't look like that was
going to happen. She was not going to be allowed to die
for her sins. For her taint. What was going to happen to
her? What did Señor Oscuro have planned for her? She
didn't know.

The servants left her alone in one of the antechambers
adjacent to the sanctuary. She had a view of the altar and of
Quetzalcóatl's statue arching over it, gold and blue feathered
wings spread wide. And on the other wall were sliding glass
doors that led to a balcony. Outside, Lucero could see the
excavation under the glowing spring water. She could sense
something there, something pure and powerful. Something
like the song and the light.

Perhaps she could be happy here for a while. Perhaps she

would get to visit that place in her dreams again. The place where the stain on her soul was almost washed away by the beautiful singing.

Almost.

13 August 2057

10

Jane-in-the-box surveyed the virtual space of her command center. A square-shaped room with riveted stainless steel walls surrounded her. Six sides of computer-generated reality, each face representing one of her datajacks. Each representing a connection, a channel to another world to which she could switch. A die-shaped virtual gateway created by the network of cyberdecks and hosts in Dunkelzahn's Lake Louise lair. Working for an ultra-rich great dragon had its bennies, especially when the dragon was a technology freak.

Jane's meat body rested comfortably at her console, six fiber-optic lincs connecting the datajacks on the back of her skull to the command ports in her terminal. But her body was just bones and sluggish flesh, and right now it felt nothing, it saw nothing. The cyberdeck cut off her normal senses in favor of those provided by her MCPC—Master Control Processor Chip.

Time to move the chess pieces, she thought. *Time to extract Quicksilver.*

On the surface of five of the steel faces shone images, four of them headcam shots from her team. The fifth face, below her, showed a shining gold door, the gateway from her private virtual space to the Matrix—the electronic universe of the world-spanning computer network.

Her team was deep in Aztlan, on site at the delta clinic in the Panamanian jungle and waiting on her word. She checked the vitals of each of them. Kaylinn Axler was the on-site team leader and highly competent from years of experience. Jane registered statistics like heart rate and respiration that accompanied the visual and audio. Axler even had a cybernetic olfactory receptor so Jane got scent from her as well. Right now, the clinic room smelled like a combination of aerosol lubricant and antiseptic.

Axler, Grind, and McFaren stood in the small white-walled room with two other people—clinic techs who were performing a preliminary scan on Axler and Grind to see what 'ware they already had. Jane had fabricated identities for them, and she had bribed a series of people to get this interview. Ostensibly to schedule cybermantic surgery.

Axler was large for a human, though nicely proportioned—long legs, narrow waist, and square shoulders. Very attractive with wavy blonde hair, doe-brown eyes, and a nice smile. Very deceptive. She liked to lull her opposition into a sense of over-confidence by using her demure physical appearance. All of Axler's chrome was discreet and extremely well-hidden. Just like any emotions she might once have had. Despite her appearance, Axler was hard and remote—an ice queen, cold and frosty at all times. Her vitals indicated she was cool and collected, not nervous at all that the clinic technician was examining her.

Grind was the other samurai. A dwarf with enough testosterone for a troll, Grind's heart raced as he waited next to Axler. Waited like a racehorse in the gate for the technician to finish up. Grind had chocolate-brown skin, scarred from too much combat, and tightly curled black hair on his head and neck. His huge muscles were augmented with synthetic materials, and Jane could swear that his male ego was bioware-enhanced. Unlike Axler, Grind's cybernetics were obvious and designed to stand out. Especially his metal arms and the articulated limb in his chest, which acted like a third arm. It was all designed to intimidate.

Both Axler and Grind already had as much chrome as they could cram into their bodies without losing their spirits, or whatever the mages called it. Jane didn't know the ins and outs of the magical mumbo jumbo, but the experts said that too much chrome could kill you. They said that a body without enough original flesh could lose the ability to hold on to its spirit.

Until cybermancy came along that was. Some delta clinics hired mages who, for the right amount of nuyen, could perform rituals that allowed the installation of machinery and metal beyond the natural limits of flesh. Beyond the pale.

This facility was reportedly one of those clinics, and Jane had managed to convince the admissions subsystem that these two had the need and the credit to undergo the procedure. A ruse to get inside.

According to their System Identification Numbers, the two samurais, Axler and Grind, were working as proactive security for Pyramid Operations, Aztechnology's California alias. Jane had found it easy to tweak the data in the California operation. Communication between it and the central megacorp was often delayed because Aztechnology couldn't legally do biz in California. Thus the transfer of data between the two went through a series of data-laundering hosts located in Malaysia and the Caymen Islands.

McFaren held the SIN for their supervisor. He was the team mage, a human with a dimpled smile and wispy blond hair that was thinning on top. McFaren was a quiet man, but a brilliant mage with a number of unique spells he'd created for himself. He seemed to be at peace with the universe as he watched the labcoats scan Axler. Jane didn't have any vital statistics on him, because he refused to wear electrodes, but she did have a jittery video feed that came through a micro-camera on his vest; he didn't have any cyberware.

The final member of her team was Terr Dhin, the ork rigger who waited outside the delta clinic. Dhin was an ork of uncommon tactical skill; an excellent pilot of almost any sort of vehicle, and an uncanny mechanic. The feed that Jane got from him was actually from the helicopter he was rigging. She got the distorted reality through the Northrup Yellowjacket's sensors and cameras. Showing nominal activity on the small airstrip outside the electrified perimeter fencing.

This was the best team Jane had ever worked with, and she'd been with them since Dunkelzahn had hired her—over five years, an eternity in the biz of covert ops and shadowruns. They operated under the legal identity of Assets, Incorporated—a real corporation secretly owned by Dunkelzahn. They were extremely competent, and Jane trusted them to get the job done. They responded to her direction even though she wasn't with them in the flesh.

Most shadowrunning teams didn't understand that Jane often had a clearer picture of their situation than they did.

That when data from the entire team was combined in her command center, she had a better conception of the reality of the environment than any one of her team. Virtual *could* be more real than real.

Axler and team understood that; they trusted Jane. It was an arrangement that gave them the ability to accomplish runs that would otherwise require a much larger, a much more unwieldy, task force.

Jane took a deep breath. Her team was in position; it was time to scan the opposition. "Three minutes to stage one," she said to them, the encrypted electronic pulses of her voice piggybacking on telecom calls to their Local Telecommunications Grid. Then, after she'd confirmed that they'd each received her message, she dove into the Matrix.

Sliding from her riveted steel box into her persona as she fell, sensation of weightlessness for an instant. Then popping into solidity as her persona hardened around her—a blonde woman with exaggerated feminine features. Tight red leather pants and matching jacket stretched across her skin. The image was obviously designed to give other deckers the wrong impression. What shadowrunner with any sort of rep would have a corporate biff for a persona?

Jane mentally punched herself from Dunkelzahn's private LTG through the fiber-optic conduits into the Tenochtitlán Regional Telecommunications Grid, breathing in the crisp digital air of the Aztlan Matrix. Most of the RTG followed the standard iconology of UMS—Universal Matrix Specifications. Planar constructs and semi-transparent geometrics glowed with smatterings of neon and chrome, a digitally precise reflection of the real-world computer systems.

Pyramidal structures littered the Tenochtitlán electronic datascape, but two were much larger than the others—giant step-pyramid constructs. Jane knew them well and avoided even passing close. One was the Aztechnology headquarters and was protected with the sort of Intrusion Countermeasures befitting the paranoid megacorporation. IC also protected the other—the Great Temple of Quetzalcóatl. Fortunately, neither was her current destination.

Jane mentally held her breath for three beats as she triggered a hidden System Access Node. A "vanishing SAN," in decker parlance. Her code worked like a fragging voodoo charm and the node materialized. It looked like a giant hand, shimmering against the black fabric of electronic space, palm outward, fingers spread wide.

Time to burn some code, Jane thought. Then she rocketed toward the giant hand. At the last second, just before connecting with the massive palm, she activated a small smartframe—a morsel of programming that would remain on this side of the vanishing SAN and trigger it after three hundred seconds if her jamming code failed to keep the hand open long enough for her to get back out. Then she was through, logging on to the SAN and blasting down the private dataline to the host's location in Panama. Chill as snow.

From the outside, the host system looked like a human body, an intricately detailed man with white skin, brown eyes, and curly hair. The man wore a tailored corporate suit that shifted colors as she circled it. Going from iridescent blue to green to shimmering red. Jane had come here once before to scan the system for Dunkelzahn, but she hadn't tried to log on.

An eerie sensation crawled across her just then. A faint burning along her skin as though she were being watched.

She spun around, attack programs at ready. But nothing was there. She probed the whole grid, but came up empty. Nothing but the cold emptiness of Matrix space.

And still the sensation stuck to her like a tingling. Like all the hairs on her skin stood straight up. She tried to shake it away, with no luck. *Must be paranoia,* she thought. *There is no such thing as a ghost in the machine.*

Jane engaged her masking utility, and her persona assumed the guise of the sculpted system, transforming from sexy biff to a large white blood cell. She watched datapackets change from the UMS octahedron into red blood cells or tiny plasma particles as the host imposed its metaphoric representation onto her deck. The data particles formed precision lines, flowing like blood into the host through holes in the wrists of the giant man.

Jane stepped into the flow and entered the body, logging on as a routine Aztechnology request for security status. The surface ice scanned her code, looking like a huge, trisected blood valve in front of her. Then it opened and let her in.

The whole process took less than half a second. Null strain.

Inside the host, the sculpted imagery continued with the body theme, but with a twist. Organs seemed to float in a soup of sanguine fluid, haphazardly connected. A massive heart pumped data packets through artery lines to all the organs. Kidneys, liver, and brain hung in the surrounding space. No lungs.

Her analyze utility recognized the different organs as subsystems on the host, supposedly in charge of different functions. She pulsed up to the brain, its ventriculated lobes looming a dull pinkish gray before her. She followed the flow of data packets and attempted to access the subsystem using her security request identity once again. *No time to lose.*

Two heartbeats passed before she was inside. *Too long,* she thought. *Might have tripped an event trigger.*

Once inside she searched for a datastore, and found it with her analyze program a moment later, hanging like a massive upside-down ganglion. She spooled out the dumbframe she had programmed, ordering it to scan for recent admissions to the clinic, while she swept over all the files by date. In less than ten seconds the dumbframe had come back with seven entries. None of them matched Ryan.

Frag me raw. Jane still had no direct evidence that Ryan Mercury, aka Quicksilver, was inside the clinic. McFaren and two other mages who had worked with Dunkelzahn had used some of Ryan's tissue to locate him with ritual magic. McFaren was sure Ryan was inside, and Jane trusted him, but she still wanted visual proof. She wanted a camera image of him.

Abruptly, she noticed something as she accessed the room logs. One of the rooms, D307, had been activated in the last day. The locks had been accessed, the machinery and sec cameras powered up. D307 had experienced a great deal of activity, but no official entry was made. *That must be it.* She decided to check the internal camera records.

A huge macrophage-like construct swooped down upon her as she detached from the ganglionic databank, trying to sleaze her way out of the brain subsystem.

"User Identify," it said.

"Decoy," she told her dumbframe. Then as she turned to the ice in front of her, transferring her bogus security clearance, the dumbframe shot past, heading back toward the datastore.

The ice moved to intercept the dumbframe. And Jane used the split-second to unleash a massive attack program against it. In the sculpted reality, her attack looked like a tapeworm, spooling out grotesquely from her persona. It coiled around the macrophage like a flattened python. And just as the ice destroyed her dumbframe, the tapeworm crushed it. The IC fragmented and disappeared.

Then she was shooting into the security subsystem before more ice could pin her down. This subsystem looked like a cancerous mass at the base of the host's spine. And she quickly learned that it was on passive alert. She double-checked her best masking and armor before attempting to give the subprocessor the commands that would let her see the camera records. Everything proceeded without a hitch until she specifically requested the trideo records for room D307.

Abruptly, a macrophage and two symbiote-looking constructs blipped into existence around her. The symbiotes looked like bacterial cells with reinforced walls and huge glycoprotein armament, and she didn't need her analyze utility to tell her that they were black ice. The utility only confirmed it, and mentioned that it was psychotropic in nature.

Fragging wonderful. Black ice could kill by inducing lethal biofeedback in a decker's physical brain. Heart stopping, brain creasing to function as the victim convulses into a series of seizures. Jane had seen it happen once, and that had been one time too many. *Psychotropic* black ice could do far worse than kill. It planted subliminal fears into the decker's mind. These ranged from relatively harmless phobias like aversion to entering the Matrix all the way up to mania and paranoia, which could result in the decker jacking out and going berserk, killing everyone in the immediate vicinity. She did *not* want this ice to touch her.

She had just the thing. One of her best attack programs. She launched it, watching the code materialize in front of her, looking like a small star, its light dim. She activated her

armoring at the same time as she ran the sunscreen utility
that protected her from the bomb. When it went off a
microsecond later, brilliant shards of light erupted into the
close space, radiating out from the lantern like a small sun.

The macrophage simply vanished under the onslaught, and
holes appeared in the reinforced cell wall of one of the symbiotes, but the other looked nearly unscathed by the attack.

Some fragging robust armor on that code.

The undamaged symbiote spooled out a tendril of DNA,
which coiled in the space above it. The Matrix equivalent of
monowire. It whipped toward her, its edge sharp as honed
diamond. She had no time to dodge, and the DNA whip
crashed into her armor. Pain shot through her shoulder, and
that section of armor disintegrated.

Two more symbiote ice constructs appeared. The system
had bounced up to full alert. *Drek! Three and a half against
one is not great odds,* she thought. *Time to hide.*

She formed words in her mind and sent them off as datapackets. "Axler," she said, "it's highly likely that target is
located in D-wing. Up one level. Room D307."

Then she executed her escape sequence alpha. First, she
retreated from the ice in a quick spurt, taking another hit
from the DNA whip as she went. Second, she activated a
barrier program, watching it form a transparent wall behind
her. It wouldn't withstand more than one or two attacks, but
it didn't need to. Its purpose was to shield and slow.

She spooled a smartframe into being next to her. The
frame's persona matched hers exactly, a dataclone, and it
was outfitted with her best evasion algorithms. As a final
bit of tinkering, she crossloaded her datatrail info so that
the smartframe would be able to backtrack and escape the
system. She didn't expect it to reach log-off, but at least the
retreat would appear genuine. It might just fool the ice.

And finally, she engaged a new masking utility that copied
the surface sculpting of the data conduit and transformed her
own persona into an exact replica of the wall. She pressed
herself close and mentally crossed her fingers. If this didn't
work, she was nearly out of options.

The symbiotes crashed through the barrier just as her
smartframe bludgeoned its way out of the security subsystem. Jane's pulse roared as the ice plowed past, not even

hesitating, flowing by without so much as a pause to analyze her.

Sweet fragging awesome! This was why she decked.

Jane waited, doing nothing for six long seconds, an eternity in the Matrix. Then she carefully ran a medic utility to heal the damage dealt by the DNA whip. The utility repaired the damage to her persona and her armor. And when she was certain that the black ice was completely gone, she slid back into the subprocessor CPU of the security subsystem. The machine had canceled active alert, supposedly because the black ice had caught and decimated her smartframe decoy. This time in, Jane did not try to access the camera logs for room D307; they were likely still too hot. Instead she executed a control slave command on the clinic's general video feed.

The CPU cranked through her request without a hiccup, and she was in, searching for her team on the security cameras. Axler, Grind, and McFaren were no longer in the examination room, and she didn't see them waiting in the large hall that served as a common area and cafeteria of sorts.

Jane quickly searched the halls for her team, but came up with nothing. Which was good because it meant they were probably hidden under magic invisibility provided by McFaren. She just hoped they hadn't been caught. If they were being interrogated in one of the high-security areas, she wouldn't be able to locate them through these cameras.

One more thing to do before logging off. Her run counter indicated on-line time was up to 245 seconds. *That cybercombat took too many fragging cycles.* It was unlikely that her jamming program would still be holding the vanishing SAN open, and she had fifty-five seconds before the smartframe issued the trigger sequence again.

She used the time to implant some data into the security banks. The retinal and print-scan data from her team members, complete with false identification. The next check against any sort of incremental backup protocol would wipe the new records, but until then, maybe Axler, Grind, and McFaren would have an easier time getting through security checkpoints.

She was just about to log off the host when she froze, unable to move. She felt pressure then, a feeling like drowning. It was as though a huge bag of wet sand sat on her chest, growing heavier and heavier until she couldn't breathe.

The blood vessel walls faded away, replaced by a conservative office-style room that materialized around her. Mahogany paneling, track lighting, classical music. The smell of wood oil and fresh-baked pastries drifted in.

"Please sit down," came a deep voice.

A chair faded into existence next to her, and she noticed that her masking no longer worked; she was in her corporate bimbo attire, wearing slick red leather pants and jacket. She probed the room with her analyze utility, but it told her nothing. Solid code, slick as teflon, dense as rock. Like hardware.

"Relax," came the voice again. "You aren't going anywhere for a while."

Jane didn't respond, and continued her search for an exit. There must be at least one.

"My name is Thomas Roxborough. What is yours?"

Roxborough? I'm fragged. Everyone knew that Thomas Roxborough was a vat case and a legend in the Matrix. Jane struggled to breathe against the invisible weight on her chest.

"It pains me that you're so uncooperative," came Roxborough's voice. "Coercion really isn't my preferred modus operandi. But if you insist . . ."

The weight on her grew unbearable, and she crumpled to the floor. Gasping for breath. None of her code worked on this system, whatever it was. Even her emergency Disconnect sequence had no effect. She tried to bring herself back into the physical world enough to actually reach with her real, flesh-and-bone hand and jack out.

No effect; her perception was firmly anchored here. She felt nothing but the constriction of breath in her chest. Pressing down on her, feeling like cold dirt on her grave as she was slowly, inexorably buried alive.

Suddenly the faint burning sensation returned. Like someone was watching her. It was a hot itch over her skin, stronger than ever. A raw-edged scrape in the back of her throat.

"What are you trying to do?" he asked, his tone harsh, the volume rattling her skull.

I'm doing nothing. It's not me.

The sensation grew, the tingling becoming burning. The burning increasing until it felt like napalm immolated her. Then it broke, like a fever, leaving only a coolness. And she noticed that a section of the floor had opened up. A swirling vortex of light and cloudy colors funneled down next to her.

Then she heard a whisper, like a ghost in her mind. "Come." It was not Roxborough's voice. Someone else was helping her.

What else could she do? It was suffocate or dive into the tunnel of light. She crawled, pushing herself with all her strength. Straining as she crept closer to the edge, the digital event horizon.

A persona appeared behind her as she reached the rim—a human in a business suit, curly brown hair. It was an exact replica of the host's sculpture. His hands reached down to grab her ankles. "Alice! I will not let you take her," he yelled at the vortex. His voice was the deep resonance of Thomas Roxborough. "Why do you care about this one? Who is she?"

But the whisper did not answer, and Jane pulled the code of her knees tight against her chest as she plunged over the tornado rim and plummeted into the vortex.

11

Latched to the old rusting ladder of the ancient amusement park tower, high in the baking night, he was a droplet of black ink against the darker palette of night sky. The burning smell of a summer fire drifted in the still heat as he brought the binoculars to his eyes. As he looked down upon the massive obsidian glass stone in the lake at the bottom of the hill. The black stone was veined with orichalcum, glowing brilliant gold as the powerful magic infused it with new life.

Screams reached his ears then. Insistent, frantic screams of a lamb in human flesh. A child? Then the pleading cries went silent with the slash of an obsidian knife. A quick cut by a white-skinned human with dark hair and a beard. His smile was cruel and mocking, his eyes gleeful and drunk with power. He was *familiar*.

The man held the child by the hair—a brown girl in the throes of puberty—pulling back her head so that the sanguine liquid of her life drained into a funnel. Her blood flowed down a narrow hose, a conduit from the child's neck, through the water to the obsidian stone at the bottom. Wispy, red clouds formed in the crystal-clear water at the end of the hose, billowing around the stone as the girl gave out, her gurgling cry dying in her throat.

Watching from high above, he felt the knife as if it had struck him instead of the child. A searing pain across his neck, a choking spurt of blood gushing to fill his throat. Before . . .

He woke, shooting up to a sitting position in his clinic bed. The cold, distant lights of the machinery along the wall to his right blinked at him in silent mockery of his nightmare. Breathe. Breathe. Sweat froze on his back.

Where do these dreams come from? He couldn't remember

anything like it. His memory was returning slowly, though. He knew his name. *Thomas,* he thought. *My name is Thomas. Thomas Roxborough.*

It was the one truth he clung to, a rock in the shifting tide of erratic memories.

The door clicked open then, and a technician entered. She was tall and broadly built, not one he recognized. Her wavy blonde hair hung around a smooth-skinned face that would have been pretty if her dark eyes had been softer, their expression less chillingly hard. Sharp-angled bulges under her lab coat sent warnings off in his mind as he watched her approach.

Something was wrong.

But what should he do about it? He didn't know.

She had reached the side of his bed before he could decide to do anything. "Ryan, it's me," she said. "Axler."

This woman knows me? And she called me Ryan. Why not Thomas?

He did not answer her, though she was obviously waiting for some sort of affirmation. Then he nodded slightly. Best to play along.

"We're here to help you escape."

We? Then he noticed that the door to his room had not closed itself completely. Something was keeping it open even though he couldn't see anything there.

"You must be drugged," she said. "Can you move?"

He nodded again.

"Good." She handed him a black cloth bundle. "Hurry and put this on before the alarms go off and wake the whole place."

He just stared at her, unsure of what to do. How could he just leave with a stranger?

"Come on!" she hissed, her voice pitched low and threatening. "We're in danger here, Ryan! You scan?"

Ryan again? Despite the hardness of her eyes, he could see that she was sincere. She cared about his safety. "I scan," he said, "but I can't go with you."

Axler's hard eyes narrowed on him. "I don't have time for this, Ryan," she said. Then she reached under her lab-coat, and there was something in her hand when she pulled it out. Too fast to see, her hand a blur as she connected with his neck.

Leaving a patch. A dermal drug patch.

"Sorry, Ryan. I don't have time to argue just now."

It only took a few moments for his muscles to relax. He sagged into her arms. His senses seemed to detach themselves from his body and he found he couldn't move.

Axler lifted him over her shoulders; she was stronger than she looked. "Grind," she said, speaking under her breath as they passed out of the room into the hall beyond. "I can't raise Jane. Can you get through?"

"No," came a gruff whisper out of mid-air. No one was there. *Magic invisibility?*

"Frag, where is she?"

Axler's shoulder hammered into his chest as she ran, out into the white and black-tiled hall. The guard at the first checkpoint looked asleep, and he did not move as they approached. His head jerked as one of Axler's invisible companions lifted it up by the hair. The man's eye was placed to the retinal scanner and the lock popped open.

"That was the hard one," Axler said, then jolted through. They passed the elevators that had taken him to see the vats. Part of himself, part of Thomas Roxborough, still there in that tank.

Or was he Ryan? *Who the frag am I? And what am I escaping from?*

Axler stepped up to another door and looked into the retinal scanner that hung on the wall next to it, muttering under her breath. "I hope Jane's codes are still working," she said. "I hope you appreciate the drek I go through for you, Ryan."

I guess I'm Ryan then, he thought. *For now anyway.*

Ryan felt rather than heard the collective intake of breath by the other two accomplices. But the door clicked open and Axler led them through. Null strain. Beyond the doors was a wide staircase, switching back every level, with no windows.

They descended two floors to level one, and Axler's retina worked again to get them through the door. And into a wider hall with several people moving along it. Ryan heard them more than saw them. His eyes were open and he could see, but he didn't have motor control of his muscles. His head swung loosely, swaying as Axler carried him.

Axler's labcoat filled most of Ryan's vision, but the people he did see caused creeping waves of nausea through him. One was close, a dwarf woman once perhaps, but now her dwarf body had been almost entirely replaced by human-sized cybernetic limbs and torso. Everything external was artificial. Except for the dwarf's hairy head. The dwarf cyborg walked awkwardly, trying to gain control over a new center of gravity.

I doubt that will ever be completely possible, Ryan thought. And as he looked around, he realized that each of these people was barely alive; each was mostly machine and many were walking hulls. Their wills only a dim shadow. It was a sudden comprehension that came through a myriad of senses, a gut feeling fed by the smell of synthetic lubricant and the queer uniformity of the cybernetic parts.

Axler ran for the double doors at the far end of the hall. Moving as fast as she could with Ryan's weight over her shoulders. Ryan upgraded his assessment of her strength and speed yet again. *She is far more than she looks,* he thought.

Grind whispered from behind them. "I still can't raise Jane."

"Jane," Axler subvocalized. "Jane, you copy?"

She waited for a few heartbeats. "Jane must be off-line," Axler said, turning back toward her invisible accomplices. "I'm going to call in Dhin without her."

"Copy," Grind said.

Axler pulled a machine pistol from under her labcoat. "Go, Dhin," she said. "You got that? Launch now."

They had reached the double doors, and Axler's retina released the lock. She opened the door a crack and propped it ajar with a foot. And waited. One beat. Two.

The ground shook from a massive explosion. And at that precise instant, Axler threw open the door and lunged out into the early morning sunlight. She ran across a narrow open space, a courtyard perhaps, rectangular in shape and filled with sculpted gardens and trimmed tropical trees. The space was bounded by the clinic wall on one side and fencing on the other three sides. Five-meter-high cyclone

fencing topped by monowire. Ryan knew the fence was electrified just by looking at it, though how he knew was a mystery to him.

Sound came crashing in on him as Axler's sharp shoulder
needled his gut. Alarm sirens blared out a keening wail.
Automatic weapons sputtered from off to the right as a
combat-equipped helicopter engaged some ground troops
who were trying to guard the clinic's perimeter.

Ryan saw the results of the explosion. A missile or mortar
shell had hit the fence at the far end of the courtyard. He saw
fire and noticed that the fence lay like twisted foil. A ten-
meter opening stood over scorched earth. But the gap was
crawling with security, and Axler made for the opposite
fence.

"Ow!" came a voice that Ryan didn't recognize. A second
later two people became visible. The one who had spoken
was human, wearing blue jeans and MIT&T tee shirt. The
other was Grind, a dwarf whose arms had been replaced with
cybernetic attachments. A third arm, slightly different in
shape, telescoped from the right side of his chest. Grind's
afro hair was black, and his face was rough with scars. He
knelt in front of the fence and produced a tiny circular saw; a
machine gun was slung over his shoulder.

The human looked up into the air, holding his hands out in
a cryptic gesture. "There's a mage in the astral here. Just a
sec." McFaren seemed to be looking at somewhere else as he
made cryptic gestures in the air.

Ryan concentrated, trying to figure out what the mage was
doing. And suddenly he saw it. The world shifted for a
second, shadows and light lengthening and contorting into a
strange world that looked sort of the same, but very different
as well. Rainbow hues and colors of light radiated in prismatic beauty from every living thing.

Then he saw the mage, hovering in mid-air like a fiery
phoenix. A flash of energy arced from McFaren and
slammed into the mage. The phoenix shimmered under the
onslaught, flickered, then winked out. *Powerful spell*, Ryan
thought.

"That one's gone, but they're more coming," said
McFaren.

"I'm through." That was Grind.

"Let's haul hoop." Then Axler was dragging Ryan through the hole in the fence. Gunfire rattled off to his left; sirens rang out. Ryan caught a mouthful of dirt as Axler lifted him again. Her shoulder slammed into his gut as she sprinted across the thirty meters of clear dirt to the edge of the jungle. She pushed into the thick undergrowth, seeking cover, then dropped Ryan to the moist jungle floor, behind the trees.

"Dhin, can you see us?"

"Got ya clean in the sights, Grind. Want a missile up the yin yang?"

"Maybe some other time, chummer. Now, how about a lift?"

"On my way."

The helo swung around toward them, rocking and tilting under its rotors as it dodged fire. It was nearly clear when a missile launched unexpectedly from somewhere on the roof of the clinic. It rocketed through the drifting steam and smoke of the battle. Ryan watched as the missile connected with the flying hull of the helicopter, catching it in the midsection and exploding, ripping away metal in a white-hot flash.

"Dhin!" called Axler, watching from just inside the jungle.

Gouts of flame blew away the engine casing. Smoke and fire venting like demon's breath as the helo faltered. Then a final attack hit, deadly fast, a magical hellblast centered on the cockpit, warping the macroplast shielding, incinerating anyone who was inside.

The helicopter stalled and fell. It exploded before impact, jets of flame and shrapnel blowing out of the engine. Then the hull of the craft came down hard, bouncing against the clinic wall before crashing to the ground with the agonizing sound of ripping metal.

Nobody could have survived that, Ryan thought.

"Drek!" Axler said. "I sure hope Dhin wasn't in there, or it'll be a long trek home."

12

The spirit Lethe hung in astral space and looked down upon the Dragon Heart—a solid, pulsing orb of immense power that rested in the center of an ornately carved circle. The lines and shapes of the circle had been etched into the smooth stone floor of the small chamber. Intertwining runes formed the perimeter, while intricately designed dracoforms filled the interior.

The physical design gave rise to a translucent blue and silver curtain in astral space. The hypnotic weave danced and moved, blending and shaping around the Dragon Heart. The item itself was made of a magical metal, a dull bronze color and shaped like a real four-chambered heart. Its surface was smooth and flawless, embedded into the stone, flush with the floor, right at the very center of the etched circle. The design immediately surrounding the heart was a petroglyph of a great dragon. The image had been cut into the stone with such detailed strokes that Lethe recognized the dragon and knew him.

Dunkelzahn.

But Dunkelzahn was dead. Lethe had learned of his death by overhearing conversations. He had learned of the great explosion in a physical place called Washington FDC. But when he had gone to investigate, he had discovered a storm over the explosion site—a magical storm centered over the crater created by a bomb. At least that's what people said.

The storm had looked like a vortex of purple lightning and magenta clouds. It spanned worlds, from the physical to the astral and into the metaplanes, as though the fabric of universal reality had been torn in that tiny spot. There was no sign of Dunkelzahn, no trace or echo of him that Lethe could detect.

Now, deep in Dunkelzahn's lair, Lethe looked down at the Dragon Heart. It was his last hope to help Thayla. Perhaps Dunkelzahn's participation wasn't absolutely necessary, perhaps Thayla could use the Dragon Heart to stop the darkness from spreading.

There was only one problem; Lethe could not touch the item. Since leaving Thayla, he had grown, learned that he had many abilities, many powers. Like when he slipped past the spirits and metahumans who guarded the lair. He could move through the hypnotic curtain and interface with the power of the Dragon Heart. And when he did, it felt something like the power of Thayla's song coursing through him. The same but different; the song of the Dragon Heart was rougher, coarser. And he could tap into its power if he tried; he could use it to expand his awareness. He could use it to manipulate the temper of the ward, the very nature of the magics that made up the dragon's lair around him. But Lethe avoided using the Dragon Heart; it was like wielding the sun. Awesome and terrifying.

But despite all his new abilities, he still could not touch the smooth metal composite of the item. He had no way to physically manifest and pick it up. So it remained on the floor, firmly entrenched in the physical world. Useless to him. Useless to Thayla.

Time passed as Lethe considered his dilemma. He could try to enlist the help of another spirit or a metahuman with magical power, but he didn't know any who would come to his assistance. He didn't know *anyone*. Except Thayla. And she couldn't leave her place at the bridge.

Maybe another dragon? he thought. But he had no way of knowing if the other dragons could be trusted.

How much time passed before the group of metahumans entered the small chamber Lethe had no way of knowing. Four of them, tall and thin, moving quietly. Suspiciously.

Two of them glowed brightly with jewels and flares, showing power in astral space. Mages or shamans, Lethe guessed. But the others were mundane, anchored in the physical. In fact, part of each one was transparent, patches of blank spirit as though they had lost parts of themselves. Lethe saw that they appeared to have metal and plastic

permanently implanted into their bodies. He had seen a few
others like that, but none so much as these two.

The two mages surveyed the perimeter of the circle, step-
ping along the edge as they peered at the hypnotic weave of
the translucent curtain. At the ripples in the fabric of space
created by the Dragon Heart.

"This is where the tracer said we should find it," one said.

"Can you break the ward?"

"I said I could, didn't I? Just watch the entrance, Liner."

"How long?"

"It'll take time, even with both of us working on it."

The two mundanes stood by the entrance to the chamber,
while the others started to work on the hypnotic curtain. One
removed a bag from her belt and pulled fistfuls of green sand
from it. She spoke some words over the sand, using
Sperethiel—the language of elves. *"Tan'ath lie armma diesk
cycampeth waregram'cen."*

Lethe understood the words. "Obscure the power of this
ward. Dull the images, the potency of what you cover."

The other magician had fashioned a spell, looking in astral
space like an elaborate key made of fire and lightning. He
was trying to integrate the key into the weave of the ward's
curtain. Time passed as the spell advanced and retreated,
advanced and retreated until it had opened a small hole in
the ward.

The woman threw the green sand through this hole, the
grains filling up the etched images. The fluctuating curtain
grew less solid there, darkening where the sand covered
the petroglyphs. Until there was a narrow tunnel through
the ward.

All the way to the Dragon Heart.

"I'm in," said the woman.

"About time," Liner said.

The woman created a simple spell that Lethe watched
eagerly. The spell reached out and lifted the Dragon Heart
from its place, cradled by a bower of magic. Telekinesis. If
Lethe could learn that magic, maybe he could move the item.
He watched the item float on the spell's current, hovering
over the trail of green sand, through the tunnel—the weakened space in the ward—and out into her hands.

"Got it." She carefully turned it over in her two hands for a minute, mesmerized. The Dragon Heart looked large in the elf's cradling grasp, easily the size of her head. "Seems to be solid orichalcum," she said. "Sheila will be pleased."

"Does it include the charmed orichalcum we sold to the wyrm?"

"Most likely, but it's impossible to tell now. When this item was created, the tracing charm was destroyed."

"The item is active?"

"Most certainly."

"Good. Let's go," said Liner.

"Yeah, I'm getting edgy," the other mundane warrior agreed.

The mage put the item into her shoulder bag and nodded to the others. Then they were gone, moving rapidly through the twisting tunnels, the maze of corridors in the depths of the lair. Lethe followed, unsure of what to do. Should he stop them? Should he follow them? Who were these people?

Something happened then. An alarm sounded and many guards and spirits came. Total confusion. Shots fired and lots of magic. Lethe watched attentively, keeping close track of the Dragon Heart, but he did not interfere. The elves who had taken the item made quick time out the maze of tunnels to a narrow staircase that climbed up through the rock.

They killed anyone who tried to stop them, something that seemed wrong to Lethe. The meaningless destruction of lives. They were nearing the exit, preparing to fight the small group of guards, when Lethe caught sight of someone . . .

Someone different.

She was an elf, seemingly, and she was in a position of authority. Lethe was inexplicably drawn to her. Such charisma, such beauty.

She stood in an adjoining corridor at the center of a group of people. Drawing him to her with her commanding presence. In the physical, she was unadulterated, lovely. Elegant with her porcelain skin, emerald eyes, raven-black hair.

She was fully in command of those around her as she spoke to an ork, tall and dark with more of those blank patches in his corporeal spirit. "What's going on, Jeremy?"

"Brooks says that a small group has infiltrated the lower levels," Jeremy said. "But the treasury seems untouched."

"Where are these culprits?"

"We've lost them," Jeremy said. "Temporarily."

"Let me know when they're caught. I want to know why they were in the lower levels."

"They must have been after some of the treasure," Jeremy said. "But were scared off."

"Maybe."

I must talk to her, Lethe thought. *I can tell her about the Dragon Heart and the elves who took it.* But, unlike Thayla, she did not hear his emotions when he tried to talk to her, and she seemed to have no awareness of any world beyond the physical.

Maybe I can use a physical body to speak with her? The thought came and he acted on it without hesitation. He surrounded the spirit of Jeremy, engulfing the ork's aura as he entered the metahuman flesh. He tried to be gentle with the fragile spirit, careful not to completely swallow Jeremy's will.

Lethe filled the flesh as the ork's spirit shrank into a nothing, until it was safely absorbed by Lethe. He had taken total control of the body. This frail flesh that the metahuman spirits called home. Seemed so vulnerable. So weak.

The flesh of this creature felt heavy and slow. He saw the warped and distorted image of the physical world through the ork's eyes, heard the dulled sounds through his ears. The flesh was clumsy and awkward compared to Lethe's pure spirit form. And had some unexpected side effects; the smell of the lovely elven woman had an arousing effect on the ork's body which Lethe found not unpleasant.

Very strange, totally unexpected.

"I must speak with you," he said, the words coming out clumsily through the ork's mouth. But they didn't sound like Jeremy's. The inflection was different enough that the elf turned to him.

"What is it, Jeremy?"

"I have taken over Jeremy's flesh," Lethe said. "Just to make contact with you. My name is Lethe, and I am what you call a spirit."

She took several steps back and glanced with suspicion at the gun on Jeremy's hip. "What do you want . . . Lethe?"

"What is your name?"

"Nadja Daviar," she said.

Nadja Daviar, Lethe thought. *No, nothing.* He had hoped that hearing her name would click some memories into place, but nothing at all had come back.

"I can tell you about that which you seek," he told Nadja.

"What do you mean?"

Jeremy's body was growing warm from Lethe's influence. "The people who came here, in the lower levels. They took the Dragon Heart."

"The what?"

"The Dragon Heart," Lethe repeated as sweat broke out on Jeremy's forehead. "You don't know what it is?"

"No."

"An item created by Dunkelzahn. I need to bring it to Thayla."

"Dunkelzahn never told me about any such item."

Several magicians had surrounded Lethe by then, and some security guards had their weapons drawn, pointed at Jeremy's body. Nadja's aura was a maelstrom of intense emotions, but none of that showed on the surface. She spoke evenly, "What have you done with Jeremy?"

"He's here," Lethe said. "I've just possessed him for the moment. I will leave soon, but I felt compelled to speak with you. I come from a place of light and song, a barren place made beautiful by the voice of a goddess known as Thayla. Her song is protecting the world, this world, from imminent destruction. She sent me to find Dunkelzahn and the Dragon Heart to help her."

"Dunkelzahn is gone," Nadja said.

Sweat turned to steam on Jeremy's skin, and a burning smell surrounded him. *I must release this flesh soon,* Lethe thought. "I have heard of Dunkelzahn's death," Lethe said, "and that is why I need your help. I cannot manifest to carry the Dragon Heart, and even if I could, I don't know how to get it across the barrier that separates your world from mine."

Nadja shook her head slowly. "Lethe, I don't know . . . you sound sincere, but I know nothing of this Thayla. And Dunkelzahn never mentioned any Dragon Heart. What you are telling me sounds like an elaborate ruse. A trick of some sort to get some of Dunkelzahn's treasure."

Her eyes were like fragments of deep green stone, and

Lethe could almost see a hint of the fury inside. "But even if it weren't a trick," she said, "I don't think I could help you. My security forces will catch the thieves and whatever they took, including this Dragon Heart, but I simply can't act without investigating your story. Many people want part of Dunkelzahn's inheritance and will go to great lengths to get it. I'm very sorry."

Jeremy's body collapsed to the floor just then, his skin bursting suddenly into flames. His heart exploded in his chest, and with one lurch, one convulsion, Jeremy died. Lethe was forced to leave the necrotizing flesh. And Jeremy's spirit came away with him, unraveled from its physical counterpart. The ork's spirit shredded and fled, disappearing in the gentle astral wind.

In the physical, the ork's body lay dead and growing cold as the people crowded around. It disturbed Lethe profoundly. *That was not supposed to happen.* He had no idea what to do next. He had lost the Dragon Heart. He had killed an innocent metahuman.

And besides all that, Lethe thought as he watched the sad look on the face of Nadja Daviar as she bent down to inspect Jeremy's body, *I have alienated the only possible ally I might have had.*

13

Falling, falling.

Jane-in-the-box plummeted into the digital vortex. Her persona pulled apart into its constituent data bits by the tornado of light and static. A whirlpool of purple threads—lightning without thunder. Only the deep hiss of random patterns.

Then it was gone, and Jane found herself standing on a street corner. She was in her physical body, her real body—thin as a rail, skin and bones, unwashed brown hair matted like a bird's nest on top of her head. She felt frail, her bony knees threatening to buckle as she nearly collapsed to the ground. She needed food and a shower.

What happened? Where am I?

Tall buildings of concrete and mirrored glass reached up into a night sky around her, but there was no traffic on the city street. Street lamps illuminated the sidewalk, reflected in silver streaks that rose up the chrome windows of the buildings. But there were no people. Only Jane, a gentle breeze, and the absolute silence of the vacant city.

Abruptly, someone touched her shoulder.

Jane spun to see a young woman, human, about twenty-five years old with shoulder-cut blonde hair, fair skin, and ocean-blue eyes. She wore black jeans and a plain white halter top. "Sorry to startle you," she said, taking a drag on her cigarette. "Welcome to Wonderland. I'm Alice."

Jane took a step back. *What the frag?* Wonderland was a Matrix legend. *I'm still jacked in.*

The virtual reality around her was so real that it was indistinguishable from reality. An ultraviolet space. She could even smell the cigarette smoke. Jane had heard rumors that UV spaces existed, but had never experienced one. She hadn't given the rumors much credence, and she'd never believed in Wonderland—the infamous place inhabited by mysterious constructs and lost data.

Jane looked at Alice. "Are you slotting me?"

Alice laughed. "No," she said. "I'm not 'slotting' you."

"Did you . . ." Jane began. "Were you the one—"

"Who saved you from Rox?" Alice said. "Yes, that was me. I like you, Jane. I like what you're doing. But I hate Rox even more. Do you remember the Crash of '29?"

"I was too young to deck then," Jane said. "But I know about it."

"I was part of Echo Mirage."

"What?" The members of the Echo Mirage team were the first to use direct interfacing with computers. The first deckers. They were the guinea pigs who did battle with the virus that crashed the worldwide computer network back in 2029.

"I was in Rox's system when I encountered the Crash entity." Alice's voice broke momentarily.

"What happened?"

Alice steeled herself, her physical appearance seeming to grow more dense, if that was possible. She took a slow drag on her cigarette. "Never mind," she said. "It's simple really. I hate Rox, and I like you. I didn't want him to get you just then."

Jane didn't know what to say. "Uh . . . thank you."

Alice fixed Jane with a hard stare, her sea-blue eyes crystallizing to a frozen gray. Jane found that she could not move to look away.

"I did not rescue you lightly," Alice said. "It took a great deal of effort, and much sacrifice. Rox's system is one of perhaps five in the world that are protected from me. For the present at least."

Jane found she could not respond.

"In return for saving your life, I will ask something from you in return," Alice said, then a smile graced her lips. "Not now, but in the future."

Alice's smile hovered in Jane's mind, endearing and attractive, but haunting, overpowering, and not to be denied. "Goodbye for now, Jane-in-the-box."

Alice's words whispered in her mind for several seconds

after the silent city had faded around her. Then Jane was back in her riveted steel box, and the image of Alice's smile had dissipated. Wonderland was gone, and Jane wondered whether the shock of her encounter with Roxborough had induced a hallucination of the whole thing. It had been so real, like nothing Jane had ever seen on even the most detailed of sculpted systems. She hadn't known she was even in the Matrix.

"Jane!" came a voice through one of her links. "Do you copy? Jane, where the frag are you?" It was Axler.

"I'm here," she said, bringing herself back into focus. "Give me the status."

"Status is that we're fragged up in the yin-yang down here. The helo went down. I was hoping Dhin had switched to Plan B, but I can't raise him, so he must've gone down with the helo, and we're pinned down so we can't make the T-bird."

Jane scanned her other feeds, seeing Axler's mistake immediately. "Stand by, Axler," she said. "I'll have you out in nanos."

14

Ryan saw the world at a slant; his eyes open, his head hanging at an awkward tilt because the drug in the dermal patch on his neck prevented him from lifting it. The fiery afterimage of the helicopter crash glowed in his mind as he watched Axler and the others crouch in the cover of the jungle's undergrowth. Security forces from the clinic were scrambling across the open area and beginning to penetrate the thick greenery.

"Jane, how are you going to get us out?" Axler yelled, even though she was speaking through her internal communications. "They've hemmed us in. We can't get to the T-bird."

Just then Ryan heard the roar of an autocannon and the scream of jet engines as a Thunderbird blew into the space in front of them and mowed down the security forces. The Thunderbird was a huge vehicle, easily twice as large as the helo that had crashed a few minutes earlier. But the T-bird was an LAV, a low-altitude vehicle designed to move below radar. Meant for extended use in hostile territory, it was painted in camouflage greens and blacks and shaped like a bullet that had been flattened lengthwise. It floated on the thrust of six jets that pivoted independently.

And as it flew past, the trees brushing its belly, the autocannon blew the trees to splinters as it tried to close off the sec forces. The noise deafened Ryan, the destruction phenomenal. "Axler," came a voice. Ryan barely heard it through McFaren's audio headphones. "Axler, do you copy?"

"Dhin, is that you?" Axler said. "Where the frag have you been? Thought you'd bought the proverbial vatfarm when the helo went down."

The T-bird banked around for a final sweep of the security forces, which had scattered before its onslaught. "I switched to Plan B as scheduled. I was in the T-bird, rigging the helo by remote control," Dhin said. "But the explosion caused massive feedback in my vehicle control rig, and I lost communications for a minute."

"All right, cut the chat," Axler said, then she turned to Grind and McFaren. "You two ready?"

"Been ready for five minutes now," McFaren said. The human looked pale, barely able to stand as he concentrated on his magic. "I've never seen so much juju tossed about like it was nothing. Luckily, only two of the really powerful mages seem to care about us."

Grind just nodded, then lifted his arms as the T-bird descended, mowing down any remaining trees with its weapons. It took only fifteen or twenty seconds before it settled on a precarious mound of chunky pulp. Grind's metal arms were cold against Ryan's skin as the dwarf carried him up to the sliding side door and into the vehicle.

Then the door slammed shut, and Ryan was thrown against the corrugated metal floor as the T-bird lurched into the air. Grind's metal arms lifted him into a chair that faced away from the near wall, and the dwarf used his third arm to pull the safety harness over Ryan's shoulders, buckling him in as the vehicle accelerated away from the fight. Or at least Ryan assumed that was what it was doing as it swerved and dodged.

"Grind, get to the cupola and man the assault cannon," Axler yelled. "We're not in the clear yet."

But the black dwarf was already climbing into the rear compartment, strapping himself in and plugging his hands into the control panel. "On it, chica," he said.

That brought a quick glare from Axler.

The central chamber of the T-bird was snug, with four chairs along the walls facing in toward cargo tie-downs. Only McFaren sat in the chamber with Ryan. The mage was limp, his body held in the chair only by the straps of his safety harness. Axler was in the back with Grind. Ryan could see Axler's left side through the open compartment door as she sat at her console, and Grind's boots were visible on the

stem of the cupola's high chair. Dhin was in the cockpit that
Ryan assumed was through the small door on his right.

"Incoming missile," came a synthesized voice over the
speakers. "Ares Macrotechnology model CH45ET200A,
Cheetah. Radar guidance with heat-seeking backup."

"We've been painted." Axler's voice.

"Activating stealth mode in two seconds," Dhin said
through the speakers.

"Flare balloon ready," said Axler.

"Mark," said Dhin.

"Flare away. Jamming chaff away."

"Stealth mode engaged. We are running cool."

Ryan felt the T-bird slow, and it immediately grew
warmer inside the compartment. Then an explosion broke his
ears and rocked the T-bird around him. The straps dug into
his shoulders as the vehicle shook, but it was all over in a
few seconds and everything seemed to be intact.

"Yes!" cried Grind. "Dodged that fragger."

"Nice flying, Dhin," Axler said.

"They seem to be letting us go," Dhin said. "For the
moment anyway."

The speakers filled with a new voice, one Ryan thought he
recognized, "We won't give them the time to send aircraft.
Fly straight to the Canal Zone. I should have new identification for you within the hour."

"Copy that, Jane-in-the-box."

"How's the cargo?"

Axler looked up from her console and glanced through the
open compartment door to survey Ryan. "Alive, but he's
been through some major drek, Jane. He's not himself. I had
to dose him and carry him out."

There was a pause. Then, "I was afraid of that," Jane said.
"I'll get a doc ready to scan him when you get in."

"Copy, we'll keep him safe."

The T-bird ran steady and smooth now. And after a few
minutes of silence, Axler and Grind returned to sit in the
central compartment with Ryan and McFaren. McFaren sat
up, said, "We're being followed in the astral. I sent some
spirits to slow them down, but it might be a problem." And
without waiting for a response, he fell asleep.

Axler took the chair next to Ryan and pulled the derm

patch from Ryan's neck. "You should be able to move in a few minutes," she said. Then she removed some handcuffs from a black nylon bag on the wall, and she anchored his wrists and ankles to the chair.

Grind watched her, a pained expression on his ruggedly wrinkled face. "Is that really wise—"

A look from Axler stopped him. "Why didn't you want to come with us?" she asked.

Ryan found that he could move his mouth. "You know me?" he said.

Axler's hard shell softened slightly. "Yes," she said.

"How?"

"We've pulled some runs together. You don't remember?"

Ryan avoided answering that question. He didn't want to reveal any more than he had to. "What were you rescuing me from?" he asked.

"That information has not been made completely available to me," Axler said. "Jane only feeds us what we need to know. Better for us, better for her, I guess." Axler gave a little laugh and a smile settled into the hard lines on her face. "All I do know is that you were working undercover inside Aztechnology. I always thought you were a crazy fragger.

"A while back," Axler continued, "we extracted a research scientist from Fuchi and transferred him to the Azzies. The name of the target was T.W. Saint John—a genetic expert or some such drek. It was you, though we didn't know it at the time. We transported the body in a fake cryogenic chamber.

"Didn't learn that it was you until Jane filled us in yesterday, just before this run. I've pieced it together like this . . . Somehow you infiltrated Fuchi under the Saint John identity, probably replacing the real researcher. Then Jane hired us to get you out of Fuchi and into Aztechnology, and got the Azzies to pay handsomely for the whole run. She probably knew they already wanted Saint John, and chose that identity, merely tweaking the photos and records to make your cover believable. Jane can do some pretty fragging amazing things in the Matrix.

"Your cover must've been blown somehow, and the Azzies brought you down here to the delta clinic."

"How long ago was this transfer from Fuchi?"

"No more than three months."

"And you knew me before that?"

"Yup. We go *way* back."

Grind gave a harsh laugh at that.

"What?"

"I can't believe you don't remember the night we . . ." Axler gave him a knowing smile.

"Really?" Ryan found her physically attractive, but she seemed too frosty to let anyone inside.

Axler shook her head. "No, just a stupid joke," she said. "But I'm not drekking you about going way back. We've known each other for over five years, which is a long, long time in this biz.

"The first time I met you," Axler went on, "you pulled *me* out of drek up to my Nikons. I was only nineteen. I'd been running for Jane two years already, and I thought I was invincible. But I let my emotions cloud my judgment, stopping to help a young kid.

"I wasn't going to stop at first, but he kept yelling for help. Screaming that he was dying. He was a fragging bystander, an innocent who'd caught a stray round, probably one of mine. The opposition was dead and backup was several minutes away. I had plenty of time to slap a patch on him."

Ryan watched Axler's fists tighten and her teeth clench together. "Or so I thought. The boy was an illusion designed to delay me while their security mage targeted my heart with his laser sight. A fragging Mossberg CMDT shotgun. Would have blown a fist-sized hole in my chest at that range. Except that you'd come with me. You saw the illusion for what it was and nailed the mage with a narco-dart. Saved my hoop."

Axler sighed. "It's funny, before the run I'd argued with Jane about letting you come along. I told her you'd be a liability. That I didn't need your help. McFaren and Dhin and I could handle it. Grind joined the team later.

"I didn't want to trust you, but now I know why you came. You came to evaluate and teach, working for whoever Jane works for. I don't know how or why, but after that run Jane started giving us higher-paying jobs. More dangerous, more intricate. And much more lucrative.

"Sometimes you would come along, and when you did, we all learned. You had combat skills we'd never seen before; you knew about infiltration and undercover work. You're one of the best physical adepts I've ever worked with. You told us you followed the Silent Way, using magic for stealth and spying, disguise and behind-the-scenes operations. I must say it was a pleasure anytime you joined our team."

Ryan had been concentrating on Axler's story. It felt true, but he didn't remember it. The *feeling* was right, but the details were lost in his mind. *So where are my physical adept abilities now that my memory is gone?* he wondered. *And who do I work for? Jane? And what about Thomas Roxborough? Where does he fit in?*

What did they do to me at that clinic?

"I think we can trust him," said McFaren coming out of his "sleep." "He seems more confused than insincere." He winked at Ryan. "I've been watching your aura," he said. Then he turned to Axler. "Also, we've lost the mages who were following. Temporarily at least."

"Good," she said.

McFaren nodded, then his head fell against his chest again, though his breathing was different than before so that Ryan thought he might actually *be* sleeping this time.

"When can I speak with Jane-in-the-box?" Ryan asked.

Axler unlocked Ryan's cuffs. "Soon," she said. "She'll be sending a plane to our base. You're one of the only people I know of who has ever actually met Jane in person."

As if on cue, Jane's voice came over the speakers. "Got the codes," she said. "New identities everyone. Scan and commit to memory. You have approximately twelve minutes."

"Twelve minutes to what?" Ryan asked, directing his question to no one in particular.

"Border crossing," Axler said. "Out of Aztlan and into the Panama Canal Zone."

"Are they going to let us out?"

Axler smiled. "Doubtful," she said. "But Jane has a plan, I'm sure. Don't you, Jane?"

"Always," came the voice from the speakers. "And this one is particularly clever . . . but it's also tricky and complicated. Pay close attention."

15

"We're all here, Mr. Roxborough," came Meyer's voice, cutting into Roxborough's privacy like a sharp weapon. "We can proceed as soon as you're ready."

Roxborough clamped down on his desire and shut down the pleasure program. That would have to wait until after his business was completed. He moved his awareness so that he looked through the board room's surveillance system. He wanted to assess the mood of the participants before activating his simulacrum.

Meyer and Riese sat in their respective chairs. Meyer's long elven face looked only slightly less bored than normal as he leafed through some ancient book on the arcane. *An actual physical book,* Roxborough thought, savoring the musty smell of it through the room's olfactory receptors. *How quaint.*

Unlike Meyer, Riese was edgy. Her petite body held a barely confined rage as she muttered into her pocket computer. Franklinson was also present, looking nervous and frightened despite his huge size. Franklinson was a troll and the clinic's head of security. He wore the traditional tan Aztechnology uniform with the Jaguar Guard shoulder flash that held a tiny silver pin of Quetzalcóatl to denote his rank of major. Franklinson's record was remarkable; Roxborough trusted him implicitly. Roxborough tried to reassure himself that Franklinson's nervousness didn't necessarily imply that Ryan Mercury was completely unrecoverable.

I've seen enough, thought Roxborough. He activated the room's hologenerators and appeared in his seat at the head of the cherrywood table. At the sound of the hologenerators, everyone turned toward his chair. "Good afternoon," he said, as his simulacrum solidified. "We have a crisis, I take it. Franklinson, what is the status?"

"We've lost the infiltrators," the troll said. "And the man they took." Franklinson gave Roxborough an inquisitive stare, which said that he didn't like being kept in the dark about any potentially sensitive situations at a site he was in charge of keeping secure. Roxborough didn't think it was crucial that Franklinson know the exact nature of all the experiments. They had had that discussion one too many times and neither had budged.

"They took a human who is very important to us," Roxborough said. "His name is Ryan Mercury, and he was a spy. It is important that he be caught. I'd like him back alive. What are the chances of picking them up again?"

Franklinson paced around the table. "They escaped in a Saeder-Krupp Phoenix II LAV. Very fast and hard to spot on satellite images, but I think they were making for the Canal Zone border. I can contact the security there and have them double their surveillance coverage. If they try to cross there, I'm sure we'll get them."

"I hope so," said Riese, "because that man represents a huge investment of time and effort. He was nearly ready for—"

"Don't forget money, Miss Riese," Roxborough interrupted. "The bottom line." But that's not what he was really thinking. Mercury was his best hope to get out of the vat. *That body was perfect.*

Riese was still talking. "The loss to the advancement of metahuman science would be devastating if we can't monitor what happens as the treatment runs its course."

Franklinson stopped pacing. "Like I said, there is an excellent chance we'll catch them at the border."

"Good," Roxborough said. Then he turned to face the elf, Meyer. "I know you wanted to abort this subject a long time ago, and I may yet give you that chance. I'd like you to prepare your team for a ritual magic execution. Can you do that?"

A sardonic grin formed on the elf's thin face. "For Mercury?"

Roxborough nodded.

"Yes," Meyer said. "We have the tissue samples. It should only take a few hours to prepare."

Riese jumped in, looking right at Roxborough's simulacrum. "Why would you want to kill him?"

"I don't want Mercury dead, but I can't allow him to escape," Roxborough said, then turned back to Meyer. "If the border patrol fails to intercept our beloved experiment, proceed with the ritual magic execution. I want him back here or dead."

Because, he thought, *I can't take the chance that he'll escape with my personality, my memories.*

My secrets.

16

Inside the Thunderbird, rocketing just above the jungle canopy, Ryan contemplated his past. He seemed to have two distinct histories. One he was beginning to remember. He had been in a different body—a fat, weak body plagued by fatigue. Still, he'd been a powerful man. Respected and rich. Important, until a terrible disease had tried to strike him down.

The other past was a mystery that he had no recollection of. These people had known him: Axler, Grind, Jane-in-the-box, and the others. He had been a warrior of some sort. Perhaps a thief. Certainly a dangerous person with a questionable sense of morality.

Random memories had been coming to him from his Roxborough past. Disjointed and without context. In one, he looked at the face of an elf slitch . . . What was her name? She wore a business suit, perfectly pressed, and her face was as hard as chiseled diamond. Immutable. She had short-clipped blonde hair and was an excellent executive. He respected her for that.

Sheila Blatavska. The name jumped into his head. CEO of the Atlantean Foundation—an organization that was more extensive and wielded far more power than it had a right to. It was dedicated to the rediscovery of lost civilizations like Atlantis, and in the course of its mission had discovered a number of ancient, and supposedly very powerful, magical items. According to his sources, Blatavska had major backing from elves of both the Tirs, and possibly from some dragons.

In the memory, she said, "I would like you to consider this trade. A few of the items in our inventory may be useful to your . . . predicament."

"And in exchange," he said, "you want permission to conduct archaeological digs in the two specified locations?"

A tight smile crossed her face. "I had hoped you might be able to make your cohorts reconsider my request to participate in the San Marcos dig as well."

"I'm sorry, I can't do that. My influence in that regard is minimal."

"But you control a large share of—"

"You seem to have an exaggerated view of my influence." Roxborough smiled. "Anyhow, forget about the San Marcos site. It's not available."

The elf merely nodded.

Roxborough continued, "I will send my head mage, James Meyer, to inspect these items you spoke of, and meanwhile, I will get you the digging rights for the other two locations. Deal?"

"There is another possibility," she said.

"Yes?"

"Have your mages perfected the orichalcum tracing rituals?"

"Perhaps," Roxborough said. "Why?"

"Well, to be frank," she said, "we haven't worked out all of the problems and were hoping to use the rituals soon."

"What for?"

"Ah, my dear Mr. Roxborough," Blatavsky said, giving him a smile. "Do I detect interest?"

"What do you want the rituals for?"

"Dunkelzahn has been purchasing vast quantities of orichalcum through various fronts, and we suspect he is in the process of making something very powerful."

"And you want it." It was not a question.

"Of course," she said. "We'd like your help with the rituals . . . if your mages really can do the tracing."

"What do you offer in exchange?"

"We will show your mages how to perfect the spirit transfer that you so desperately crave."

The memory dissipated in Ryan's mind. When had that been? he wondered. How long ago? It frustrated him that he had no context for it.

Now, inside the rumbling shell of the Thunderbird, he took a deep breath. The tension of Axler and the team was high, and that mood had infected Ryan. One missile hit, and they would all be indistinguishable from the shrapnel.

"Border guard is requesting security clearance codes," Axler said. "Put-up-or-shut-up time."

"Transmitting the codes now," came Dhin's voice. "Let's hope Jane comes through again."

"How're we hoping to get past their security?" Ryan asked.

"The codes were stolen from one of Aztechnology's own T-birds," Axler said. "Top level, according to Jane, and beyond question. I just hope they don't know that they've been copped."

"It's going to be a real short trip if they do," said Grind.

McFaren slept, or looked as though he was sleeping. Ryan knew that he could be projecting into the astral plane, watching for spirits or mages. The T-bird banked right and slowed a little.

"We're three klicks from the Canal Zone," Dhin said. "I'm bringing us over nice and easy, like Jane said."

"The codes?" asked Grind. "Did they accept the codes?"

"No data yet."

"Isn't it taking too long?" Grind said, his voice edged with anxiety. "They should've cleared us by now."

"Stay on course, Dhin," came Axler. "Don't stray until you see some offensive enemy activity."

"Copy," Dhin said. "Holding course."

"But—"

"Codes confirmed," came Axler. "Repeat, I've just got a routine confirmation."

Dhin came on. "Copy and second that. We're clear for exit from Aztlan."

"I don't like it. Too much delay," said Grind.

Jane-in-the-box's voice came on. "Neither do I. Stay alert, chummers. This could be an ambush of some kind."

"Copy," said Axler. "Staying sharp. Full radar sweep."

"Incoming fighters!" came Dhin's voice at full volume. "Repeat, incoming bogeys. We have company."

"Fragging ambush is right!" yelled Grind. "There are four Azzie warbirds vectoring in."

Axler interrupted, "They'll try to take us down on this side

of the border. So as not to risk international war in the Canal
Zone."

Jane's voice filled the cabin. "Plan Beta," she said.
"Immediately. Go to Plan Beta."

"Acknowledged," said Axler.

"Copy." That was Dhin's voice.

Ryan was thrown into the hard foam of his chair as the
T-bird banked abruptly right and opened up to full throttle.
Jets screamed as they angled south toward the Gulf of
Panama. He pushed himself upright in the chair. "Anything I
can do to help?" he asked.

"Can you operate a minigun?" came Dhin's voice over the
speakers.

"Not sure," Ryan said. "I think so."

"Then get back with Axler and Grind. Sit in the cupola and
fire at the enemy when they come close enough."

Ryan moved into the rear compartment, which was
slightly smaller than the central chamber and filled with
more equipment for monitoring adversaries. Axler sat at a
console, keeping track of the defensive weaponry while
Grind sat on a tall seat, looking out through the clear
macroplast of the assault cannon's cupola.

The minigun's cupola was just aft from there. Ryan moved
up the short ladder and settled into the seat as though he'd
been born for the task. And as he looked at the controls, he
discovered that he did know how to operate the gun. Instinctively he put his hands and forearms into the long, power-
assisted reticulated metal gloves and practiced swinging the
minigun's barrel around.

"Don't get comfortable, Ryan," Axler said. "We bail in
two minutes."

"If we're still alive," said Grind.

"Right."

Ryan caught the radar tactical superimposed on the
head's-up display and slued the big gun barrel around toward
one of the incoming jets. They came fast, from near the
border. Gaining on the T-bird, which was going full out
toward the southern coast of the narrow isthmus. Ryan
wasn't sure what Plan Beta was, but one thing was clear; the
bogeys would catch up with the T-bird before it reached the

coast. And even if they did get to the bay first, they'd be easy to target over the water.

"One minute, thirty seconds to bail," came Axler's voice.

An alarm siren sounded. "We've been painted," said Dhin. "Hold on!"

The T-bird cut left suddenly, then dove into a narrow ravine in an effort to confuse the jet's missile lock. But the T-bird wasn't built to outrun a fighter; it was slower and less maneuverable. Their only chance was to stay close to the ground and hope that the trees and hills would cover them.

Ryan strafed one of the jets as it flew by when Dhin abruptly decelerated. The minigun roared, a staccato barrage of sound as the heavy slugs flew. The tracer rounds formed a solid white line to show the path of the bullets. Then the jet was gone, and Ryan knew he had missed. It had all been way too quick.

"Sixty seconds to bail," Axler said.

"Launch!" cried Dhin. "We've got heat coming up our hoops."

"Can you hold it off until we reach—?"

Jane came on. "I've contacted the rebel mercenaries," she said. "They're in position and will wait three minutes before scattering."

Dhin was yelling now. "That missile is going to fry us in fifteen seconds unless Axler can take it out or confuse it."

"I'm on it. I'm on it."

The ravine around them gave way to low hills covered by jungle. In a minute they'd be out over the water. Technically out of Aztlan. If they survived the missile hit.

"Chaff away now," Axler said.

Dhin pulled the T-bird into a short climb, and Ryan braced for impact. None came. But he didn't hear any explosion. "Blew past us," Dhin said. "Chaff confused its radar."

"Yes!" said Ryan. He found himself enjoying this.

"Don't celebrate!" Dhin said. "It's coming back around, and two more just locked on."

"Launch detected," came the computer.

"Bail in ten seconds," said Axler, standing up from her console to step into the central compartment and open the side door. Wind rushed in, and the scream of the T-bird's jets rasped in Ryan's head.

Grind and McFaren joined her, ready to jump. "Move, Ryan, move," Grind said. "We've only got one chance at this."

Ryan climbed down the minigun cupola and stepped up to the open side door. The jungle sped by just beneath them, the top of the canopy nearly brushing the base of the T-bird. The T-bird slowed suddenly, hovered for a second, then dropped. Ryan's stomach lurched as the big machine fell precipitately, down into a small clearing in the jungle that had been covered with camouflage netting.

"Now, Ryan, jump!"

Ryan followed the others out the side door, and Dhin came close behind them. Throwing himself out head first. Falling, falling. An odd feeling of déjà vu crept over Ryan as he fell, as he flipped slowly in the air.

Falling, he saw the T-bird's huge jets spew fire. The machine lifted suddenly and accelerated into the sky, trying to continue its course southward. It didn't even reach the edge of the clearing before three missiles impacted with the reinforced steel frame, ripping it open. Blowing it into flaming hunks of red-hot metal.

Gone in an instant of violent chemicals. Vaporized.

The explosion's fireball singed Ryan's hair as he tucked himself into a ball. Shrapnel and sparks rained down around him. He landed in a huge camouflaged net, suspended from the trees at the edge of the clearing. The landing wasn't soft, but he was no worse for it. No bruises, no scrapes.

When he rolled out onto the jungle floor, he saw that he and the others were surrounded by men and women in jungle camouflage. Mercenaries, Ryan guessed. The rebels that Jane had contacted. One of the mercs draped a poncho over Ryan's shoulders to hide him, and they were off through the jungle.

As they walked, Ryan catalogued their guides. He guessed there were no more than fifteen mercs, most of them unaided by cybernetics or magic, but all well-trained in combat and field techniques. Axler told Ryan that these mercenaries worked with smugglers who brought in contraband from ships in the Canal region, across the border for eventual sale in Tenochtitlán. They were just as happy smuggling live contraband the other direction for some extra pesos.

Ryan heard the jets fly over once or twice as they hiked the kilometer to the border, but he couldn't see the aircraft through the jungle canopy, and he suspected the jet riggers would have just as hard a time spotting the camouflaged mercs. The jungle canopy was just too dense. They slowed to a snail's pace as the undergrowth thickened up ahead, and as Ryan watched, the people ahead of him simply disappeared through some sort of veil. Vanished into the shadows.

Then Ryan too passed through the illusion. On the other side was a steeply sloping ravine covered over with vines and trees and undergrowth. It would be nearly impossible to see even without the magical illusion. The ravine cut down about twenty meters, the path at its base surprisingly level and well worn. Until it became a paved passageway. Concrete and cinderblock formed walls on either side and finally they entered a tunnel.

There was a guard at the tunnel entrance who detained them momentarily, speaking with one of the mercenaries before allowing them though. The underground passageway got them across the border and into the Panama Canal Zone. Out of Aztlan.

Axler stayed close to Ryan during the journey. She seemed to be in good spirits as the mercs gave them new clothing to change into—California navy uniforms. They would be disguised as personnel operating off the *Exeter* helicopter carrier. Axler explained that California Free State had no navy to speak of, but its ships had been kept in use by the government and could be "rented" by the highest bidder. In this case, that meant Jane.

Their journey on to the *Exeter* went without a glitch. The mercenaries left them at a narrow beach on the south coast, where a small helicopter picked them up and flew them out over the water. Ryan was exhausted, but he felt almost safe again, though he didn't know why he should. The flight to the deck of the ship was brief, and as he stepped out of the helicopter, he was surprised to be greeted by one of the officers.

She was human, standing nearly as tall as Ryan. Broad shoulders and black skin. Her hair was cut utilitarian short. "Are you Quicksilver?" she asked.

He paused for a second, considering. Then he said, "Yes, I think so."

"Telecom for you," she said. "Urgent from Nadja Daviar."

"Thank you," he said, but he was wondering, *Who is Nadja Daviar?*

"You can take it below decks," she said. "This way."

Ryan followed her, with Axler and the others behind. He felt safe for the first time in a long time. He hadn't really felt safe in the clinic, though he was still not sure why. She led him down into the ship, through gray metal corridors, past gray metal rooms, until she stopped at a gray metal door.

"In here, Mr. Mercury," she said.

He stepped into the room, which was tiny, with only a narrow bunk and a fold-away tabletop. There was a telecom screen built into a wall, however. He touched the screen to activate it.

A woman's image appeared. Elven, with pale skin and black hair. She was beautiful and commanding. Deep green eyes sparkled under the sharp lines of her black brow. "Ryan," she said. "I've been worried about you, even though we agreed I'm not supposed to do that sort of thing." She smiled. "Are you all right?"

Ryan staggered back. She knew him intimately, that much was obvious. But he didn't remember her. There might be something familiar about her, but as much as he tried to remember, he came up blank. *What had their relationship been?* He didn't know how he was supposed to feel about her. *Had they been friends? Lovers?* He didn't know.

What he felt for her now was nothing. A void of emotion.

He could tell, too, that she would be hurt if she knew the indifference he felt toward her. And it scared him that he felt pleasure in withholding his feelings from her. It seemed to be true that the Ryan Mercury she knew would not lie to her.

But the new Ryan Mercury understood things in a different way. The new Ryan Mercury—the man with two pasts—knew that lying now might give him an edge in the future. This woman's concern for him, and his feigned interest in her, might just be the perfect way to manipulate her.

17

In front of Thomas Roxborough stood a boy of Mayan descent. Beautiful, golden brown skin, smooth and soft and without blemish. His large eyes were the color of café au lait, and his thick black hair had been cut short about his ears. His name was Alberto, and he was a Matrix creation from Roxborough's fantasies.

He was a reflection in Roxborough's mind, a virtual sculpture of his desires. Alberto was young and robust and muscled in all the right places. A boy who might, if he were real, grow up to have a body like that of Ryan Mercury.

Roxborough allowed himself a moment of pleasure in the thought, and was about to indulge his fantasy when he was interrupted by a call from Franklinson. Roxborough sighed; the boy would have to wait. He touched the boy's lips with his finger. "Pause," he said, and the boy's virtual presence froze. He would stay that way until Roxborough returned.

Roxborough looked in on Franklinson, his huge, ugly body sitting in the security room, surrounded by screens. A closed-circuit rigger was jacked into the console next to the troll. "Yes," Roxborough said, activating his screen icon.

"Sir," said Franklinson as he sat upright in the chair, "I believe we have prevented your spy from escaping Aztlan territory, but he is dead."

"Tell me about it."

"Four of our fighters intercepted them near the Panama Canal Zone border and shot them down. Their craft sustained massive damage when it impacted with the ground and exploded. We could find no survivors."

"Did you find the body?

"I'm afraid not. Everything was blown apart and burned

beyond recognition. We might recover some bone fragments. I'll let you know."

"Has a mage assensed the wreckage?"

"Yes, but the results are inconclusive, as are most things magical." Franklinson was not known for his trust of shamans and mages.

Roxborough frowned. "It is possible, then, that Mercury and the others escaped. Perhaps they weren't aboard when the T-bird exploded."

Franklinson's face remained impassive. "Possible," he said. "But not likely."

"Still, I will have Meyer continue his ritual magic, if only to determine whether Mercury is alive or not."

"Yes, sir," the troll said. He did not look happy.

Roxborough wanted to return to his encounter with the boy, Alberto, but he couldn't just yet. He activated the cameras in the sub-basement ritual room. Dim blue and violet light shone on the walls. Tall candles of black and red wax burned around the perimeter of a large ritual magic circle, their flames filling the chamber with the scent of anise. The circle itself had been created with chicken blood from fresh sacrifices, dripped from a cured goat stomach that Meyer used for all his ritual circles.

Meyer and two others sat cross-legged inside the circle, each one at an apex of an equilateral triangle that had been drawn in black ink on the duracrete floor. Roxborough did not want to interrupt, but Meyer must have noticed the cameras coming on because he addressed Roxborough.

The elf looked up at one of the cameras. "We're just about to begin the ritual," he said. "Unless you have news that will allow us to forgo this and get on with our real work."

"I'm sorry," said Roxborough. "Franklinson is not one hundred percent sure that Mercury is dead. I need certainty."

Meyer nodded. "You'll get it. If Mercury is alive in the world, we'll find him. If we do, we'll destroy him."

"Good, good," said Roxborough. "That's what I wanted to hear."

"Then we will begin." Meyer turned to speak with the others and soon they were lost in a trance-like state. Roxborough watched for a minute, then left them alone. Ritual magic wasn't much to see, unless you could look into astral space. But it was quite effective.

It was with that thought in his head, the sensation of completion that came with a job well done, that Roxborough returned to his fantasy. To Alberto and his lovely gold-brown skin. Roxborough touched the boy's naked body, making him come alive and smile as he looked up with large, dark eyes.

"Now," Roxborough said to the boy, "shall we continue?"

18

In the small cabin on the *Exeter,* Ryan looked at the beautiful elven face on the telecom screen. Nadja Daviar. The gray metal room was an oppressive monochrome around him. "I'm just a little disoriented," he said. "It's been a rough day."

"Well, it's not over yet," she said. "You must get here as fast as possible. Jane's team will fly you to Lima, where you'll all catch a suborbital to Seattle. There, Jane's group will take you to their compound, and I'll have transportation waiting for you there."

And as she spoke, a spark of recognition flared inside Ryan. Something about her inflection or the way the corner of her mouth moved. The one endearing flaw in her otherwise perfect body. He couldn't quite pin down what it was.

"The whole trip shouldn't take more than four or five hours," she said. "I'll see you tonight."

"Good."

"Yeah, I have to make sure that all this nuyen I'm spending to get you out hasn't gone to waste. Nothing personal."

"Of course not," Ryan said. Nadja seemed guarded about something. *Is she nervous about seeing me?* he thought. *Perhaps.*

"See you later then," she said, but did not disconnect.

"Goodbye, Nadja," said Ryan, then cut the line.

Axler stepped in next to Ryan. "We've got to roll," she said. "Now." And she rushed him back up top and into a waiting helo—a big, double-rotored kind that flew them south across the water toward Peru.

The next four hours went exactly as Nadja had described. A suborbital jet awaited them on the tarmac when they landed in Lima. The logo emblazoned on the fuselage proclaimed it to be owned by Gavilan Industries, and they were the only passengers. Ryan wondered how Nadja or Jane had arranged that.

The flight to Seattle passed quickly. Ryan thought about Father—Roxborough's father actually. He remembered the large man, his red beard and balding pate. Father had been a moderately successful entrepreneur, and young Thomas Roxborough rarely saw him while his mother was alive. It was only after she'd died in a terrorist bombing in London that Father had taken an interest in shaping his son's life.

Ryan remembered one time when Father had promised to take him to an Arsenal football match at Highbury Stadium. Little Tommy Roxborough had been looking forward to seeing his favorite team play. A real live match! He'd been waiting for weeks in anticipation. Father said all he had to do was complete his programming homework, which he did brilliantly.

But something had come up at Father's work, an important meeting with the execs of another corp, Ryan couldn't remember which, and the promised match passed without Roxborough. Father had told him later that his meeting had made them over a million nuyen. Business, Father had said, was always more important.

It wasn't until years later that Roxborough truly understood what he had meant. Roxborough had been in the final stages of foreclosing on Tennessee Nitro Technologies—a company that owed him a sizable chunk of nuyen—when he learned that Father was in the hospital, dying of VITAS— Virally Induced Toxic Allergy Syndrome. Roxborough couldn't pass up his opportunity to destroy the company and put millions into his account. Timing was crucial.

He decided to postpone his visit to Father in the hospital.

Father died before he made his visit. But Roxborough was sure Father understood, even in those final moments, that his son had his priorities straight. Roxborough knew Father would be proud. He threw a fantastic funeral for Father. All the important people came.

Now, the suborbital shuttle was landing in Seattle. Ryan stretched and took a deep breath, trying to shake off the eerie feeling that draped over his body like a blanket of shivers.

The postures of Axler, Grind, McFaren, and Dhin relaxed

somewhat after they stepped off the suborbital and onto the
concrete of SeaTac airport. This was close to their home turf.
They obviously felt much more safe and secure here, though
as Ryan looked around, he got the sense that Seattle could be
extremely dangerous.

A small jet took them to the compound, which Axler
called Assets, Incorporated. It was a small airstrip in Salish
Shidhe, the Indian nation that covered land previously
known as Washington, Idaho, and British Colombia. Assets,
Inc. lay hidden in the mountains above Hells Canyon, and
Ryan gathered that it served as Axler and Company's base of
operations.

The compound was bounded on one side by a sheer rock
face that stretched up into the sky, and on the other by a
precipice—a steep cliff face that fell into the canyon, over a
kilometer to the bottom where the Snake River wound its
way, a narrow, green ribbon in the distance below. The
perimeter of Assets, Inc. was fenced, and there was a corrugated steel warehouse of some sort, but Ryan didn't get time
to inspect either. He was ushered straight into another jet,
larger and more luxurious this time, complete with its own
pilot and security guards.

Axler had grown even colder toward him as their mission
had come to an end. Jane had paid them through a deposit in
their Zurich Orbital account, and Axler was all business.
Grind and McFaren shook Ryan's hand just before he
stepped aboard, but Axler simply said, "Good luck," in her
ultra-chill way, as if from a great emotional distance. Then
she'd turned her back on him.

Biz completed. No attachments desired.

The security guards took position in the rear of the jet and
Ryan was left alone in the plush cabin. Luxury and loneliness enveloping him.

Still there was some hope as the jet flew him out. They
were taking him to meet Nadja, the woman who might have
some answers about his past. A woman who he knew, but
didn't remember. What was his relationship with her? He'd
find out soon enough.

They flew north, and Ryan learned that they were going to
Dunkelzahn's lair in Lake Louise—a dragon's lair. The
rigger pilot knew him. Her name was Barb—a sleek-looking

elf with brown locks that hung to her nicely shaped behind. She told him that he worked with Black Angel and Dunkelzahn, that he was "jacked in" with the higher-ups.

So I work for a fragging dragon, he thought. *It's all becoming perfectly clear . . . Not!*

Ryan finally decided just to see what happened. It would all come back when he was least expecting it. He sat back in his seat and tried to relax by looking out the window at the passing landscape. The peaks of the Canadian Rocky Mountains stood majestic and raw, speaking to Ryan in a primal language as he gazed out the window. The ancient stone at once forbidding and enticing.

The plane landed on a short airstrip built on a high plain between two peaks. The sun reflected a blinding white off the snow-covered glaciers; the silver-blue glass buildings lower on the slope of the mountains sparkled like cut gems. It was awe-inspiring. Stark and beautiful.

She stood on the cold runway waiting for him to disembark. She was surrounded by guards, her black hair blowing wildly in the chill wind. He wrapped the coat they'd given him tighter around his body and stepped down the short staircase to meet her. Up close, he sensed that she was a very powerful woman. Confidence and poise radiated from her presence. From the sureness of her stance. The way she stood was inviting in a conspiratorial way, yet held a solid immutability. She would listen, but *she* would make the final decisions.

As Ryan set foot in front of her, that manner all but melted. She stood slightly taller, but her frame was insubstantial compared to his. She looked down at him with wet eyes. Then she smiled. Broad and genuine. He could see the desire in her expression, smell it on her. And he wasn't surprised when he felt a reciprocal desire for her. She was extremely attractive.

"You've changed," she said.

Ryan nodded. "Yes. I can't remember much about who I was."

"I'm so sorry, Ryan." And as she reached to put her arms around him, pulling him into a tight embrace he realized he'd been longing for, he felt a spark of familiarity. The details of the moment coalesced into a whole, the many tiny

individualities coming together to remind him of a time
before.

They had known each other; they had embraced like this
before. But it had been a parting embrace, and they had both
been coldly resolved to accept it. The smell of her, so close
to him now, brought the emotions cascading back, confusing
and disconnected from memory.

An image came into his mind of the sun, peeking over the
flat, cobalt blue surface of the ocean. The memory. The sky
was a watercolor of yellow and pink from the dawn. The air
was warm, the tiny cove empty as Ryan stood and stared out
across the ocean.

She had come up behind him, putting her arms under his,
wrapping them around his chest. Nuzzling him with her nose
against the side of his neck. A shiver passed through him, an
electric shock from her touch. But already he was clamping
down on his emotions. Already he was forming the inner
fortress that was necessary for his continued survival, his
continued devotion to Dunkelzahn.

I must be an island, he told himself.

He didn't look at her. "Black Angel called," he said. "I've
got a mission."

Her hands went slack.

"I'm sorry," he sad. "I don't . . ."

Her voice was flat, almost a monotone whisper. "I thought
we had two weeks," she said.

"Yes, but—"

Her voice rising as she spoke. "They promised us two
fragging weeks!" She let go, and he turned finally.

Her arms were crossed in front of her chest, over the loose
cotton robe that was blowing in the morning breeze. Her
hair, recently disheveled from sleep, flying about her. The
heat of her anger flushing her white skin.

She is the most beautiful thing in the world, he thought.
But I cannot let myself love her.

I will not!

She saw what he was thinking. They had talked about this;
they had been worried that this might happen. He wanted to
go to her now and hold her, more than anything he had ever
wanted to do for himself. But he didn't work for himself. He

worked for Dunkelzahn, and love did not fit in with that work. It got in the way.

On an assignment, he couldn't be responsible for anyone besides himself. He didn't want anyone to care about him; he just wanted to complete his mission. That was all that mattered. That was everything.

"When do you leave?" she asked.

"Ten o'clock."

"Then you'd better get packed," she said. "Join me in the café if you have time for breakfast." Then she turned and walked away in silence.

Now on the airstrip, Ryan held her tightly. He didn't want to release her; he clutched her close, his only tie to a past that seemed to be his own. He put his head in the hollow of her neck, and was surprised to find himself shaking from the power of holding her.

Too soon, she released him. "We must hurry," she said. She took his arm and escorted him across the tarmac to a low concrete building. "We've got to get you into the lair's protective circle. I suspect they'll try to find you by ritual magic. The lair should hide you from them."

Ryan nodded, and allowed himself to be led. The circle of guards closed ranks around them as they approached, then entered the steel doors of the building, moving through blue-tiled hallways and taking an elevator down into the mountain. Nadja submitted to a retinal scan in order to allow the elevator access to the lowest level.

And when the elevator came to a stop, deep inside the mountain, when the double doors opened, a tall elven woman waited in the center of a hewn stone corridor. Her skin was dark brown in stark contrast to her white hair, which she had pulled back into a tight ponytail so that it followed the sharp line of her skull. She smiled broadly when she saw Ryan, obvious relief on her face.

"Quicksilver," she said. "Good to see you back in one piece."

Ryan couldn't help but smile. "It's good to be back," he said. "I think."

She puzzled over that for a second. Then she went on, "Dunkelzahn left some instructions for you," she said. "I've put them inside the chamber. Let me know if I can help."

Nadja pulled on Ryan's arm. "We've got to go," she said. "Their mages could get to you even here."

He followed Nadja down the corridor and into a huge vaulted chamber. A silver statue of a dragon stood at the very center. "We're going to seal you in here," she said. "The walls are layered with a fine weave of enchanted orichalcum and a layer of elemental earth. Plus who knows what protections Dunkelzahn had."

"Where is Dunkelzahn?"

Nadja stopped abruptly and faced him. "You don't know?"

"Know what?"

She paused; whatever she was about to say was serious. "Dunkelzahn is dead."

"What?" Ryan was surprised. How could a great dragon be dead?

"He was killed."

Ryan knew the news should have done more than surprise him; it should have shocked him. It should have reached into the very core of his spirit and shattered it. Should have devastated him. He knew this by Nadja's delivery, by the myriad clues he'd picked up about his relationship to this creature—Dunkelzahn. He and the dragon had some sort of special connection, a bond that went beyond normal social interaction. He had loved Dunkelzahn.

But now, he felt nothing at the news of the dragon's demise. He did not feel remorse or anguish. He did not feel relief or joy or sadness.

He did not *feel* at all.

"An explosion in Washington . . ." Nadja trailed off. "Four days ago, just after the inauguration. I can give you the details later. Plus, I'd like to discuss the phone conversation you had with him just before he left the party."

"I don't remember it," Ryan said.

"There might be some things we can do to help you with that," she said. "But now I think we should seal up the chamber. You'll be safe in here."

"When will I be able to come out?"

"When our mages have detected a ritual sending. I have to return to Washington tomorrow for the reading of Dunkelzahn's Will. If your mission parameters allow it, maybe you'd like to come with me for a few days?"

"I think I'd like that," he said, and he wasn't at all surprised to find that he spoke the words in all sincerity.

She smiled. "Goodbye for now, then." She leaned to hug him, but he pulled her into a more intimate embrace, moving his face close to hers. She turned to look into his eyes, her lips brushing across his cheek. He kissed her, pressing his lips against hers. She fell into it willingly, parting her mouth slightly. Relishing the momentary intimacy.

The moment passed too quickly, and Nadja pulled away, trying to maintain her air of dignity and control with the guards looking on. Ryan got the feeling that this public display was uncharacteristic of his past self. Then she was gone, and the thick stone door swung closed, filling the large opening with a grinding crash. He was sealed inside.

Ryan concentrated to focus himself. He felt he was on the verge of remembering who he was, on the edge of beginning the long slide into himself. Maybe Dunkelzahn's last message to him would provide the final push. The dragon had obviously been important to him.

Ryan walked to the center of the chamber and stood next to the dragon sculpture. It was bright silver and looked almost liquid in the chamber's light. Nearly Ryan's size, it stood on its hind legs, head extended toward the ceiling, mouth open as if to breathe fire, tail arcing left behind it. At first Ryan thought it was a statue of Dunkelzahn, but up close, he realized that it couldn't be. Unlike Dunkelzahn, the dragon in the sculpture had no forelegs, only wings.

Ryan instinctively reached up to touch the statue. The metal felt surprisingly warm, and as his hand brushed the surface, a form flickered into existence, a spirit trapped inside the sculpture. The shining platinum surface rippled from the spirit's motions, almost seeming to move the statue.

"Ryanthusar," came the spirit's deep voice. It was a tone and tenor that Ryan found disturbing. Like a ghost's voice. "Listen carefully, my servant. This next mission is the most important I have ever entrusted to you . . ."

19

Lucero stood on the open air balcony, high up the side of the San Marcos *teocalli*. The stone under her feet radiated warmth from the day's heat. The night air hung still and hot even this late. Atop the hill directly across from her, Lucero caught the silhouette of the old amusement park tower, stabbing up into the sky like a stiletto dipped in black blood. Directly below it was the spring-fed lake; it glowed a blue-green from the submerged floodlights. In the center of the lights was a cut stone of obsidian black, and around that were crews in scuba gear with excavating machinery.

Lucero felt the power of the magic coming from the lake. It beat around her like a living drum. Whatever Señor Oscuro was doing there must be creating some powerful juju. Lucero hadn't lost all of her magic, but enough of it was gone that she rarely assensed things without great difficulty.

The spring site emanated power; it touched her and beckoned to her. It brought her hope that she might wield the mana again. That she might be as she once was, a manipulator of life energy. A mage.

If only I had another chance, she thought. *I would not accept the taint. The addiction to blood magic. The desperate need that stains my soul.*

Two temple servants came to her side, and bade her follow them. Her presence was required for another exposure. She followed them into the sanctuary, paying her silent respects to Quetzalcóatl as she passed the sculpture of him. A small group of young adepts and trainees stood in sacrificial robes, entranced by Oscuro, who waited for Lucero at the altar. They did not know that they were to be sacrificed. Or perhaps they did know and were eager to give up their life energy for the god they loved so dearly.

A thin, tight smile graced Señor Oscuro's face, barely discernible beneath his black mustache and beard. He was hopeful; his eyes showed intense eagerness to proceed with the ritual. He held out a strong white hand for her, and as she approached, she focused on that hand, on the individual black hairs that protruded from the back of his fingers. Like tiny snakes; she imagined them writhing over his skin, all of his hair transformed into living flagella.

The image passed, and Lucero climbed up onto the altar, the chill of the stone passing through the thin cotton cloth beneath her. She lay completely still as Señor Oscuro opened her robe, spreading the sides of it so that the front of her body was naked. She did not look down at her own flesh, the hideousness of the scarred skin. She focused her gaze on Quetzalcóatl, on the god's brightly colored feathers shimmering in the yellow light. He seemed almost indifferent to her inside the statue.

Oscuro started his spell, summoning the first adept. Holding the girl's head at the proper angle to give the knife easy access to her throat. Lucero saw the cut, the ceremonial obsidian blade opening the girl's neck, the welling of her blood. It pooled on Lucero's stomach, filling the room with the iron tang, before Oscuro dropped the dead girl and spread her blood over Lucero. Over the scarred flesh of her breasts, stomach, and thighs.

The liquid was warm and sticky for a second. Then Lucero lost consciousness and was flying through the astral. Crossing over the threshold to the metaplanes, past the guardian blood spirit. On her way to the place of light and song.

She came to a stop in the place. She knew that she stood on the hard stone of an unfinished bridge, but she could not see her feet. The light was so bright and white that she could see nothing else. And the music, the song of the woman whose name she did not know, was beautiful, clear, and crystalline in its pitch, exact in timbre. Lucero loved that voice.

The dark stain of her blood tie was the only blackness there. And as Lucero stood, basking in the ocean of light and sound, the stain began to spread again. Like last time, it welled forth from Lucero's heart, a black ooze that darkened the space immediately around her. It grew until a ragged shell had formed, a tattered swatch of bloody cloth on white linen.

Suddenly, Lucero felt a surge of power so immeasurable that she could not fathom it. Oscuro had formed the connection to the submerged obsidian stone. The Locus, they called it. The extra power was helping her darkness grow, making her thirst for the blood magic again. Lucero did not care, as long as she could stay and listen to the voice. But the voice was growing more and more distant as the power grew, the connection to the Locus.

As the darkness around her gained strength, Lucero became aware of the precipice, of the huge crevasse between the narrow outcropping where she stood and the other side, a wall of stone in the distance. And she felt the presence of creatures, of nightmare entities with frightening power, held barely in check by the strength of the song. They wanted to come across, she knew. They wanted it more than anything, and they would stop at nothing to accomplish that. Her presence made them happy.

Then, as suddenly as the first time, the dark stain was washed away in a flood of light. Her power could not hold out against the sheer impenetrable beauty of that voice, of the song that resonated deep inside Lucero. Touching a chord, a harmonic thrum through the core of her spirit.

Throwing her back into the physical world.

Lucero woke on the altar, her naked body slick with blood from the sacrificed adolescents, the adepts and trainees who had given their life energy so that she could stay in the place longer.

Oscuro's face hung above her, hair and beard as black as soot, eyes like chips of coal in his head. But he smiled down at her, flashing white teeth. "Well done again," he said. "The Locus helped, but it is still too weak. Next time we will assemble the Gestalt."

Lucero nodded her understanding, and sat up. Oscuro wrapped a clean white sheet around her. She had never felt better. Energy pulsed through her body, making her ecstatic. Like fire in her veins.

Power. Close to what she had felt when she'd been part

of the Gestalt. It was enough to make her forget that she hated her addiction. That she abhorred the stain on her soul. She climbed down from the altar, and made her way out of the sanctuary and to her chamber so that she could wash herself. The rush inside her would fade, she knew, and so she enjoyed the sweet ecstasy of it, the pure pleasure of invincibility.

But through the burning ambrosia of her high, she felt a twinge of yearning. A desire that was growing stronger and stronger. It was the desire to return to the place of light and song. To simply listen to the beautiful music. She would do anything to stay there forever.

Anything.

20

Roxborough slept, dreams of walking through the clinic's hallways fluttering in his mind. He was physical in the dream. Inside a real body, alive in the world of atoms and molecules. Of flesh and steel.

Sometimes, when he dreamed, his mind moved through the clinic's computer system, like sleepwalking. Murmurs and fragments of sentences would come from the speakers throughout the clinic. His face would fade into the trideo and telecom screens like an electronic ghost, spooking the patients and workers alike. Some said the clinic was haunted. On rare occasions, even his simulacrum would come to life in the boardroom when he slept.

Roxborough didn't care really. The more his workers feared him, the better. And his Matrix technicians said that nothing could be done, short of disconnecting him from the virtual reality when he slept. And for Roxborough, that was not acceptable. He had a phobia of being permanently cut off. The fear that came in the moment of absolute absence of sensory input before the computer recognized he was awake.

The black void of silence, of nothingness, was like a womb of suffocation. And that moment stretched on. And on until Roxborough panicked, thinking he was permanently disconnected from the world. Thinking he would have to spend all of eternity in that void, unable even to kill himself. Going slowly, inexorably, insane.

So he left himself connected to the host while he slept.

Now, something woke him. A gentle beeping that indicated a telecom call. Roxborough saw that it was Meyer. His elven face showed fatigue and satisfaction. He'd been hard at work on the ritual magic for six hours.

"Yes," Roxborough said.

Meyer took a breath. "We're finished," he said. "We didn't find him. Mercury is either dead or so well protected that it's beyond our power to locate him."

Roxborough nodded. "Well done," he said.

Meyer smiled. "Thank you."

"What are the chances that he's alive, but protected?"

"Slim to none. The only places we can't see are inside very powerful magical wards, well beyond the capability of the runners who took him. Unless he's in space; we can't detect anyone outside the manasphere."

"Thank you, Meyer," Roxborough said. "Get some rest. You deserve it."

Meyer nodded and disconnected.

Roxborough was pleased. Meyer was the most powerful mage he had known, a man who took pride in his work. If Ryan was alive, Meyer would have located him. The likelihood that Mercury had found his way into space or inside a ward was extremely improbable. Statistically insignificant, in Roxborough's opinion, and could be ruled out. Roxborough had made a fortune by using statistics and odds. Numbers never lied in the long run.

It was with those satisfying thoughts settling in his head that Roxborough prepared to fall asleep again. But just before he entered the dream state, his Matrix interface indicated another incoming telecom call. This time it was Darke. Not someone he could ignore.

"Darke, my friend," Roxborough said. "What can I do for you?"

"Cut the drek, Roxborough. Where's Mercury?"

"Dead."

Darke narrowed his eyes. "Are you certain? My sources tell me he escaped."

Roxborough sighed. He had never been able to root out Darke's informants. "Your sources have not misled you," Roxborough said. "But my security forces have destroyed their vehicle, and my mages could not locate him with their ritual magic. He is dead, as much as it saddens me to say so."

"I'm sure your sec forces are top-notch, and I know Meyer and the others are powerful mages. I fragging trained them." The intensity of Darke's stare nearly made Roxborough draw back.

Roxborough held his ground. He couldn't let himself back down or show fear. He couldn't let himself feel fear. That would mean admission of defeat, and long ago Roxborough had vowed never to give in.

"But," Darke went on, "we're dealing with someone who specializes in undercover work—infiltration, disguise, and escape. Mercury is far more dangerous than you realize." Darke's black eyes seemed to look into Roxborough's mind, measuring him molecule by molecule. "Mercury doesn't fit into the statistical models, Roxborough. He lives in the extremely slim margin outside the numbers. I told you he worked for Dunkelzahn. Did it occur to you that a dragon's lair might have a protective circle powerful enough to block the ritual detection?"

"Dunkelzahn is dead."

"Yes," Darke said. "But his lairs have not been destroyed. They still may provide protection to those who were close to the wyrm."

"Okay, so he might have survived," Roxborough conceded. "I don't like it any more than you do. What do you want me to do? Meyer used up the ritual tissue sample we had. Where should I tell my people to look?"

"Do nothing. I'm tired of your incompetence. I will assign a small team to locate his body, and if he lives, they will eliminate him."

With that the line went dead.

Roxborough tried to get back to sleep, but couldn't. Darke had no right to ridicule him like that. The man held no official position in the corp. Darke was merely a lackey for Juan Atzcapotzalco, the president of Aztechnology. Or, more accurately, Atzcapotzalco's puppeteers; the man hadn't been fully functional for years. But Roxborough also knew that he risked everything if he went counter to what Darke wanted. The man had too much power, and until Roxborough had a body, there was little he could do to undermine that power.

Slowly, Roxborough drifted into a fitful sleep. Nightmare images came to him, and the clinic's speakers and monitors sounded with his howling. His ghost image contorting with his screams.

21

Ryan stood on the stone floor of the enchanted chamber, watching the liquid silver surface of the dracoform statue. A spirit had come to life inside the flowing metal sculpture; Ryan sensed its presence. It must be a trapped guardian spirit of some sort. White track lighting kept the room bright around him as he stepped back away from it.

The spirit spoke to Ryan in a voice that was both familiar and alien. *It must be Dunkelzahn's voice,* he thought. And yet that could not be. Dunkelzahn did not speak the same way that people did.

"I have created a magical item called the Dragon Heart," the spirit said. "The item is a large, heart-shaped object made from pure orichalcum." The spirit gave an eerie laugh. "It is quite powerful, and you might be able to use it to augment your abilities. But that is not its purpose, Ryanthusar.

"You will find the Dragon Heart in a warded chamber off the central passageway on sublevel 5. The door is marked with an astral sigil. You will be able to pass through the ward without hindrance, but do not let anyone in with you or you will both be struck down.

"Your mission is to take the Dragon Heart to the metaplanar site of the Great Ghost Dance and give it to the one whose song protects the spike. She is called Thayla. I will repeat this once, Ryanthusar, because it is so important. Retrieve the Dragon Heart and deliver it to the metaplanar site of the Great Ghost Dance—the bridge that must not be finished.

"In order to complete your task, you must enlist the service of a powerful mage who knows the ritual that can carry you and the Dragon Heart into the metaplanes. This mage must also be absolutely committed to this endeavor. Of all my friends, only two fit these criteria—my old friend Harlequin and Ehran the Scribe. Harlequin would be my first choice; he knows Thayla and has vast experience, albeit tainted by his own hubris. Finding Harlequin might be difficult, however. Jane-in-the-box may have some ideas about how to find him. Ehran is competent and will be easy to find. He is one of the Princes in Tir Tairngire. But help from him will be harder to win.

"And you must win. Accomplishing this task is paramount. I have taught you of the cycles of magic, but no one has dared manipulate them as they do now, bringing this age to the brink of destruction so early in the mana cycle. The discovery of a Locus by Darke may be the single most devastating event in all of history. If the metaplanar chasm is breached before we are ready, we will all suffer. All beings will die.

"*All* beings.

"My fellow dragons are overconfident, thinking they can hide in their lairs as they have always done. But when the Enemy comes, the monsters will be able to use the technology of our own time to locate and breach our lairs. No sentient creature is safe this time. When the mana level gets high enough, the chasm will grow narrower and narrower until the Enemy can cross without any bridge. But there will be no hiding this time. Technology changes everything. No magic can protect against it.

"There will be no hiding this time. There will only be war. We must build up our defenses; we must gain the time we need to build up *our* technology so that we have the ability to fight the Enemy when it can cross. But to gain that time we must protect our natural defenses. They must not be allowed to fail, and the Dragon Heart will ensure that they don't. Thayla will know how to use it. Get it to her before it is too late.

"Goodbye, Ryanthusar. And good luck. You have always had it, and you will need more than your share for this mission."

The spirit flickered inside the enchanted statue, then disappeared when it was done speaking for Dunkelzahn. Message delivered, it was set free.

Ryan merely sat in stunned silence. *What have I stumbled*

into? Who was I that I should be entrusted to complete such a mission?

Do I even care?

Ryan sat thinking about that for a few minutes, and had just realized that he didn't know whether he cared or not when the large stone door swung open. He had cared, before his ordeal with Roxborough, he was sure of that. But now? Now he wasn't sure. Now he wondered if it even mattered. Dunkelzahn was dead. Perhaps the whole mission was pointless.

Nadja entered the chamber, followed by four guards. "Rhamus, our head mage, tells me that he has detected a ritual sending from the location of Roxborough's clinic. It should be safe for you to leave the chamber now, hopefully."

"Good."

Nadja started to say something, but stopped herself. Instead she said, "Now what?"

"You mean the mission?" Ryan asked, then understood instinctively why she had stopped herself; she wasn't always privy to knowledge of his activities.

"Yes," she said flatly.

Well, Ryan thought, *things are different now.* How could he expect to begin such an undertaking without his memory? He needed help, and he knew no one he could trust better than Nadja. He didn't need to tell her everything, just enough to make her feel included. Just enough to get her help on some important things.

"Do you know of an item called the Dragon Heart?" Ryan asked.

Nadja stared at him for a minute, a barely discernible expression of suspicion on her face. She seemed surprised that he was telling her about his mission. Then it passed and she said, "Yes. Only recently we had a security breach connected with that item."

"What?"

"A team of burglars stole it from one of the chambers near the treasure." She paused, thinking. "The warding and protection on that room was very strong. They obviously came well prepared for it."

"They got away?" Ryan found it hard to believe that anyone could steal something from a dragon's lair.

"I'm afraid so. But something else strange happened that you should know about. During the burglary, when security was trying to track down the infiltrators, a free spirit of some sort came to me. It possessed one of my security men, telling me that it had been sent by a being called Thayla and talking about something called the Dragon Heart. Insisting that it must deliver the Dragon Heart to a barren place of light and song. It sounded like lies at the time, and then the spirit killed my sec man, burned him up before my eyes." Her voice cracked at the end; she obviously cared for the dead man.

"It's true," Ryan said. "My mission involves the Dragon Heart, and I must find it."

Nadja's eyes went wide. "Oh, *that's* what it means," she said.

"What?"

"There's a line in Dunkelzahn's will," she said. "To Ryanthusar, I leave my heart . . ."

"Oh," was all Ryan could say.

"He must have meant the Dragon Heart, don't you think? And now, I've let it slip through my fingers. I'm so sorry, Ryan."

"It's not your fault," Ryan said.

"But it's obviously very important. What do you think this spirit wanted with it?"

"If he wasn't lying to you," said Ryan, "then the spirit's mission is the same as mine."

Nadja's face went slack. "I'm sorry, Ryan," she said. "I wish I'd known that spirit was telling the truth."

"Would it have helped you get the Dragon Heart?"

"No."

"Then don't fret it," Ryan said. "The Dragon Heart will turn up. What I don't understand is why Dunkelzahn included it in his will?"

"He was a bizarre old wyrm," she said. "And perhaps a bit paranoid. The will was updated constantly, just in case. He left you some other things, too, not mentioned in the public will, including Assets, Incorporated."

"What?"

"The corporation that employs the runners who got you out of Aztlan." Nadja frowned. "I wonder why Dunkelzahn never mentioned the Dragon Heart to me."

Ryan knew that last was a rhetorical statement, but he responded anyway. "Did the dragon tell you everything?"

Nadja smiled at him. "No, but I believe I knew more about his agenda than anyone else. Except maybe Jane-in-the-box. I was his voice, his connection to the public. It's just a little surprising to learn about another aspect of his plotting, and to discover that he kept me totally uninformed about it."

"I'd like to talk to Jane," Ryan said. "She might be able to track down the Dragon Heart."

"Yes," Nadja said. Then she smiled broad and full, beaming at him.

"What?"

"Nothing really," she said. "It's just that you're so motivated, so driven. You haven't changed at all."

But he had changed; he didn't feel driven or motivated. He felt lost and out of control. As far as he could tell, he had almost nothing in common with his rapidly growing picture of his previous self. His physical adept abilities were mostly gone, only a fraction of his magic remaining. His connection to Dunkelzahn, which supposedly had made him an unquestioningly loyal minion, no longer existed.

He admired the dragon, but he didn't idolize him like the previous Ryan supposedly had. He would no longer blindly follow orders; that was for robots and automatons. Ryan's dedication to this whole quest was waning. Even though it was obviously very important, he couldn't find any reason of his own for putting his life on the line. He just didn't care that much. He *couldn't* care until he'd figured out who he was.

In fact, the only thing he seemed to have in common with his former self was an affection for this attractive elf, Nadja Daviar. She had hired people to save his life. She was warm and open, and so damned sexy it nearly drove him to distraction, clouding his judgment. But there was more than all that, or at least he thought so. Nadja and he were alike in some basic way that separated them from others.

And that is why, after a medical exam proclaimed him to be well and fit, he made arrangements to travel back to DC with her. She had important business, what with the Will reading, the Scott Commission hearings, and preparations for becoming Vice President of the UCAS. But she wanted Ryan to come along, to be her temporary companion.

He was inclined to oblige her.

Ryan had no home. Even the room in the lair that he used was temporary, and was occupied by someone else now. His previous self had led a transitory existence, always on the move. He had never collected memorabilia.

For Ryan, now, that meant there were no clues about who he had been. Who he was. It seemed that his previous self had been a chameleon, a mimetic creature able to adapt to any situation and environment. That helped him infiltrate and spy on corporations and governments. That had been his most distinctive trait, versatility.

Now, however, it left him nothing to latch onto, no distinctive characteristics. Nothing except the elf who loved him. Nadja was the closest thing to an anchor in his life. And there was no way he was going to let her get away.

22

Burnout stood, alert and focused, scanning the darkened room of the rundown restaurant where Ryan Mercury had been tortured. Musty blue wall-to-wall shag carpeting, patterned with gray diamond patches. Old curtains the same color, hanging from threads. Tables and chairs of rotting wood scattered like defunct cyberware. Bone-dry aquarium, filled with spider webs.

Burnout concentrated hard to keep his attention on what the people around him were saying. There were three others close by, talking and planning. They weren't speaking to him directly. In fact, they spoke about him as though he weren't there.

He was used to that, and he didn't care. Because much of the time, he wasn't aware of them anyway.

Two others stood inside the room's perimeter. Burnout had catalogued them by their heat signatures, had isolated their weaknesses and was ready to destroy them if it became necessary. They held weapons and therefore they might need to be neutralized.

"Burnout! Pay attention!"

The voice of Slaver came as if from a great distance, like a cry from outside, even though the man stood right next to him. Burnout turned his head, feeling the nagging itch in his neck again. Psychosomatic, he'd been told. None of his original neck muscles or nerves remained, all of it replaced with synthetic tissue and microhydraulics. He nodded to Slaver to indicate that he was listening.

Slaver was his commander, someone he knew he had to protect. Someone he had to obey. Slaver was a mage and short for a human. Much shorter than Burnout, who no

longer thought of himself as human. Burnout was easily the
size of a large ork and weighed more than a troll.

Slaver's head was bald, covered only by an elaborate
tattoo of a coiled snake that began at the apex of his scalp
and spiraled out in greens and blacks and blues. He wore a
loose-fitting jumpsuit of tan silk, ridiculous clothing that
offered no protection against ballistics but let him move
freely, which Slaver insisted was important for his spell-
casting. There was a Jaguar Guard shoulder patch on the
jumpsuit, and for a moment Burnout lost himself in the fili-
gree detail of the jaguar design on the patch.

Burnout had been a powerful mage like Slaver. In a past so
distant, so alternate and removed from his current state that
Burnout remembered it not as part of himself, but as a history of someone he knew well. It was like channeling the
spirit of another person, or a past life. Burnout had loved the
mojo, had lived for astral conduit, the electric thrill of
pumping all that juice through a tiny circuit to blow the
living drek out through some poor slot's nostrils.

Then one day, his edge had dulled. He was a step too slow.

He'd gotten some cyberware installed to compensate. Mistake. Slowed his magic even more. The after-spell drain
started taking its toll, and soon he found himself spending a
week recovering from a two-hour run. That wasn't for him;
he never took a back seat. He'd always been the best of the
best, and so he got more and more cyber. He got training,
learned how to kill people. He became a street samurai, one
of the best. Until the Azzies gladly accepted his indentured
servitude in exchange for state-of-the-art cyberware and top-
of-the-line training. A career in killing in exchange for his
soul. And finally, ultimately, that's what they took. His soul.

He couldn't remember when his past died and he became
this incarnation. Two months earlier? Two years? His
internal calendar would show it, but he didn't care. Now he
was more machine than man; he was like a rigger for his own
body. It was a thing of terrifying beauty.

He couldn't stand to see his own reflection. And the awful
thing was that he still loved the magic, and he could sense it
when it was near, like the smell of good food—subtle and
alluring. He was drawn to it instinctively.

That was why he put up with the heaps of drek Slaver

piled on him. He hated Slaver, and one day the human mage would push him too far. One day Slaver would go the way of all Burnout's opponents—straight to Hell.

Burnout finally managed to snap his concentration back to the conversation. The human with the black hair and beard spoke to Slaver in a commanding tone. "Mercury is alive," he said. "My sources in Lake Louise report that he's there. You will find him and destroy him. Is that perfectly clear?"

Slaver bowed obsequiously. "Of course, Señor Oscuro."

"I have provided a rigger and a diplomatic Aztechnology rotorcraft to use as you need."

"Thank you, Señor."

The other being, which stood next to Slaver on the opposite side from Burnout, was not metahuman even though it looked vaguely like an elf. It had skin the color of dried blood, covered with large black pock marks that moved across the surface. Its head was bald, and the cartilage of its nostrils had been flayed into strips and peeled back where Slaver drew blood from it for some of his spells. Very gory, though Burnout was not affected by that. Its name was La Sangre, and it was a blood spirit. Bound and allied to Slaver. Like Burnout, the spirit was not allowed to speak.

Then the conversation was over and Burnout had missed most of it. Not that he cared one way or the other. He'd recorded it on his cybercamera so he could replay or search any section of it if necessary.

"Let's go," Slaver said, then muttered silently, "Imbecile."

Slaver must have thought that Burnout couldn't hear his fragmented whisper. Or maybe he didn't care. But Burnout cared; he was no imbecile. He was merely *distracted*. It was a condition that went along with the fragging territory. *If Slaver couldn't handle it, then Slaver could . . .*

Burnout let the thought trail off as a rush of warmth filled him as an injection of his happy drug hit him. The chemical substance that kept him in line. Hatred was a good thing. The docs said it helped keep him alive, helped to keep his willpower up. But they didn't want him to overdo it. Thus they put the drug on an automatic injector. Measured his adrenaline or some such drek, and if he wasn't in a combat situation, it kept him from going off and massacring innocents.

Took some of the fun out of being such an awesome killing machine, but the rush was pretty nice.

Burnout moved to join Slaver and La Sangre as they walked outside to stand on the shore of the lake. The excavation was in full swing. Burnout could see that they'd almost completely unearthed the huge black stone.

Burnout knew the rock was magical, and the arcane glow of it was like a beacon to him, drawing him in like a cybernetic moth to a blow torch. He couldn't move; he must have it. Frag everything else. The rock held his future. It could restore his magic with its power.

The hypnotic rippling of the black surface drew him in, until he realized that he'd left the other two standing on the shore. He was chest-deep in water, walking further in.

A memory came to him then. They always came when he lost control. They wanted him to stay anchored in his new body, this horrid amalgamation of wires and fibers and metal. He thought of his mother, her face bright, smiling as she patted his head. He was eight years old, or maybe nine. She turned to him and said, "I'm so proud of you. Highest score again. You're always the best at whatever you do . . ."

The warm rush he felt in his memory was barely discernible from the drug in his system. Getting high on praise.

"Get back here, you idiot!" Slaver yelled. "We've got to go."

And by the time Burnout had come back to the present, there was a magic barrier of some kind between him and the stone. The allure of it was lessened by the barrier, but the stone's power was immense and the barrier couldn't completely mask it. Still, Burnout tried to focus, tried to ignore it and join the others.

A half-hour later, when they were in the helicopter, flying north toward Canadian American States territory, Burnout asked what they were going to do.

"You'll like this mission," Slaver told him. "We get to kill someone. Someone named Ryan Mercury."

14 August 2057

23

It was mid-morning when Ryan climbed into the Lear-Cessna Platinum III jet with Nadja, her aide Gordon Wu, Carla Brooks, and some security. They were headed to Washington.

The ride was smooth and relatively quiet, so Ryan decided to try to get some sleep during the flight since Nadja was dictating instructions to Gordon Wu. Busy working. This was a working trip for everyone on board except perhaps Ryan. Since Dunkelzahn's death, their work load had increased exponentially.

Ryan reclined his chair as the jet took off, noting that the wide leather seats were much more comfortable than the hard plastic of the T-bird's seats. It seemed so long ago that he'd been asleep in the clinic bed, a prisoner without knowing it. And now . . .

Now he was another kind of prisoner—a prisoner to Dunkelzahn's mission. Something wouldn't let him give it up completely even though that is what he most wanted. *If I get things moving,* he thought, *I'll at least have tried.*

Ryan activated his wristphone, placing a secure call to the LTG that Nadja had given him for Jane-in-the-box. It took a few moments until encryption and decryption protocols synched, then he was looking at Jane's persona on the screen.

She looked like a blonde corporate bimbo in red leather. Very stylized and unrealistic, but attractive in an absurd cartoony way. "Quicksilver," she said. "I trust you're well?"

Ryan smiled. "Thanks to you," he said. "I'm alive at least. Though my problems seem to have just begun."

Jane nodded, shifting to biz mode as she realized that this

wasn't intended to be a social call. "So, what can I do for you?"

"Do you know of the item called the Dragon Heart, which was taken from the lair yesterday?"

"I have followed the report of its theft," Jane said. "That's all I know."

"I must track down who took it and where it is. It's urgent, and I don't know who else to ask."

Jane's persona smiled. "I'm flattered," she said, then gave a little giggle.

Ryan winced. He didn't remember ever meeting Jane, though Axler said that he was one of the few people who had actually met the decker. He had the feeling that in the real world, she wasn't at all like this image. She was very intelligent, very savvy and smart. Cunning. This persona must be a front, an image designed to trick people into underestimating her.

Ryan's assessment of Jane was based on his conversations with Axler and later with Nadja. The decker seemed to be an invisible entity in the Matrix. Even though she was extremely accomplished, few in the Matrix knew who she was because she never posted as herself. Nadja had told Ryan that Jane had been doing Dunkelzahn's decking for many years, and she had acted as sort of an über-fixer. She had done a good deal of the management of the dragon's shadow ops, tracking the activities of other fixers, who never realized that they were working for Dunkelzahn.

Ryan liked her instinctively. "I wasn't intending to flatter," he said, "though I will if it'll help." He laughed. "This is important, Jane. Please, just do what you can."

A cartoon smile drew itself across Jane's icon. "I'm on it, Quicksilver."

"Thanks." The line went dead.

The jet landed about an hour later, coming into a Washington that had been nearly closed down by riots and martial law. Dunkelzahn's death had caused outbreaks of rioting across the UCAS. All the major cities had been affected. On one side, there were many taking out their frustration because they'd idolized the dragon. And on the other, those who hated him were celebrating his demise by destroying property, looting, and fighting his supporters.

The new president, Kyle Haeffner, had declared martial law in the Federal District just a few hours earlier, calling in the Knight Errant and Ares Arms security forces to help the FedPols quash the rioters. So far, according to Nadja, they'd made little progress.

National Airport was eerily quiet as Ryan made his way from the jet, across the tarmac to a private helo. It was midmorning, the sun hot in the sweaty Washington sky. Too hot for comfort. Air traffic seemed extremely light, and while security personnel were abundant, the regular airport workers were sparse.

Abruptly, automatic gunfire sputtered in the distance. Ryan spun to assess the situation, suddenly feeling exposed. Out in the open. But Brooks and her guards surrounded Ryan and Nadja. And the gunfire, he realized, had come from more than a kilometer away. He'd heard it distinctly, but his hearing was better than the others'.

My abilities are slowly returning, he thought. *Of course I don't even know what they were. I can't remember my training.*

Nadja was greeted by some corp suits, and she spoke with them for a few minutes before continuing on to the 'copter. Maybe they were from the government. Ryan couldn't tell. Nadja gave them some instructions about removing and handling the cargo on the jet. A few things of Dunkelzahn's were going to be given out the next day after the reading of the dragon's Last Will and Testament.

The flight to the Watergate Hotel was short. Nadja normally stayed at Dunkelzahn's estate in Georgetown, but the reading of the will was scheduled to take place in the Watergate Grand Ballroom tomorrow. With the rioting, they figured it would be safer to avoid unnecessary traveling.

Ryan convinced the pilot to fly past the front of the Watergate once before swinging around and landing on the roof. He wanted to see the blast site. He hoped it would spark something inside him, memories or emotions, feelings about Dunkelzahn.

The area was surrounded by a crowd of people—tourists, mourners, media hounds, and even worshippers who considered Dunkelzahn a martyred saint. The blast crater was larger than Ryan expected, a massive hole in the center of the boulevard, isolated by temporary construction fencing.

Above the crater hovered a prismatic cloud that looked to be made of light and energy. It writhed and morphed, roiling like an undulating droplet of oil trapped inside an invisible sphere of water. It was obviously magical in nature, and Ryan could actually see its astral reflection when he concentrated.

It looked exactly the same in astral space.

That, he knew, was very strange. Even frightening. It was as though the fabric of physical space had been torn away just at this spot. As though the barrier to astral space had been eliminated here, so that this manastorm, as they called it, looked the same in both planes of reality. Why else would it give off light in the physical world?

Ryan was just speculating. It was an unknown phenomenon, and even Nadja's best sources had yet to determine its true nature. He was disappointed that seeing it did not help him remember. All it did was leave him with a sense of awe and wonder at the power of something that could destroy a great dragon like Dunkelzahn.

The helo took them to the rooftop, and from there hotel security escorted them to a suite. The space was elegant and simple, large with a living room and office, plus two bedrooms. After Nadja had dispatched all the suits and corporate types, she asked security to step outside to give her and Ryan some privacy. Then she sat on the couch and took off her shoes. "I hate these fragging things," she said.

Ryan smiled. It was the first time he'd heard her speak with anything less than perfectly proper language, and he found it endearing. She was letting her facade slide away for him, a gesture of intimacy. He sat down next to her. "Do you want me to massage your feet?"

She smiled. "Don't start something you're not prepared to finish."

Ryan picked up one of her feet and set it in his lap. Her skin was cool under the calluses of his palms. He rubbed them, putting pressure on the muscles, focusing, trying to force them to loosen. To relax. He found he could make his hands grow hot if he tried, and he suspected that this ability was based in magic.

Nadja sank back into the cushions. "What happened to you in Aztlan?" she asked.

"I don't remember much. Some sort of personality transfer. Thomas Roxborough wanted to use my body for his mind."

"I'm sorry."

"Does it bother you?"

Nadja thought for a minute. "I don't know if you're Ryan or not."

"Tell me about Ryan . . . about myself."

Nadja smiled. "We're connected, you and I," she said. "There's something fundamental that bonds us to each other, something that will never change. I don't know what it is, really, but even Dunkelzahn assured me it was true. It often manifests as luck, sometimes as premonitions, dreams, and such." Nadja shook her head. "Am I making any sense at all?"

Ryan didn't answer. He was overcome with the sensations of her—the tenor of her voice, the animal essence in her smell. The slight disarray of her hair, stray ebony strands floating over her face. The delicate freckling on the bridge of her nose could only be seen up close, and it was this accumulation of tiny flaws—the endearing defects in her perfection—that reached into the base of his brain and kindled a desperate lust for her.

He breathed deeply, drinking in the smell of her as his skin tightened. As he felt pressure in his groin and the faint tingle of anticipated pleasure.

She touched his arm with her fingertips. "How much do you remember?" she asked.

"About us?"

Nadja nodded.

"I don't *remember* that much," Ryan said. "But I sense a great deal."

"What do you sense?"

"That we care for each other, that we're intimate, probably lovers. That we have a deep relationship besides that."

Ryan was barely finished with the sentence when she pulled him down against her, moving her face close to his. "Right in one," she whispered, shifting her hips to take the weight of his. He came into her embrace, his broad chest against hers, crushing her into the cushions of the couch.

She looked up into his eyes, ran her delicate hands through his hair. She blinked in slow motion, so close he saw his own irises reflected on the surface of her pupils. Her hands reached up under his shirt and dug into the broad muscles on his back as he placed gentle nibbling kisses against her throat, up along the back of her delicate jaw, to her pointed ear.

He raised himself up to look at her, and she stared into his eyes, brushed her lips lightly against his. He focused on the curve of her upper lip as he kissed her, as she parted her mouth and sought out his tongue with hers. The taste of her sparked recognition in Ryan, so familiar. So exquisite.

She pulled away slightly, teasing him. But Ryan caught her mouth with his, kissing her hard. A brutal loss of restraint, before backing off into a softer, deeper kiss. He was desperate for her. "I must have you now," he said.

She responded by tearing his shirttail from his pants, up and over his head. Then she was running her hands over the broad flanks of his back, pushing down below his waist, ducking under the edge of his pants to touch his bare skin.

He rolled her over, and they fell to the floor, her on top of him, her skirt up around her waist so that she could straddle his hips. Ryan focused on the swell of her breasts beneath her silk blouse, and he reached up to them, delicately brushing their outline. Nadja began to unbutton her blouse, but Ryan couldn't wait for her. He put his hands between the buttons and ripped the blouse from her body.

He experienced the first vision as he tore her skirt away and pushed his own pants off. A memory from his Ryan past. He and Nadja in Maui, walking hand in hand along a private beach under a moonless sky. Stripping their clothes off and swimming in the dark, clear water. Playing in the surf. Making slow sweet love under the outdoor shower.

Now, in the hotel suite, they were naked on the plush blue carpeting, rolling like desperate teenagers. She was below him now, desire on her face as she arched her back. Her naked legs open to him, her thighs slick and hot.

He moved against her, involuntarily. All control gone.

"Now," she whispered.

He entered her.

She moaned and bit down on his shoulder, her finger nails cutting into the skin of his buttocks. She wanted it rough, hard.

He moved faster. Giving her exactly what she wanted.

Something was happening in his brain. More visions, memories. They began to come as he climaxed. Flooding over him in waves.

He saw the huge sinuous form of Dunkelzahn, a magnificent glowing worm in astral space. Then the image was gone, and he smelled cayenne pepper and baking bread—a goulash meal he'd shared with Sergeant Matthews during a Desert War training exercise.

And the memories continued after, as Nadja bucked violently with her orgasm. Fragments of his life crashing through his brain.

He heard a rumbling roar in his memory. He was very young. An image of Dunkelzahn descending like a fiery bird of prey flashing through his mind. Descending to rescue him. Then he heard a cry of pain, a different scene, much more recent—a few years ago at most. Axler crouched down to help the crying kid who'd caught a stray bullet. Scenes from his life coming back at random.

Now, Ryan lifted Nadja in his arms and carried her to the bed. She drew him down to lie next to her, then rolled on top, straddling him. He put his hands on the rising swell of her breasts and pinched her large brown nipples as she guided him into her. They made love again.

The memories came on. He experienced his love for Dunkelzahn. His training and his many missions; Ryan remembered everything in those hours. He remembered his mission to Aztlan, his discovery of the Locus, his report to Dunkelzahn right before the helicopter came, right before the cyberzombie took him out and drugged him. A shudder passed through Ryan as he lay next to Nadja tracing a delicate circle around the brown oval of her areola as she fell into asleep.

Ryan remembered himself completely.

24

Lethe longed for Thayla's voice, pined for the touch of her song. He missed her—she who had named him. But his mission was far from complete, and he would not return to her without the Dragon Heart.

Tracking the item had been harder than Lethe had expected. He had felt its power when it was in Dunkelzahn's lair, so its astral resonance was imprinted on him. Therefore, he should be able to find it anywhere in the manasphere.

But its aura had been masked, disguised by the metahumans who had taken it from the chamber in Dunkelzahn's lair. They had dulled its astral resonance. Weakened Lethe's ability to follow its trail through astral space. But his sense of the Dragon Heart was extremely keen. The tracking had been more time-consuming and difficult, but Lethe still smelled the tendrils of mana that the Dragon Heart left behind. The delicate eddies and currents it created in astral space.

The elves who took it could mask the Heart itself, but not its effect on the astral landscape. Lethe had followed the trail with a growing awareness that this Dragon Heart was an extremely powerful object. Its very presence reshaped the astral background. The effect was slight, very subtle, but Lethe could see it, and he could follow it.

They had taken the Dragon Heart to a place called Eugene, in an elven nation known as Tir Tairngire. In the physical world, the building that held the item looked old, but sturdy. Constructed of concrete and riebar, brick and steel beam. The inside was crawling with spirits and mages playing with enchanted items. There were more items, of various power and potency, at this one location than Lethe had known to exist.

After watching carefully for a time, and trying to avoid detection, Lethe came to the conclusion that the mages and spirits where conducting research on these items. Testing their power and ability. Trying to elucidate the various histories by magically tracing the object's past. Who used it? What for? When?

The basement housed training facilities for what looked like an army, though Lethe was less than well-schooled in the combat practices of metahumans. Lethe recognized the elves who had taken the Dragon Heart talking with more elves. In fact, everyone present was an elf. In the physical world, everyone wore similar black combat armor—close-fitting, but flexible. And they all had something else in common, markings Lethe hadn't noticed before. Each elf was tattooed with a crescent moon under a long sword and a banner.

Lethe honed in on astral resonance of the Dragon Heart, and finally found it in a warded chamber two levels up from the training facility. The ward looked strong in astral space, an electric blue and green glass sphere around the item.

Suddenly, alarms were sounding. He had been detected. Lethe turned to see a line of air and fire elementals coming toward him. "Do not approach me," he said. "I will leave soon, and I do not wish to hurt you."

The elementals ignored him. They had been bound by mages and were forced to obey them. They rushed toward him, trying to surround him. Engulf him.

Lethe extended his will toward them. And as he focused his thought, they disappeared, banished to their home planes. But they had caused him delay. Others would be coming. Mages and shamans, perhaps powerful enough to threaten Lethe. He didn't know the extent of their ability.

He fled for the moment, leaving behind the Dragon Heart. And leaving too his hope to see Thayla soon, and bask in the beauty of her song.

25

The Washington night was like a sauna, hot and humid around Ryan. He took a deep breath and leaned forward against the concrete banister of the suite's balcony. Far below, to his distant left, the manastorm crackled and sprayed its rainbow light on a crowd of people.

"Can't sleep?"

Ryan turned to see Nadja coming through the sliding glass doors to join him. She wore a pearl-colored silk robe, almost transparent. The protruding tips of her nipples pressed against the sheer fabric. But it was her crooked half-smile and the deep, hollow line of her clavicle, showing in the open collar of her robe, that brought a smile of delight to his face. She was truly savory.

"No," he said. "I've remembered everything."

Her eyes widened. "Really? Are you *you* again?"

"Mostly."

They stood in silence for a few minutes, her arm around his waist. He enjoyed her presence, but his mind was elsewhere. He was watching the manastorm as though Dunkelzahn might spring back into existence if he wished hard enough.

Ryan remembered now first meeting the dragon. He was a boy, just seven at the time, living in the El Infierno housing projects of California Free State. The memory was absolutely clear in his mind. The midnight sky was bright with reflected city light, the noise of traffic subsiding when he heard the chatter of automatic gunfire. A scream came a second later, sounded like his mother, but the pitch was too high. Like the screech of a bird.

He ran; he needed to get into the tenement.

He heard his mother again, yelling hysterically. She was

still alive. He could reach her in time. His heart pounded in his chest, throbbing in his ears as he pushed bare feet against the pitted asphalt. Graffiti-stained concrete walls blurred by on his left.

"Shut up, slitch!" came a voice he recognized. It was TB, the leader of 'Hood Watch, the most powerful gang in the projects. "Quite whining and tell me where he is." The man clipped his words, spitting them out like bad food. "Or you'll end up like your do-man here."

Then Ryan was through the opening and inside. His mother knelt on the hard tile floor five meters away, facing away from Ryan. Next to her, on the left, stood a tall ork holding a submachine gun to his mother's head. On her right, face-down on the floor was his father, blood spreading in a dark stain beneath him. He wasn't moving.

Ryan froze. He couldn't help his mother. He turned to run. Only to be caught by another member of the gang who came up behind him. "Looky, TB. Look what I got me."

"Then I guess we don't need this slitch anymore," said the ork with the machine gun. He pulled the trigger.

Mom's body jerked forward, falling to the floor, lifeless. Blood leaked onto the threadbare carpeting.

"Let's go," TB said. "I want that reward."

They covered Ryan's mouth with duct tape and bound his hands and feet before carrying him outside. Into the hot night. But despite the heat, Ryan felt chill inside. Shivers shook through him, and he couldn't stop shaking. Tears welled in his eyes, and he almost blacked out.

Suddenly, the sky brightened above them. Ryan came crashing to the asphalt as the gang members dropped him. He looked up to see a huge dragon filling the sky. Fire erupted from its mouth, shimmered along its blue and silver scales as it descended.

The gangers ran, scattering like leaves in wind. Ryan watched as the dragon burned or ate each one of them, and he braced himself when the creature approached him. But the dragon did not harm Ryan.

Hello, Ryanthusar, came the dragon's voice in his head. *My name is Dunkelzahn, and I have been looking for you. Will you come with me?*

Ryan's bonds broke, and the tape tore from his mouth, telekinetically. "Yes," he said, mostly out of fear.

Dunkelzahn scooped the young Ryan up in his talons and flew off into the night sky. Taking Ryan to his lair in Lake Louise.

A few years later, Ryan had asked Dunkelzahn the reason his parents had been killed.

Dunkelzahn had turned to the boy, who stood defiantly next to the dragon's huge size. *Both good and evil exist in the world, Ryanthusar. It is something you will have to learn. And it is part of the wonderful complexity of the universe that sentient creatures, for the most part, contain a mix of both. It is a rarity to find anyone totally good, or totally evil.* Dunkelzahn paused, leaving the young Ryan puzzled.

"But that doesn't tell me why my parents were murdered," he protested. "What I mean is—"

It is not what we feel that defines us. It is how we act, Dunkelzahn continued. *Those who killed your parents succumbed to the evil side of themselves. And they acted upon that. But they were not intrinsically bad people, no one is. They had families and protected many from violent acts by others.*

Young Ryan merely blinked. Dunkelzahn spoke like this often, and Ryan found it somewhat alien and very hard to follow.

Remember what I am telling you, Ryanthusar. There is an evil voice inside us all. Listen to yours and come to understand it, for it is a crucial part of you. But always remember, who you are is defined by how much you act upon what the evil voice tells you.

It wasn't until many years later that Ryan learned the specifics of his parents' murders. TB had been paid to capture Ryan and deliver him into the hands of Aztlan priests. He discovered that certain people were naturally adept at manipulating the arcane energies of this world. Those people could be detected and trained.

Dunkelzahn told Ryan that he had the potential to be one of the most powerful living magical beings, and that is why Aztlan sought him out. That was also why Dunkelzahn had been looking for him. To offer to train him. Ryan had been with the dragon ever since.

Now, on the balcony of the Watergate Hotel, overlooking the manastorm where Dunkelzahn died, Ryan was in shock. *Could Dunkelzahn truly be gone? How could it be?* The thought of it tested the limits of his mind. He could barely comprehend it. Such a powerful creature, such a noble personage. A true hero of this time, and in Ryan's eyes, one worthy of devotion and unquestioning commitment.

Who could have done this? And why?

That wasn't what Ryan was supposed to be wondering, he knew that. Dunkelzahn wouldn't want him to waste time thinking of revenge. Dunkelzahn would have wanted Ryan to complete his mission, nothing more.

Something caught his eye just then, a flash of red light in the sky. He looked up, his jaw dropping as the scene came into being. A dragon streaked across the sky, racing down like an immense eagle toward its prey. Red flames blasted from its nostrils as it descended, the fire trailing behind it in twin tails. It wasn't Dunkelzahn, Ryan knew, but it looked like another Great Western. Lofwyr? Or another?

A long, melodious bellow announced the arrival of a second dragon, off to the left. An Eastern Great, this one, green scales and shorter wings, sinuous as it flew. Like a snake in the air.

The two met just over the manastorm, their speed dizzying, leaving streaks of fire, one red, one green. Another arrived, a feathered serpent this time. And another Western. They flew around the site of Dunkelzahn's death, spiraling past each other as they rocketed into the sky.

Ryan felt magic come from their dance, increasing as more and more dragons arrived to join in. The dance was held in absolute silence at first, made all the more poignant by the fact that the rioting and fighting had stopped across the city, at least as far as Ryan could hear. People were mesmerized by the sight.

After a few minutes, twelve or thirteen dragons, by Ryan's count, were flying in the sky. All species were represented. Nadja stood next to him and watched in silence and awe. Their dance was raw and powerful, magical and intricate. Light and heat radiated from the tapestry of motion they created.

Bellows and cries reached Ryan's ears then. The dancing

dragons had broken their silence. The roars shook Ryan to the bones. There were screams of anguish and outrage. Howls lamenting their fallen kin, taken from his mortal coil against nature. Visceral outcry against such an affront.

Anger and sadness coursed through Ryan at the sight. His knees quavered and gave out.

"You all right?" Nadja helped him to his feet.

Ryan didn't answer. *No,* he thought. *Nothing is all right. Nothing will ever be all right.*

Tears welled in his eyes as he watched the dragons continue their dance. Such power, even individually, now combined into a truly awesome force. Such wonder and beauty in their dancing flight.

An homage to one of their own, fallen before his time.

It struck Ryan again, and he nearly fell a second time. The significance of this display. Dunkelzahn was truly dead; his own kind knew it. All hope of the dragon's return drained out of Ryan, and it took his will with it.

He found himself wishing he hadn't remembered himself. His past seemed so fragile now, shattered and in ruins with the death of his master. *When I didn't care,* he thought, *I was stronger. I was my own strength. Now . . .*

Now, who will sweep down and rescue me? Now, where will I find the strength?

The Great Dragon Dance went on for several hours, and by the time it was over, Ryan's head was buried in Nadja's sweet-smelling hair, tears streaming from his eyes. She was his pillar now. With Dunkelzahn gone, she was his only support.

He found his strength a few minutes later, part of his Roxborough past coming to his aid. Memories of his disease and the treatment for it, the submergence into the vat. If he could live through that treatment and the certain knowledge that he would never come out of his vat, then he could live through anything. He had never given up, never relied on anyone besides himself.

Ryan wiped his eyes and escorted Nadja back inside. Back to bed. They held each other for a while, and soon she was sleeping soundly. Ryan lay awake next to her, thinking about his two pasts, about his mission, and about the new emotion that was welling up inside him.

Anger.

Anger toward Dunkelzahn. Rage toward the creature who had let him down in the end, leaving him alone. Isolated for the first time in his life.

26

Jane-in-the-box paced around her electronics, trying to pump some blood into her bony limbs before jacking back into the datastream. She took another bite of her ham and swiss croissant, a special gift from the cook, Enrico—a troll with a huge gut and a penchant for French cuisine.

Her trid interface beeped, indicating that her smartframe had completed its scan-and-evaluate cycle. And found a match, she noted. "Fragging sweet," she said. There was no one else in the huge chamber, and her words echoed off the hewn stone walls of the cavern. Jane often spoke to herself when she wasn't jacked in. It kept her company and helped to organize her mind.

After Ryan's call asking her to dig up any information on the location of the Dragon Heart, Jane had scanned the security video to try to get an ID on the perps who had lifted the Dragon Heart. One of her image-recognition routines that searched for distinctive markings picked out a tattoo on the partially exposed forearm of one of the runners. A woman, and probably a mage, based on what she was wearing.

The tattoo was a crescent moon, under a flapping narrow banner and a sword. On the banner was a word, "Tal'shai." Jane had laughed aloud. This was almost too easy.

She'd programmed another frame to search the datanets for several variables, including a match or partial match to the tattoo, and any known elven shadowrun teams with the rep or resources to pull off a run against the high security of the lair.

Now, Jane jacked in, entering the oh-so-familiar virtual space of her riveted steel box. Six sides of brushed gray metal animating around her. The results of the smartframe flowed in the dataspace in front of her, and as she scanned it, she separated the data into two bins, hits and misses.

The smartframe had found the tattooed word in Jane's online Sperethiel dictionary. It meant "black widow spider." That didn't narrow down the choices at all. Any elven runner could go by that name. But as Jane continued her scan, she reprogrammed on the fly to modify the smart frame to narrow its search parameters as she rejected the bogus and reinforced those her gut told her were on target.

She found the trend at the same time as her frame. A dead elf with the same tattoo had been discovered by Seattle Lone Star. Except there were no words on the banner. This one had a small black symbol—three triangles with their points almost touching, slightly offset from center. This dead elf was male and didn't look like any of those who'd taken the Dragon Heart.

The Lone Star report said that the tattoo identified the deceased as security for the Atlantean Foundation. The smartframe had searched the personnel files of the Atlantean Foundation, but there were no security personnel listed. Jane knew they got their security from the Mystic Crusaders, an enigmatic organization whose purpose Jane did not know.

"Very interesting," Jane said to herself. She knew that the Atlantean Foundation collected artifacts and powerful magic items. Even if the Mystic Crusaders were mysterious, it was likely that the AF was behind the theft. But where had they taken the Dragon Heart?

Jane prepped to enter the Matrix. She would do some digging into a few of the Foundation's hosts, and see if there had been any deliveries of a special nature in the past twelve hours. She chuckled to herself. This was going to be fun.

There was only one detail that nagged in the back of her mind. Conspiracy theorists claimed that the Atlantean Foundation was run not just by elves, but by immortal elves. Elves whose existence had never been proven, but who were said to have been born thousands of years ago. Jane believed that one or two immortal elves did exist; she'd done enough decking for Dunkelzahn that she *knew* certain things. But she didn't think they were behind the Atlantean Foundation. There was no direct evidence to show it.

At least she hoped not. These immortals were extremely

powerful and cunning. Even Dunkelzahn had respected their power. If they had the Dragon Heart, even Quicksilver himself, Dunkelzahn's greatest operative, would be severely outmatched.

27

In the cold of the Canadian Rockies near Lake Louise, Burnout stood as still as a statue, taking in the scene. He stood on an icy slope overlooking a small airstrip that had been chiseled out of the mountain. Forty-two minutes earlier, Burnout and Slaver had descended from the helicopter, coming down on hoist wires into a small clearing nearly a kilometer away. The rigger had remained inside the hovering machine, waiting for the completion of the mission—the death of Ryan Mercury.

Now, the late-evening sky was moonless and dark, but not to Burnout. His eyes self-adjusted to the low light. The few sodium lamps outside the mirrored glass buildings next to the airstrip flared brightly on his cybernetic retinas, streaking his vision with cold blue-white.

The perimeter was marked by a three-meter-high wall, topped with looping monowire, security cameras, and rail-mounted drones that tracked back and forth, no doubt wired into a closed-circuit simsense rigger who could activate their weapons with a thought. Periodically, one of six guards walked the perimeter inside the fence. The guard was always leashed together with some sort of animal. A dog or a paranimal. Something with a good sense of smell, no doubt. The guards had light body armor under their uniforms, and carried pistols and Ares Cascades.

"Burnout, capture one of the guards." Slaver's voice came as if from a great distance away, like out of a dream across a windy lake. But Burnout heard, and it was all the prompting he needed. He moved. Quickly and quietly, picking a spot where the sec cameras would have a harder time seeing.

He knew he was normally an easy target for astral creatures, but Slaver had supposedly masked his aura as much as possible. No matter. There was nothing more he could do about it now. *No hesitation,* he told himself. *No second thoughts.* Just the quick fluidity of this mechanical body.

He passed down through the pines, crossed the short clearing like a ghost of metal, and reached the wall. He jumped as he came close, using all the strength of the hydraulic jacks in his legs. He cleared the wall and the mono-wire and the track with ease, landing without a sound on the other side. Looking around for a microsecond, he honed in on a guard walking away from him. *Target lock.*

Then Burnout was moving toward him, taser in hand. The dog saw him first, spinning toward Burnout just as he loomed up behind the guard. The taser made a tiny springing noise, and the beast fell with a small yelp.

The guard didn't even get that far. He moved as if in slow motion, his hand not yet reaching his weapon.

Burnout's palm came across the guard's mouth, clamping down tight before abruptly pulling back. Jerking the man off his feet. Burnout had to stop himself from snapping the man's neck. Slaver had said capture, not kill.

The man's pupils widened when he saw Burnout, and he tried to call out. His cries were muffled, and he stopped completely when Burnout placed the barrel of his silenced Predator II to his face. A quick, hard punch to the gut knocked the man's wind out and left him gasping while Burnout sealed his mouth with his stash of fiber tape, then bound his hands and feet with the same.

Two more things. First, the dog. A quick twist broke its neck. Second, escape. That might be a little tougher.

Burnout glanced around. No disturbances, no trace of alarm. He jacked up the gain on his hearing, but came up with nothing more than the sound of a helicopter motor clicking as it cooled and the amplified hum of his own microhydraulics.

The guard thrashed a little when Burnout picked him up and slung the man's bulk over his shoulder. Made holding difficult. Burnout was not happy. *This human must be controlled.* Burnout quietly set the guard on the ground, then grabbed the man's foot with one hand. He used his other hand to place a hard sideways punch to the guard's knee, snapping the bone in several places.

The guard's scream was nicely muffled. Very effective tape. And he didn't squirm so much when Burnout slung him up to his shoulder the second time. Burnout jumped back over the fence with his human cargo. Then he raced off into the trees. No sound from the drones. He had made it out.

"You broke his leg?" Slaver asked when Burnout dumped the guard in the snow.

Burnout just nodded.

"Was that necessary?" But Slaver didn't let Burnout respond. He knelt down next to the guard, putting its hands on the man's face. The man's chest heaved as Slaver scanned his mind with magic. The screams of agony stuck in his throat.

After a few minutes, Slaver looked up. The guard had passed out. "Mercury is no longer here," he said. "He left with Nadja Daviar. They went to Washington FDC."

He rose and dusted himself off. "Now kill him and let's go," he said to Burnout.

Burnout bent down and grabbed the man's head with a iron-grip. He was already unconscious, so this wouldn't hurt. Besides, this was the most effective and humane way. A sudden brutal twist snapped the man's neck, severing his spinal cord. He was dead instantly.

28

The anger percolated inside Ryan, simmering just below the surface as he watched prismatic light wash over the wall above the bed. The colors coming through the window from the manastorm outside—fine wavy lines of red, orange, yellow, blue, and violet forming mesmerizing patterns on the antique white paint of the suite.

Dunkelzahn was dead, gone? It slotted him off. How could the dragon be so fragging vulnerable? How could he not see it coming? Stupid fragger!

Nadja sprawled next to him, sleeping soundly. Innocence showing in her slack expression. Serenity in her restful slumber.

Not so Ryan. He couldn't sleep. Too much going on in his head. Too fragging much to think about.

Nadja's peace wormed its way into his mind. Why was *she* blessed with the ability to forget her worries while he could not?

Ryan had never slept well. Neither of his past selves had restful, natural sleep. As Roxborough, he'd been able to rest only by taking drugs or drinking alcohol. As Ryan, his sleep had been induced by magic, a forced rest period that was often interrupted by a crisis of some sort.

Now, he had neither the desire nor the inclination to induce that state. It wouldn't be the child's sleep that Nadja enjoyed. It would just be maintenance.

Ryan was coming to realize that he was no longer the same as either of his past selves. He was not the subservient creature that Ryan Mercury used to be. If anything he was more like the old Thomas Roxborough inside. Tougher, more resilient mentally. He relied on no one but himself for emotional support.

Ryan decided he wanted to be like that. And he knew suddenly that it did no good to maintain his anger toward Dunkelzahn. It was counterproductive. Stupid even.

The plain and simple truth is that Dunkelzahn just doesn't mean that much to me anymore, Ryan thought, trying to convince himself that it was true. It was a trick from his Roxborough past. Therapy through devaluation. And it worked wonderfully.

Ryan took a slow breath. The constriction in his chest had come first with the realization that Dunkelzahn was truly gone, the grief he had felt. The tightness had intensified when his grief had given way to anger. Now it was gone, and he could breath almost normally.

Dunkelzahn is no longer a part of my life. I must move on.

He felt much better already. *I don't need the dragon,* he thought. *I can be an island. I need no one.*

He looked down at Nadja, at the lovely hollow of her neck white against the blue satin sheets. Black hair around her head like a pool of dark ink.

An image came into his mind then. A memory?

The woman in the vision was different, but the position of her body was the same. Lying on her back, head tilted slightly left. The arch of her neck so alluring, the skin of it soft to his touch. Dark pool of hair around her head.

Then he imagined his fingers brushing over her throat, delicately so as not to wake her. Wouldn't want to disturb her peaceful repose. He imagined encircling her neck with his two hands, palms angled out, thumbs hovering over her trachea. The marks he made didn't show right away—the bruises that would form where he grabbed her suddenly and squeezed, pressing the ball of his thumbs into the soft spot of her throat, just below the jaw.

In the vision, the dark pool changed from hair to blood. The thick coppery fluid gushing from the split in her skull where he had been forced to slam her head against the bedpost. And in the silent moments after the small struggle, before the bruises faded into view, she lay there exactly as if she slept. Just as peaceful. Just as serene.

Mocking him from beyond the pale.

The vision passed, and Ryan shook his head. Nadja lay there, untouched and very much alive. It wasn't a memory, he knew now. It was a fantasy from Roxborough's distant past. The woman's name was Eva Thorinson, someone he knew back in college. She had been his girlfriend for about three months. Three very intense months.

He had fallen in love with her, but she not with him. She had wanted him only for sex and money. She had *used* him! Ryan felt anger at the thought. She had used him and had left just when he'd proposed moving in together. Eva had stared into his eyes, her face set in stone, and she had told him that she felt trapped by him.

Ha, that he scared her. Of all the stupid fragging lies. He treated her like royalty, bought her anything and everything she wanted. That ungrateful slitch! He wanted to kill her, but he'd never had the confidence he could pull it off.

Nadja's neck glimmered in the prismatic light. Beckoning him to touch it. She would do the same as Eva. No doubt in his mind. This elf whore would use him for this worthless mission, and keep him for sex, but afterward, he would be forgotten for the next man. For someone who could stay at home.

Wait a minute, Ryan thought. *What am I doing?* He drew his hand back; it had been hovering just over her throat.

He could kill her easily; he knew many ways. Crushing her trachea would be painful, but suffocation was appropriate. Roxborough knew what that felt like. Now she would too.

He reached out with his hand, holding it just over her neck. The move would have to be quick. Decisive, and powerful. No hesitation. No second thoughts.

Ryan lowered his hand a fraction of a centimeter. Still not touching, but so very close. So close he could feel the warmth of her skin. He could detect the microvibrations of air as her breath passed in and out of her throat.

Ah, that delicate throat. So fine. So fragile. How could he bring himself to mar such beauty?

His wristphone beeped, and he jerked his hand back. Silence. No movement from Nadja.

It beeped again and he slid out of bed to answer it. "This is Quicksilver," he said, his voice low.

"Jane."

"Verify, Jane."

Her identification code came through and registered on his wristphone. "Good," he said. "It's late. What do you have?"

"The stat-feed from your phone indicated you were awake," Jane said.

"So I am," Ryan's response was too quick. "Get to it, chummer. What've you got?"

"I've got some leads on the item you're looking for."

"Are we secure?" he asked.

"Yes."

"You know who stole the Dragon Heart?"

"I believe so."

Something entered the room just then. A presence that Ryan felt like a palpable energy, even though he couldn't see anything. He spun around, searching the room, but he saw nothing unusual. Nadja still slept peacefully despite his low conversation.

"Hold on," he said. Ryan concentrated, shifting his sight so that he could see into the astral plane. The astral came into view, blinding him. In the center of the room shone a brilliant gold beacon of astral energy, dimming and brightening as he looked at it.

A spirit?

Ryan adjusted his astral sight in an attempt to take in what he was seeing. Around the yellow sphere of energy was a nearly transparent fluctuation, a distortion of astral space like a heat shimmer. Flashes of energy arced out from the glowing center through the distortion, like gold lightning. Ryan couldn't tell if the shimmer was part of the entity in front of him or an effect of the central core, but the distortion passed through the walls and out of Ryan's sight. Too large to fit into the confines of the room. Ryan had never seen an astral creature this big.

What the frag—?

29

Lethe hovered in the hotel suite, looking at the man in front of him. In the physical world, the man was large for a human, and extremely fit, with strong muscles, all natural. He stood completely naked except for a small device on his wrist into which he had been speaking. His hair was reddish brown, his eyes were blue, strangely adorned with silver flecks that gave them a metallic look.

In the astral, a war flared inside this man. His aura was strongly magical, and there was a foundation of solidity, but within that foundation it seemed that fluctuations were forming. Discontinuities that Lethe could see plainly. This person was something other than he seemed, and was changing by the moment.

The human seemed to be able to perceive Lethe's presence. Perhaps Lethe would be able to communicate with him without having to possess someone. Maybe he was like Thayla in that regard. Lethe extended his will. "You can see me."

"Yes," said the human.

"You can hear me?"

"What are you?"

"I am what you call a spirit," it said. "My name is Lethe."

"What do you want?"

"I want to talk to the elf, Nadja Daviar."

"Ryan?" It was Nadja's voice. She was waking up.

"There is a powerful spirit in the room, Nadja," Ryan said. "Calls itself Lethe."

Nadja bolted upright in the bed. "What does it want?"

"To talk to you," Ryan told her.

"Last time it talked to me, someone died."

"That was an accident," Lethe said. "I had never possessed

anyone before, and I did not realize what would happen. I am truly sorry."

Ryan relayed the words to Nadja.

"This is the spirit I was telling you about," she said. "The one who told me about the Dragon Heart theft."

"You know of the Dragon Heart?" Ryan asked.

"Yes. I seek it."

"Why?" Open suspicion in the human's voice.

"A woman named Thayla asked me to bring it to her," Lethe said. "She is protecting the world from destruction, but there are those in this world who try to erode her defenses."

The human looked stunned. "Incredible," he said.

"What do you mean?"

"I have been given the same task."

"By whom?"

"Dunkelzahn," Ryan said.

Excellent! Lethe thought. *An ally! This human must be competent enough to complete the task if Dunkelzahn gave it to him. . . .* "I'd like to help," Lethe said. "I know where the item is."

"You do?" Ryan said. "Where?"

"The elves who stole it brought it to a city called Eugene, in a land known as Tir Tairngire. It is in a heavily guarded building where many items are kept and studied."

Ryan lifted his hand and spoke into the device. "Jane, this spirit says it knows where the Dragon Heart is.

"Where?" came a tinny, synthesized voice.

"A well-guarded building in Eugene, Tir Tairngire."

Jane did not respond immediately, perhaps considering the possibilities. "That scans," she said finally. "It could be right."

"What've you come up with?"

"The runners who took the Dragon Heart belong to a group called the Mystic Crusaders. I don't have much on why their organization exists, but one thing they do is provide security, and runners, for the Atlantean Foundation."

Lethe knew none of this, but Ryan was nodding his head.

"I know about AF," Ryan said. "Go on."

"You do?" Jane sounded surprised. "Did you get your memory back?"

Ryan smiled. "It's been a mixed blessing, believe me."

"Anyway, I did a surface run on the AF main host. They do have a research facility in Eugene. It's one of three highly secure sites. The majority of their facilities are warehouses, office buildings, and low-security museums. I scanned their shipment logs, but came up blank. According to their data-banks, they haven't checked in a new item for over two weeks."

This Jane woman is very resourceful, thought Lethe. *A definite asset.* "Even if they've moved the item," he said to Ryan, "I will be able to find it."

"How?"

"I don't know exactly. I'm attuned to its signature and can locate it by the signs of where it passed. Do you understand?"

Ryan shook his head. "I've never heard of anything like that, but it sounds a little like ritual magic."

Nadja slid across the bed and stood up, wrapping her silk robe around her. She came over and put her arms around Ryan. "What are you talking about?" she said. She couldn't hear any of what Lethe said, and this human hadn't been translating everything.

Ryan turned to her. "I think Lethe here is going to help me find the Dragon Heart," he said.

"The spirit's data is consistent with mine," Jane said. "I'm not going to be able to pin it down further than three possible places. Might as well try Eugene first."

Ryan nodded. "Let's do it then. Who can we get for backup?"

"How about Axler and her team at Assets, Incorporated?"

"Can they pull it off?"

"They got you out of Aztlan, didn't they?"

"I suppose they did," Ryan said. "Nearly killed me a few times, too."

Jane's tone was dead serious. "They're the best I know."

"Okay, are they available?"

"I think so," said Jane.

"Check it out, would you?"

"Sure thing, chummer."

"Thanks, Jane," Ryan said.

"See you down the screaming highway," Jane said, then disconnected.

Lethe listened, fascinated by the conversation. Intent on piecing together the meaning. He thought he understood what Ryan said, but he found that his perception was greatly enhanced by his ability to see Ryan's astral image. It gave him clues about meaning and sincerity. But deciphering Jane's idioms and slang spoken in a fake voice from an electronic universe was nigh impossible.

Ryan looked at Lethe again. "Will you come along?"

"I see no way you can stop me," Lethe said, meaning no disrespect. But as soon as he said it, a puzzled look crossed Ryan's features. His aura flared blue for a moment.

Ryan laughed. "Why would we want to?" he said. But Lethe could tell that the laughter was forced. Ryan was less than one-hundred percent sincere. Lethe saw that as a fatal flaw. Ryan was competent; he was willing. But was he committed? Was he prepared to risk his life for his mission?

Lethe judged not. Lethe determined that Ryan could end up a liability. Lethe would go along for now. He would help Ryan get the Dragon Heart. But he was wary. He knew a time might come when he and Ryan Mercury would be at odds. When that happened, Lethe would be ready.

15 August 2057

30

In the dim pre-dawn light, Burnout stood on the roof of the Howard Johnson's across the street from the Watergate Hotel listening intently to the sound coming from the laser microphone. The roof guard lay dead a short distance away, a trickle of blood leaking from the side of his open mouth. Burnout had shot him from the Aztechnology diplomatic rotorcraft as it descended to land on the helipad. The night flight from Lake Louise had brought them here, and now a reward was soon to come. Burnout could smell it.

Slaver sat next to him, cross-legged in his idea of street clothes—loose-fitting Guatemalan pants, brightly striped in purples and yellows. His shirt matched, very reflective and simple to spot even at night. An easy target in combat. Slaver's tattooed skull gleamed in the prismatic light coming from the street below, the coiled serpent seeming to dance in the shifting rainbow.

The light originated from the magical phenomenon that hovered over the center of the road below. The manastorm, Slaver had called it. An eerie sight that reminded Burnout of astral space, the world he could no longer see. Reminded him of his lost dream.

The manastorm had been setting the blood spirit, La Sangre, on edge ever since they'd come near it. The spirit said nothing, but he obviously seethed at Slaver, who had sent the spirit over into the hotel room at first. La Sangre had come back in terror, ranting about an invisible spirit in that room, a spirit with such power it could banish him with a thought. Now, La Sangre huddled next to the knee-high cement ledge and whimpered.

Burnout saw hatred of the mage in the spirit's eyes, and it wasn't the first time he'd seen that. Burnout wondered if

Slaver knew that the spirit wanted to kill him. Now, Slaver seemed to ignore the increasing discomfort his ally spirit felt in the presence of the manastorm. Slaver had asked for silence so that he could listen.

The laser microphone used a light beam to detect the vibrations on the window glass of the hotel suite across the street. Any sound that hit the glass was amplified by the microphone that Burnout held in his hand; the servo mount built into his wrist kept the heavy device steady. The curtains of the chosen room were drawn and any view inside was obscured.

Several voices came through the speakers. Two voices seemed to be coming from the room, one male and one female. Another voice sounded technologically created, like it came from a telecom or a trideo. Burnout had heard the male's voice before; it matched the pattern in his memory of the human he'd fought with back in San Marcos. In the helicopter. This one fought very well, surprisingly quick and stronger than he looked.

His name was Ryan Mercury.

He was the man Burnout had been ordered to kill, and his voice filled Burnout's head like a ghost of static, and it took all Burnout's concentration and effort to remain still. The man was close, just across the wide space, inside the hotel.

"Yes, Jane?" came Mercury's voice.

"I've got Assets, Incorporated on line," came another voice, tinny and barely audible. Burnout assumed this was Jane.

"Good," Mercury said. "How do I get transportation to their compound?"

"I've reserved you a suborbital seat to Seattle, diplomat class, of course. Axler will meet you when you land. She'll escort you to the Assets compound."

"Are she and the others ready for the run?"

"By the time you get to the compound, they'll be prepped."

"Good." After a pause, "What, Lethe?" Then, "Okay, right away."

There was nothing for a moment except for the sound of fingers tapping on a keyboard. Burnout felt an itch in his mind, a need to fulfill. To kill this Ryan Mercury. He was here now. No time to waste. This one was fast, quick. He might be gone anytime. He might slip away.

"The male voice matches our target," Burnout said. "We should kill him now while he's—"

"Shut the frag up!" Slaver said in a harsh whisper. "I'm trying to listen here, you complete imbecile! I need to make absolutely sure it's him before we can proceed. Spirits hang you."

"But—"

"Just shut up and hold that laser mike steady!"

Burnout felt the hatred surge inside him. He had already verified the target's identity. Slaver was becoming a liability to their mission. He would have to be neutralized so that Burnout could proceed with the assassination. Burnout's aim on the laser mike wavered, sluing to the left.

Static screamed in the speakers as the laser raked across the glass. Slaver glanced up at Burnout, another spiteful reproach on his lips.

Then the drug filled Burnout's body with pleasure, and he remembered his life of magic, back in his teen years when he ran free with his friends. He dazzled them with a levitation spell he'd learned from old man Getty.

Slaver's abuse didn't matter. Nothing mattered.

Burnout got the laser focused again. But the suite was silent now. The conversation had ended. Mercury had left. They had lost him.

"Fragging slot!" Slaver said. "If that was really Mercury, you just let him get away."

Burnout merely stood there and thought of his past. Pleasant memories. The drug coursed through him, warming him from inside. It didn't matter what Slaver said. Even though Burnout knew the mage was wrong, he would stand and take the blame. If they'd acted instead of waited, Mercury would be dead now.

But that didn't matter. Slaver was right. Burnout was wrong.

And Ryan Mercury was alive, but not for too much longer. It was the promise of another fight with him that filled Burnout with a rush of adrenaline. This time the fight would be to the death, bloody and gruesome. This time there would be no capture orders, no restraints to keep Burnout from inflicting death upon the man.

There would be no injections of gamma-scopolamine to immobilize the body. There would be nothing that could save the man's flesh. There would be only broken bones, gushing blood, and one eviscerated human corpse.

31

Ryan settled in his seat as the suborbital descended into SeaTac. He'd been contemplating what had happened in Washington. He'd nearly killed Nadja, had come to the edge of destroying the one person he still had feelings for. And for what?

He didn't really know. And that scared the drek out of him.

A shiver shook him. He had some serious problems to work through. Bits and fragments of his Roxborough past were coming back to him at unexpected times; they made him act erratically. That last one had nearly cost him Nadja's life. *I'll have to be very careful,* he thought. *And strong, so that I can see right from wrong.*

Ryan was anxious for action. It had been only three days since he'd been rescued, and he was already getting jittery from lack of motion. That had been one of the major reasons he'd decided to go ahead with the Dragon Heart mission, at least for now. To combat the boredom. And to *move,* to act. He was a physical adept; his life was defined by action and physical activity. Excessive stasis gave him too much time to think.

Too much time to relive Roxborough's memories.

The shuttle plunged out of the stratosphere like an aerodynamic rock, the slope of its descent frighteningly steep, though the ride was very smooth. Soon Ryan was on the ground and being greeted by Axler at the terminal.

She gave him a cold smile, the doe-brown color of her eyes matching her tasseled suede jacket. She looked good in street attire, though her posture was aggressive, almost hostile. Par for the course. She was hard and wasn't about to show any hint of weakness.

She pushed a strand of blonde hair out of her eyes. "Dhin is waiting," she said.

"Great to see you too," Ryan said. "I'm fine, thanks for asking."

Almost brought a smirk to her face. Then she stifled it and turned to face him. "Look, Ryan, I'm not one for small talk and chitchat. You want that, get yourself a biff."

"Whoa, it was just a fragging joke, *omae.*"

"And I'm not your *omae,* chummer."

"Got it," Ryan said.

Then she laughed, and it was a genuine, friendly sound. Ryan found it refreshing, but then he saw the opportunity to take control of the conversation. Part of Roxborough's training flooded him, wouldn't allow the chance to slide by. He cut off her laughter. "You've got everything ready?"

Her laugh broke off abruptly, and she glared at him. "We're still getting data from Jane."

"Fill me in on what you've got."

"Not here," she said, and he noticed her guard was back up, her body language all biz. She had jacked up reflexes, possibly a move-by-wire system to get such smooth motion, such control. He also suspected that her muscles had been replaced with synthetic fiber. She didn't *look* that strong, but she carried herself as though she could humble a troll in hand to hand.

Ryan didn't doubt that she could. He remembered how she'd carried him out of the delta clinic with null strain.

Strictly speaking, however, all her cyber was hidden. Her eyes looked natural; her skull showed no obvious signs of surgery; even her flesh-toned datajack was discreetly hidden under her hair. It was all part of her plan to lull opponents into thinking she was a biff. Just before she wasted their hoops.

They passed through a security check and out into the private aircraft area. Seattle had been hit pretty hard by the same rioting that had spread all across UCAS after Dunkelzahn's death. Air traffic was down to minimal, but Jane must have been working hard because their credsticks got them through with ease.

Dhin was sleeping in the cockpit of the modified Hughes

Airstar helicopter when they approached. "Hoi!" Axler said, slamming the door after she and Ryan had climbed aboard.

Dhin jerked awake, nearly banging his big, warty head against the rigger console. "Frag, Axler," he said, wiping some gray drool from his chin. "Don' do that."

Axler gave a short laugh. "Just get us moving," she said.

"Hells Canyon tour?"

"Yes, Assets compound."

As Ryan strapped himself into a torn vinyl chair next to Axler, Dhin powered up the rotors. And a few minutes later, the blades thrumming rhythmically above them, Dhin lifted the helo, taking them up steeply. He angled up and out, then kicked in the jets, and they blasted into Salish-Shidhe territory.

The Cascades shone in the afternoon sun, white snow caps above forested slopes. Several of the highest peaks were rounded since the massive eruptions that occurred in conjunction with the Great Ghost Dance forty years ago. Ryan had been only five years old when that had happened—four peaks erupting simultaneously in the most massive display of ritual magic ever. The Native Americans had gotten fed up with the oppression against them and had called on their shamans to stop the government troops threatening to destroy them. Many, many shamans sacrificed themselves to power the ritual, or so the rumor went, and all that magical power was channeled into the volcanic Cascades.

Nothing since could compare.

Once the Hughes Airstar had cleared the peaks, and they were flying safely along the far northern edge of the Columbia River Gorge, Axler contacted Jane. The water shone a pristine blue on their right, and across its wide flow were the hills of the elven nation of Tir Tairngire. The elves had a reputation for paranoid border patrol, which was why Dhin kept the helo well inside the Salish Shidhe edge.

We'll be going there soon enough, thought Ryan, and a thrill of excitement channeled through him. Their run tomorrow would take them deep within the borders of the elven nation. It would be a dangerous run, and they would need all their cunning and stealth to pull it off. It was just what Ryan needed.

"Jane," Axler said to the telecom screen. "Ryan's here.

We're enroute to the Assets compound to rendezvous with the others and plan the run."

"I've got some details on the Atlantean Foundation's building security," Jane said, her voice flat and without emotion on the helo's speaker.

Ryan activated the telecom screen next to his seat, and saw Jane's ridiculous blonde bimbo persona looking out at him. All red lipstick and sparkling eyes, huge bosom and hourglass hips under pinstripe business suit. He almost laughed, but instead he said, "Ready for download."

A series of graphics flooded into the telecom's memory. There were maps of Eugene and surrounding area, enlargements of the research park area along the Willamette River, with one of the buildings bolded. There were photos of the outside from almost every angle, plus Jane had reconstructed a three-dimensional model based on the photos.

Ryan was impressed. "Excellent work," he said. "Very thorough."

"There's more," Jane said. "I couldn't get a floor plan, but I did manage to snag the original blueprints from a very old databank—in the city's archives, of all fragging places."

The blueprints appeared on Ryan's screen. "How old?"

"The building is forty-two years old, but the Atlanteans have only had it for seventeen. I would say the blueprints are unreliable at best. A lot of interior modifications could have been made. I couldn't get current floor plan schematics without risking tipping their security. I can try if we deem it's crucial."

"Hopefully we won't need you on site, virtually speaking, until the actual run," Ryan said. "Lethe might be able to help us determine what remodeling they've done. He's been inside, remember."

"I know, but . . ." There was hesitation in Jane's voice. "I don't completely trust that spirit. What do we know about it?"

"Good point. We don't know drek."

Axler joined in. "I don't want it along," she said. "It could get us all killed."

Ryan turned to her. "I don't think we have a choice. The thing is way too powerful to stop. If it wants to come along, there's nothing we can do."

"McFaren might be able to trap it, or bind it or something," Axler said.

Ryan just laughed.

"What?"

"Maybe," he said finally. "But I seriously doubt it. Lethe is the most powerful spirit I've ever encountered."

"We just need to be aware that its intentions may not jive with ours," Jane said.

"Agreed."

"Where is it anyway?" asked Axler.

"I don't know," said Ryan. "Last I saw it was early this morning in FDC."

"I'm right here," came a voice that nearly sent Ryan jumping out of his seat. He looked into the astral plane to see the blinding glow of Lethe. Only a tiny part of the spirit fit inside the helicopter, but even that small fraction was enough to chill Ryan. Like ice water in the very marrow of his bones.

32

The dwarf male shifted nervously in his fancy chair, blonde leather, high-back with dark finished wood-grain wings. Burnout was used to the reaction. Some people just didn't like what he had become, a perversion of humanity and robotics.

The dwarf man's name was Wynar Smith. He was a fixer, based in the Washington DC area, and as such he was very well connected, accustomed to a life of comfort, of dealing with powerful corporate execs. He had hired the shadow-runner, Kaylinn Axler, and her team for several runs. Or so Slaver had learned from his contacts. Smith knew about Assets, Incorporated, the place where Ryan Mercury had gone. And sooner or later, the fixer would give up that information. It was just a matter of time and torture.

Burnout knew all these factlets, but they didn't come close to encompassing this quivering lump of dwarf flesh in front of him. Wynar Smith was afraid to die, and Burnout could smell it.

It smelled pathetic. Still, Burnout stood behind Slaver and the blood spirit ally, waiting for the order that he knew would come. The information first; he had to remember that. They had to get the information before the man's throat could be ripped from his neck, his bloody windpipe yanked out by his Adam's apple. Yes, Burnout would have to wait.

"I want the location of Assets, Incorporated," Slaver said, pacing. His short body was only slightly taller than the frightened dwarf, but Slaver held himself with confidence, that made him seem much larger. "I'm willing to make a deal if necessary, but I must have it."

"I . . . I . . . You must understand, I can't tell you that. If it ever gets out—"

"What?" Slaver asked. "They'll kill you?"

Wynar Smith glanced around him furtively, scanning the bodies of the street samurai who served as his bodyguards for signs of life. Burnout and La Sangre had killed six of them, two mages and four chrome jobs. Good fighters. Not like this dwarf coward.

"They . . . they *will* kill me," the dwarf said flatly. "I . . . I . . . I don't want to die."

"Nobody wants that," Slaver said, an edge of false sincerity in his voice. "We just want the data. You can do whatever is necessary after we leave. Make it look like a break-in, like they threatened to kill you if you didn't tell them." Slaver paused, smiled. "Oh yeah, that's the truth." He gave a little grating laugh.

Burnout twitched, becoming impatient. This was taking too long.

"Besides," said Slaver, laughing softly. "You won't have to tell me. I've scanned it in your mind. It's situated on the edge of a deep canyon."

"You can't trick me like that," Wynar Smith said. "I won't think of it."

"Which one, halfer? Don't try playing games with me, you hear? Not the Grand Canyon? No. What about Zion? No."

"My mind is blank," Smith muttered to himself. "My mind is blank. Blankness. Nothing in here. My mind—"

"Hells Canyon?" Slaver said, then paused as he seemed to concentrate more intently. "That's it," he said finally. "Hells Canyon it is."

"You don't know drek," Smith yelled. "Hells Canyon is more than a hundred and fifty kilometers long. You'll never find it."

"Tsk tsk, getting a little uncivilized," Slaver admonished. "Burnout, can you teach him some manners?"

Burnout sprang into motion like a pouncing tiger. His laser tool was in his hand instantly as he moved to Smith's side. So fast Smith didn't have time to jump before Burnout's free hand had encircled the dwarf's ankles. Burnout jerked Smith into the air, feet first. And held him there, upside down, while he activated the small laser.

"Ah, let me down."

The laser tool wouldn't do extensive damage unless used

on the eyes, but at the highest setting it hurt, especially when
applied to sensitive areas like the genitals. Burnout didn't
think that would be necessary today. He just held the dwarf
high and stripped off his Armanté shoes and his argyle
socks. Then he began burning a heart shape into the skin
over his Achilles tendon.

The dwarf screamed as the laser burned into the skin, a
thin wisp of smoke rising along with the smell of roasting
flesh and hair.

"The location of Assets, Mr. Smith?" Slaver said.

"Frag you!"

Burnout smiled. This might be more fun than he'd origi-
nally thought. Smith's hands made dull thuds as they hit his
abdomen, but he barely registered the sensation. The heart
shape was finished, so he decided to use the laser to excise
one of the dwarf's toes, the pinkie of his left foot. It would
take ten minutes to cut all the way through.

The dwarf's screams echoed through the room as Slaver
poured himself a glass from a pitcher of lemonade that was
sitting out on the table. Then he came back over. "Don't kill
him," he said. "Yet."

It was a simple comment, and in hindsight, an innocuous
one. But it slotted Burnout off. Of course, he wouldn't kill
him. He knew that. It was *understood*. He felt the hatred rise
inside him.

"What you must realize, Mr. Smith," Slaver said,
addressing the dwarf, "is that my metal friend here is not the
brightest boy. He's very efficient at killing, and he's almost
impossible to kill, but if he gets it in his chrome skull that
you don't deserve to live, I might not be able to control
him."

The hatred flooded Burnout, filling him like an instant
tide. And this time it came so fast that the drug didn't kick in
before he'd reacted. He swung the flailing body of Wynar
Smith around like a thick flesh bat, smashing it against the
hard flagstones of the marble hearth. The white rock spat-
tered red with the impact, as the dwarf's head split like a
rotten pumpkin.

"Burnout, you fragging moron!"

"He's not dead," Burnout said, holding up the crimson-
stained body.

Slaver bit off a reply, his face taking on a look of intense concentration as he focused on the dwarf's bloody form.

As the happy drug rushed through Burnout, he held the body still as the last of the dwarf's blood dripped to the carpeting along with loosened fragments of skull and brain matter. The drug held him content, his memories and the longing for magic anchoring him in the realm of the living.

Finally, Slaver looked up. "He's dead," he said to no one in particular. "But his own thoughts betrayed him in the end. I know the location of Assets, Inc."

Burnout dropped the dwarf's body and stepped back. He knew he had violated some trust with Slaver, some fine line of command that had existed between them. Gone now. They both knew it, but he didn't know what either of them was going to do about it.

"Let's go," Slaver said, not looking at him.

Burnout nodded and followed the others out.

33

The jet-assisted Hughes Airstar blasted through the cool air over the Columbia River on its way toward Assets Incorporated. Ryan took several breaths to get his composure back. "Lethe," he said, forcing a laugh. "Don't scare me like that."

"I assure you I am trustworthy," the spirit said. "My intentions are pure."

Jane came on. "Is it there with you?"

"Yes," said Ryan.

"Maybe it can get some recon data on the target site so we can make adjustments to the blueprints. It'd be nice to have a current schematic."

"What is the electronic spirit asking?" Lethe said.

Ryan smiled at that. "She wants to know if you'd be willing to go back to the building where the Dragon Heart is being kept. We need to know the layout of the corridors and rooms so that we can use the information to modify the blueprints we have. It will help us plan out the run."

The spirit's answer was quick. "Yes." Then it was gone, winked out like it had never been there.

Ryan sighed. "Well, it's gone again," he said.

"Where?" said Axler.

"I think it's going to get the recon data Jane wanted."

"Excellent," said Jane.

"If we can trust what it tells us," said Ryan.

The rest of the flight to the compound passed quickly, the scenery spectacular as the mountains rose around them. They had branched away from the Columbia when it met the Snake River, then had followed the Snake for just over an hour, before the canyon began to rise on either side. It was like two edges of a jagged cut in the flesh of the world. Now, Dhin was taking them up and up, until they rose up over the rim of a ledge in the eastern cliff face—a narrow flat space that had been paved and made into a secret compound.

Ryan remembered Assets, Incorporated from a few of his missions before the Roxborough incident. But it seemed to have changed somewhat in the past year. Axler, Grind, McFaren, and Dhin were the only employees of the corporation that had been wholly owned by Dunkelzahn through various holding companies and false fronts. Nadja had just told Ryan that the dragon had left the entirety of Assets, Incorporated, to him in his will.

So I own all of this, he thought, looking around as he climbed out of the helicopter. There was a warehouse of corrugated steel, a concrete airstrip, some metal sheds full of weaponry and ammunition, and an underground bunker.

What a drekhole.

But what did he expect? Assets had been created by Jane-in-the-box to be a front to run a special operations team. Also known as shadowrunners. Or criminals.

Axler led Ryan inside the warehouse, which had obviously seen better days. Its panels hung askew, the metal rusting in places. Huge hangar-type doors opened into the haphazard mess of Dhin's rigger shop where oil, grease, and engine parts were strewn everywhere. Ryan saw the skeletal remains of an Aguilar attack helicopter and what looked like a mostly functional T-bird.

Axler led the way through an innocuous door in the side wall. And into a small, functional changing room. Lockers and closets full of uniforms, disguises, and body armor of all sorts lined the walls. There was an adjoining room stocked with all but the heaviest weapons and ammunition, which Ryan knew were kept in separate sheds.

Axler kicked off her boots and indicated for Ryan to do the same. He complied, then followed her through the far door and down the four flights of stairs and into the command center. McFaren and Grind greeted them as they entered the command room. It was clean and very modern, with a communications array to rival the security bay of any well-protected installation.

There was a workout floor with weights, a sparring mat, and a simsense deck to hone skills in simulated real life. There was a large trideo surrounded by couches, a kitchen and dining area, plus a conference table and desks. McFaren had a separate room, down one level, for his magical work.

Ryan quickly revised his opinion. Dunkelzahn had obviously seen fit to upgrade this base since Ryan had last been down here. Axler and team had far better facilities than he'd realized. Dunkelzahn and Jane valued them highly, and they *had* managed to rescue Ryan from a well-protected delta clinic in the heart of Aztlan—a hostile country under the best of circumstances. Ryan was starting to believe that they could actually pull off this run to retrieve the Dragon Heart.

The trideo came to life in front of him, showing Jane's three-dimensional construct of the Atlantean Foundation building. The walls were a transparent gray, and the floor plan of each level showed the interior design, at least from when the structure had been built.

Grind came up to Ryan, extending one of his metal hands. "Hoi."

Ryan shook the dwarf's hand. "Good to see you, chummer."

Grind nodded. "We've been going over Jane's data," he said. "We've got a few ideas for infiltration, but the detail on security is slim. We're hoping this spirit, Lethe, can help."

"Me, too."

McFaren joined them as they sat down on a couch. "He's not here yet," the mage said.

"He?"

"The spirit, Lethe."

"Why do you call it a he?" Ryan asked.

McFaren scowled. "I thought you would know," he said. "You've got the sight. It's a he."

"Oh," was all Ryan said. But the mage's comment bothered him, as though his perception had been impaired somehow by what had happened to him at Roxborough's clinic. The freakish duality of his mind, of his past, which made no sense unless he considered that he'd been two people up until a few days earlier.

Ryan suppressed a frown. "*He* should be back soon with the recon data."

"Let's proceed without him for now," Axler said. She held a remote in her hand, which she used to point out the outer defenses. "Now, let's get the basics down. First of all, the

Atlantean Foundation is a highly magical corporation with an interest in obtaining items and artifacts of an arcane nature. The Eugene facility is located in the Riverfront Research Park, right on the Willamette River. It's in the heart of Eugene, nestled between Franklin Boulevard and the west bank, surrounded by an arboretum of pines and maples and such. The arboretum extends for about twelve kilometers along the river on both banks. We could come in from up- or down-river and travel to the facility on foot using the paved pathways or through the trees."

"Any local heat to worry about?" asked Grind.

"Perhaps," said Axler, "but not more than elsewhere. Once we get inside the border, we shouldn't have to worry about cops, only corp security. We know the perimeter from the recent photos. Standard electrified cyclone topped with monowire."

"Any drones?"

"No drones," she said. "No cameras either. They saved those for the outer wall. There are paranimals, however."

"What kind?"

"Hell hounds," she said.

McFaren shuddered, but said nothing.

"There aren't very many, maybe five or six," Axler went on. "They patrol the space outside the building between the perimeter fence and the security wall." The pointer followed an open area just inside the outer fence. "The second obstacle is the wall," she said. "It's a five-meter-high cinderblock construction with our favorite Ares Sentinel track drones and security cameras."

"Might also be spirits and watchers, or maybe a ward there," McFaren said.

Ryan felt a presence around him, and he pushed his sight to see into the astral. Lethe had joined them. "He's right," the spirit said. "Tell him that there are air and fire elementals and several dozen watcher spirits."

Ryan relayed the information, serving as translator for the big spirit. Jane joined them as soon as she heard that Lethe had come with new data. Ryan translated for the spirit, and Jane modified the 3-D holograph in front of them to be consistent with the new information. Within a few hours, the

detail had increased tenfold, and they had formulated an
infiltration strategy.

Their plan was far from perfect, and they didn't have all
the data. Lethe had been reluctant to enter the chamber that
held the Dragon Heart. The room was warded, and he hadn't
wanted to break the barrier and warn the researchers of his
presence. So Axler and Jane and Ryan went over the plan
several times, suggesting alternatives, weighing options, and
ironing out any potential glitches.

Excitement gripped Ryan as they finalized the timetable;
he was anxious for action. He worked well with these people.
Especially Jane, who had an amazing knack for coming up
with the simplest plan, which despite its simplicity included
provisions for failure at any step along the way, and for
escape after the item had been retrieved.

Grind and McFaren dressed in their disguises, got fake
System Identification Numbers from Jane, and left right
away. They needed to be on site first. It took a few additional
hours for Ryan and Axler to prepare everything and get
underway. A thrill raised the hackles on Ryan's neck as Dhin
lifted the helo from the tarmac. Axler was strapped in next to
him, a look of stone-cold determination on her pretty face.

Ryan smiled; it was a good plan. One that took into
account almost every contingency. Almost. There was just
one thing that bothered Ryan. One intangible that could frag
everything to hell. Lethe. They were relying on the spirit for
entirely too much, and Ryan wasn't ready to completely trust
him. The spirit was alien and very powerful; there was no
way of knowing his real motivation. His real intentions.
If Lethe wanted to double-cross them, it would be far too
easily done.

34

Jane-in-the-box surveyed her sensory feeds. She was in the brushed steel cube of her box, the video and audio feeds of her team spinning around her as she changed point of view and checked the inputs from each runner.

Axler and Dhin were with Ryan in the approaching helo, the night wrapped around them like a black velvet blanket. They were vectoring down from Willamette Pass east of Eugene. Their estimated time to target was nine minutes. Jane didn't have a feed on Ryan, though she could contact him by his wristphone if necessary.

Grind and McFaren were already on site, presumably with the spirit Lethe. It had been early evening by the time McFaren had managed to get inside under the newly created identity of Dr. Jack Rinehart, a leading researcher from the Illuminates of the New Dawn magical order. Dr. Rinehart wanted protection from the Atlantean Foundation until he could cut a deal with them for the sale of an item he deemed to be very powerful.

Grind was along as his personal bodyguard, and Lethe was the item. Or at least he was supposed to make the mundane African sculpture that McFaren carried *look* like ancient magic.

Jane hoped it worked. McFaren had asked for asylum from IOND, claiming the powerful magical order would gather a group of initiates to kill him by ritual magic. The AF facility was the only place he knew whose members might be able to create a hermetic circle powerful enough to protect him.

Through Grind's headcam link, Jane could see that he and McFaren waited inside a huge circle of painted Sperethiel and chalk powder symbols. Three resident research mages were inspecting the item in the corner of the larger chamber, and so far, so good.

Besides the mages, there were only two guards with them. Lethe only had to convince them that the item was magical until Axler and Ryan got on site. A few more minutes. All feeds were strong. Time for a little Matrix run.

Jane slipped down through her virtual gateway and into the electronic skies of the Lake Louise private grid. She paused briefly to stretch her virtual muscles, then blasted out through her special datalines, and into the heart of the Tir Tairngire Matrix without a hiccup. She'd been here before, had a legit front as an investment property manager, though her host operated as a virtual machine on a powerful mainframe that was operated by a Eugene-based company called Synerman Technologies.

It was a cheap and easy way to avoid decking through the Tir's defenses every time she needed to break into the country's electronic landscape. Which was getting to be all the fragging time.

Jane popped out of her virtual host and into the Eugene LTG. Most of the structures were still standard UMS iconology—octahedrons and planar explosions of data colored blue and purple. The power company—Eugene Water and Electric—looked like a large elven hand holding two bolts of lightning in a closed fist. The lightning flashed alternately yellow and blue, but under the facade, everything was the standard geometrics.

Jane logged on as a request for a billing update, a standard octahedral datapacket. She moved in past the probe IC without hitch, then she changed tactics. Using her analyze utility, she scanned the universe of databanks and subprocessors hanging in front of her. One of the SPUs was the one she wanted.

She sleazed her way in past the tar baby IC and assumed control of the subprocessor. This SPU wasn't heavily guarded because it didn't need to be. It only monitored systems; it didn't control anything. Jane smiled. That was the beauty of her plan. She would minimize the lethality by making several seemingly innocuous penetrations that would work synergistically. Each move was easier than a direct penetration of the host, and the results would hopefully be the same.

Jane spooled out a smartframe she had programmed for this run; it would sit dormant until the time was right. Then it would trigger the system, making it look like one of the power substations was failing. If the smart frame didn't work, her next job would be much harder.

Jane sneaked out of the host, gracefully logging off, and back through the Eugene LTG to look at the research park construct. It was a windowless fortress tower made of white ivory that stretched up into the sky like a virtual needle. There was a single door at the base.

The tower construct held the security hosts for several buildings, including the AF structure. Jane knew she could get into the Atlantean Foundation host through their central system in Atlanta, but she was sure that would be harder than this. That corridor was clogged with ice and might take too long for her to punch through. Besides, she didn't need access to any interior data; she just wanted a look at their security for a few CPU cycles. Also, she suspected that this ivory tower sculpture was less formidable than it appeared. Merely a facade to scare off newbie deckers.

At least she hoped so as she moved up to the entrance. She released a huge net and intercepted a datapacket that was headed for the single door, then had her deck analyze it before letting it go. She repeated this a few times; she still had a few minutes before her dormant smartframe came out of its coma. After six tries her deck found one with the right destination code—headed for the AF security subsystem.

She kept her standard octahedral facade, but used the datapacket's destination as she approached the door and tried to log on. The system asked for a passcode and a validation, which Jane's deception algorithm provided. After a long pause, the door slid upward and let her inside.

Inside, the iconology changed and Jane followed suit. The theme was an office building, not the most original metaphor to be wasted on such a vast amount of computing power. But that didn't concern Jane in the least. She merely changed her persona to match, becoming a floating memo—one of the ancient kind written on actual paper.

She located the AF structure and surveyed it. Getting into

the central host would be difficult, though not impossible for Jane. Just potentially ugly.

She had no intention of things getting ugly, however. She didn't need to access the central host, merely the subsystem that fed data to the closed-circuit security rigger. If there was no rigger and the drones were on autorecognition—unlikely, but possible—Jane's job would be even easier.

She positioned herself, and was ready when her smart frame triggered the false alarm. A simple matter of tricking the power company's subsystem to register a faulty reading. The EWEC system sent out a standard warning message.

"A power loss has been detected in the substation that feeds electricity to your building. One of the transformers is out and will have to be repaired. Meanwhile, power will be rerouted to the auxiliary substation. There should be no interruption of service, but a slight power surge is possible. The Eugene Water and Electric Company takes no responsibility for any damage that occurs to electronic devices during this transition. Thank you."

Perfect. Jane rushed into the midst of the priority messages and data instructions that came along with the message, and sleazed her way past some hefty-looking black ice, showing in the carpeted hallway like paper shredders. But they didn't sift the incoming data closely enough; the priority status fooled them. So far, so fragging good, and now Jane felt a rush of emotion. This run was just starting to test her, though it was still far easier than her run against Roxborough's system.

So far, she reminded herself. *Don't get overconfident now.*

As if on cue, she felt the burning sensation over her skin just then. That feeling of being watched again. *Alice again? Or just paranoia?*

Jane ignored the feeling. If it was Alice, she'd talk to her after the run. If it wasn't, then Jane would have to recook all her chips to get the ghost feeling out of her deck.

Then she was in the security subsystem. It took only a microsecond to set up a delayed power surge in three cameras and one drone. The power to the electric fence would also cut out for few minutes. She had set up a blind spot in the defenses, to become active exactly when the power company switched to the new substation. It would look like a power surge had burned out the electronics.

Once the smartframe was planted, Jane instigated a full retreat, as fast as possible. She had one more stop to make before she left the Matrix. The fire station was going to be an easy target. First, however, she wanted to get back to her box and check on the run's progress.

She was almost out when Alice manifested in front of her. Then Jane was no longer in the Eugene LTG, she was no longer in the Matrix at all. She was walking on a rain-slick black road in the mirrored canyon of Wonderland City. Alice stood under a street lamp, looking up as she pulled a cigarette from her mouth.

Jane felt the rain, smelled the cigarette smoke. Everything was so real. "I'm in the middle of a run," she said. "Please let me return to my friends. They're counting on me."

Alice smiled, the firefly street reflecting in her eyes like an endless reduction of mirrored images. "I have determined how you can repay me," she said. "I will explain, briefly, then I will let you go."

Even if Jane had a choice in the matter, she never let a debt go unpaid. "I'm listening," she said.

35

"Go, go!" Axler yelled, her voice ripped to hollow tatters under the deafening rush of the helo's rotor.

Ryan let himself fall through the night air, so fast he was pushing the edge of control as he free-rappelled down the nylon rope hanging out of the hovering helicopter. He watched Axler's black-streaked face grow smaller as he slid down, his gloved hands growing hot as he channeled the rope through his harness at a furious pace.

The sky was a splotched charcoal underbelly behind the 'copter, as Ryan caught a glimpse of Axler descending her rope just above him. She wore the same gray and black-spotted camouflage that covered Ryan, with semi-flexible Kevlar body armor underneath. The silhouette of a rucksack bulged on her back, its smooth surface broken by the sharp jutting of her Ares Alpha Combat gun, her favorite weapon—an automatic assault rifle and grenade launcher in one.

Ryan snapped his focus back on himself, using his magically enhanced strength and senses to drop into the arboretum trees below. And in seconds, he was down, unbuckling the harness from the rope. Crouching, blending into the surrounding cover. He made a quick scan of the terrain from down here even though he had done the same from above.

Nothing thermal, nothing visual. And nothing in the astral except bushes and trees and brambles.

Axler landed deftly next to him and scanned the area herself. Her subvocalization sounded like a deep whisper in his ear. "Condition?"

Ryan subvocalized into the pickup taped to his throat. "Green. Let's go."

He caught Axler's nod in the darkness, and followed her as she led the way through the trees. They sneaked along the river, darting from copse to thicket until they had gone about two kilometers. There were paved paths for bicycles, and foot bridges for pedestrians. There were birds and wildlife and lots of plants. Amazing for the center of a fragging city. Of course, this *was* Tir Tairngire. The elves were notorious for their adamant protection of nature.

In this case, it worked in Ryan's favor. He and Axler closed to within thirty meters of the outer fence of the Atlantean Foundation building before they had to stop. The physical movement felt great after the long, uneventful ride in the helicopter. The Tir border patrol didn't even hiccup when they'd come across near La Grande earlier that afternoon.

"I don't like it," Axler said. "Jane's been out of touch too long."

"We wait?"

Axler nodded. "Give her five minutes," she said.

Ryan sat on his heels and looked at the building. A three-meter-tall cyclone fence marked the perimeter of the facility. Monowire looped along the top, and inside those loops cameras and electric pulse generators were placed at twenty-meter intervals. A solid inner wall of painted cinderblock ran parallel to the fence. The building itself stood a few meters inside the wall. *This was not going to be easy.*

Ryan focused himself. Centering. After a minute he looked into the astral. The building's aura glowed in fuzzy reds and greens, like a defocused Christmas tree. The high background energy made it harder for Ryan to locate the watcher spirits, but after a few minutes of concentration, he thought he'd spotted them all. Two tiny spirits that looked like floating eyeballs hovered just above the inner wall, waiting for intruders.

Ryan couldn't see any elementals or nature spirits, but he did catch a glimpse of one of the hell hounds. The paranimal was larger than a normal dog, about twice the size of a wolf, but with red eyes, and acutely aware of both the physical and astral planes at the same time. It ran along a worn path inside the outer fence, trotting past as it burned off nervous energy.

The hound stopped just then, sniffing the air right in front of them. Ryan held his breath and refocused his vision on the

physical. He grabbed Axler's arm, then held a finger to his
lips when she looked at him. He pointed toward the fence
where the hell hound paced, smelling the air.

"Axler, Ryan," came Jane's voice in his ear just then. And
even though she'd whispered, Ryan's heart jumped into his
throat. His breath quickened for a second before he used
magic to steady himself, to hone his senses down on the here
and now. *No more fragging surprises.*

"Stand by, Jane," Axler subvocalized in a low whisper.

"I had a short delay," Jane said. "But I'm on-line now.
Your black window begins in twenty seconds."

The hell hound looked out in the direction of Ryan and
Axler as they crouched like part of the foliage, unmoving.
Finally, it moved away, continuing on its pacing track.

Jane's voice sounded in Ryan's ear again. "Grind and
McFaren are ready to move," she said. "They'll wait until
you're through the perimeter. Where's the spirit?"

Ryan looked into the astral but there was no sign of Lethe.
Wait a second, he thought. The fuzziness of the building's
aura grew clearer as he looked. As if a transparent pane of
glass or a heat shimmer stood between him and the fence. "Is
that you, Lethe?" he spoke.

"Yes, I am here. You are very perceptive."

"Thank you," Ryan said, but he was wondering how the
spirit had made himself nearly invisible in astral space. Ryan
hadn't thought it possible. "You'll have to show me how to
do that sometime."

"I'm not sure if it is something I can teach," came the
reply.

"Ready?" Axler said.

"Yes," said Lethe.

"Ready," said Ryan.

"Their blind spot is between those two cameras." Axler
pointed at a space on the perimeter about six or seven meters
to their right. "We'll have to move exactly between them to
prevent the other cameras from spotting us."

Ryan looked at Lethe. "Can you take care of the watcher
spirits?"

"Yes," came the reply. "They will not see us."

Axler tensed next to Ryan. "It begins . . . now," she said.
"Let's go."

She led the way, moving in a quick crouch, along the edge of the trees for a few meters, then straight across the clearing to the fence. Ryan moved behind her, a silent, invisible shadow. Axler reached the fence and doused the links with a squirt from her Ares Cascade gun. The liquid inside the reservoir was DMSO-laced water with a modified gamma-scopolamine clip. The stuff would paralyze a human or metahuman on contact. The liquid fell on the metal fence without so much as a sizzle. No electricity here.

Axler glanced around for the hell hounds, then removed wire cutters from her belt, clipped the fence at the base, and scrambled through. Ryan followed. The sprint between the fence and the wall went without a hitch, but just as Axler's grapple caught on the top of the wall, one of the hell hounds trotted around the corner.

Ryan moved, a blur in the night, pulling out a narcotic dart before the big dog even knew he was there. The dart flew, a high-velocity projectile, moving silently in the dark. Another was in Ryan's hand before the first one struck, hard, in the hound's neck.

Ryan had not needed his magically enhanced abilities since the night he'd spoken with Dunkelzahn on his wrist-phone, high on the ladder of the amusement park tower. It felt good to use magic again. He remembered falling that night, remembered fighting the cyberzombie, Burnout. And losing for the first time in his life. That idea hung in his mind for a minute. Had he met his match in combat? He and Dunkelzahn had both lost that night.

But this is just a fragging dog. He was on the hound before it could even yelp. Ryan grabbed its nose and clamped down, closing its jaw and twisting it off its feet in one motion. Taking no chances. The animal had no time to react; Ryan was too fast, too strong. He jammed the second dart into the creature's neck and it passed out. The whole thing took less than a minute.

Then he was pulling the hound's body off the worn track before following Axler up the rope and over the wall. They dropped down into a grassy courtyard scattered with tables and benches. *So far, so fragging excellent.* The target room was through the double glass doors, and up one level in a sealed room. But when Ryan and Axler crossed the grass and tried the doors, they found them locked.

Drek! Grind and McFaren are supposed to be here to unlock this door. What could have happened to them?

Axler shrugged, then moved aside as Ryan switched to the backup plan—he would pick the lock. That would take time, however, and time was a luxury they just didn't have. He examined the lock—simple dead bolt operated by an ID scanner. The best option would be to use acid paste on the bolt.

"Jane," Axler subvocalized. "The doors are locked. Can you help us out?"

Through the darkened glass, Ryan caught a glimpse of something inside. People coming. *Guards?* He bolted to the side of the door, pulling Axler with him, pressing himself against the wall. He focused, listening to the sound of the approaching footsteps. The harsh blue-white light on the wall shone through the trees, casting twisted skeletal shadows over the tables and chairs in the courtyard. Perfect cover.

Ryan pulled a small mirror from his webbing and carefully held it out in front of him, angling so that he could see the approaching figures. There were four of them, uniformed in black and crimson, carrying automatic weapons of some kind. They were headed straight for the double doors.

"Put-up or shut-up time, Axler," Ryan said. "Four sec guards. SMGs, light body armor, swords. Possibly a mage or a shaman. Ready?"

Axler sighed, drawing her Ares Cascade and dialing the nozzle to wide spray. She nodded.

"Okay, chummer," she said, "let's grind some hoop."

36

In her virtual steel box, Jane tried to shake off the lingering sensation of Wonderland City and focus tightly on Grind's feed. Alice's request had been simple, and could easily wait until after the run, but what gave Jane the shivers was what she'd learned about Alice from her research into the Crash of '29.

The only Alice who'd been part of Echo Mirage was Alice Haeffner. There were two things that spooked Jane about that. The first was her last name. Alice Haeffner turned out to be the ex-wife of Dunkelzahn's running mate and current president of the UCAS, Kyle Haeffner. The second thing was even more creepy: Alice Haeffner was dead. She had been killed in cybercombat against the virus that had caused the worldwide computer crash forty years ago.

Jane took a deep breath and shook away the virtual goose pimples. It was time to put all that out of her mind and deal with the here and now. Right now, Grind and McFaren, under the cloak of invisibility, were stealing along the corridor a safe distance behind the four security personnel who stood between them and the doors where Axler and Ryan waited. There were three women and one man, all of the elven metatype. They were not the same four who'd stolen the Dragon Heart, but she had no doubt that they belonged to the Mystic Crusaders.

They wore similar uniforms, except that one of the women wore a dog skin draped like a headdress. *Must be a shaman,* Jane thought. The others were most likely samurai or physical adepts like Quicksilver. The datajack in the temple of one of them said he could be a rigger or a decker, but the man also carried an array of knives and at least three guns that Jane cold see through Grind's eyes.

Luckily, none of them had looked back astrally. In fact their posture seemed overly casual to Jane, as though they were taking a break. They chatted among themselves in Sperethiel.

Earlier, back in the hermetic circle chamber, Grind and McFaren had taken out the two guards with a combination of magic and precise shots to their skulls. At that exact moment, Lethe had trapped the astral projecting forms of the three mages who had been examining the African sculpture. Then McFaren had cast a physical masking spell in the room to make it look to the cameras as though nothing had happened, calling on one of his elementals to sustain the spell.

Now, hiding in the corridor behind the four Mystic Crusaders, Grind subvocalized, "Jane, any suggestions on how to get rid of these guys?"

"Let those guards open the door," Jane said. "Then hope they don't see Quicksilver and Axler passing through."

"I don't like that idea. They're off duty, I think, probably going outside for a pipe or a tea or whatever the frag dandelion-eaters do on break."

"I don't think we should try to take them down," Jane said. "Too risky. Too much noise if they fire their weapons."

"I can sustain a silence spell on them," McFaren said, "but we might become visible. The high background in here is making my magic a little unpredictable."

Axler's voice came through. "Jane, give me *something*. They're almost to the door."

Drek, drek, drek. Not enough time to plan it out right.

"Okay," she said. "McFaren, silence spell as they open the door. *Not* before. Axler, you—"

"Too late," Axler said. "They've just popped the door." Axler turned, and through her eyes, Jane saw the Cascade come up.

One of the samurai called out a warning, but her cries made no sound. And by the time she'd drawn her gun, and was starting to jump out of the way, she was doused by the spray from the Cascade. The gun was on wide disbursement and all the guards got drenched.

Next to Axler, Ryan was firing his silenced pistol. Gel rounds, Jane remembered, to stun them. Trying to keep casualties low. First the dog shaman went down with a jerk as the bullet slammed into her neck.

The male samurai dove backward, and brought his weapon up with inhuman quickness. The laser sight flicked across Axler's chest for a second before Ryan's second shot hit the man's hand and made the shot fly wide. Fine and good, but Jane wondered how much sound that bullet would make when it hit the wall.

The whole scene was like a strange simsense game with the sound turned off. And in real life, the action was over in a less than a minute. And then only another two minutes more before Ryan had taken a passcard from the paralyzed body of the dog shaman and had hidden her in the bushes with the other bodies.

Jane's chess pieces were back in position. Inside the building and prowling along the hall under a newly cast mantle of invisibility. Headed toward the chamber where the Dragon Heart was kept.

Ryan spoke then. "Lethe says we've got to hurry. Some spirits saw us."

37

As Ryan moved silently down the corridor, he shifted his perception to see into the astral. He caught the near transparent ripple that was Lethe, but there was no sign of any hostile spirits. "Where are they?" he asked.

"I banished them to their home planes," Lethe said. "They will be happier there anyway."

Jane's voice sounded in Ryan's ear. "What's the scan?" she asked.

"Lethe was able to banish the spirits," he subvocalized. "But their absence will alert their masters."

The group increased its pace, moving quickly and quietly along the corridor. Though not as quietly as Ryan would have liked. He realized that these runners were good, but they did not follow the Silent Way as he did. The mage, McFaren, was marginally adept at stealth, and Grind was more of a combat expert than a thief. Without the invisibility spell, those two would be dead by now. And Ryan wasn't about to let that happen. He needed the mage to get through the ward around the Dragon Heart.

"The door on the left—stairs," Axler said. "We go up one floor. Standard formation."

Standard formation was Ryan at point, then Axler, followed closely by McFaren, with Grind bringing up the rear. Ryan opened the door to the stairs, surprised that it was unlocked, allowing unrestricted entry to the staircase. He noticed, however, that the door would be locked the other way. Anyone in the staircase would need a passcard and a keycode to get out. Ryan pulled some tape from his webbing and placed a strip of it over the latch. Old trick, but it was simple and worked well.

A quick glance showed him that no one was on the stairs.

"Clear," he said, then edged his way in. He noticed security cameras and drone tracks. Stairwells were closed spaces and corps loved to put killer drones there.

Hope that invisibility holds up.

Ryan didn't need it himself. He had his own version, magic that helped him blend into dark places, helped camouflage him with his surroundings. Ryan gripped his silenced Walther PB-120 and climbed slowly and steadily up the stairs until he came to a door marked "2nd Floor: Thaumaturgical Research."

He looked at the lock as the others edged up behind him. He knew their astral images would show like beacons in the dark stairwell, and he hoped no other spirits would come wandering through. He pulled the ID stick that he'd removed from the body of the dog shaman and slotted it into the maglock reader.

The maglock acknowledged the card, then said, "Please enter passcode" in a man's generic voice. Ryan took the small remote receiver from Axler, and slotted its datacord into the reader's jack. "Unit attached," Ryan subvocalized. "Jane?"

But before Jane answered, Ryan heard the maglock click open. "Pull the stick out, Ryan," Jane said. "The code is R4N54CK."

"Got it."

They passed through the door and into the dark hall beyond. Ryan followed Lethe now, the spirit glowing a little brighter, though Ryan didn't know why. Maybe Lethe was doing it on purpose to make himself easier to see. Or perhaps the spirit·was reacting to the proximity of the Dragon Heart. Ryan led the others down the hall, their footsteps a delicate whisper as they moved as quietly as possible.

Lethe stopped just shy of an intersection with another hall, coming from the left. "It's down this corridor," Lethe said. "But there are guards."

Ryan signalled the others to stop and maintain silence, then pulled out his small mirror and used it to glance around the corner. Two elves stood in front of a set of double doors. They wore body armor covered by black and crimson uniforms. Ryan subvocalized to Axler. "Two guards," he said, "alert and armed with SMGs and Supersquirts. There are also cameras and locked double doors."

"Prepare for alarms from here on out," she said.

"Yes, but let's try to take them out quietly."

"Agreed," Axler said. "Everyone ready? On three, two, one . . . Go!"

Ryan and Axler stepped around the corner, Axler unloading with her Cascade. The DMSO-laced chemical sprayed over the two elves before they could react. Ryan delayed his strike until he saw their reaction. One crumbled immediately. The other reached for his gun, his reactions obviously chipped.

Ryan focused his magic to knock the man's hand away, and unleashed his distance strike. The elf's hand jerked back, hitting the door behind him. Then the chemical took effect and he fell, slumping on top of his companion.

Time clicked into slow motion as Ryan ran for the double doors, moving at his fastest speed. The doors were made of plate steel and would be difficult to blast through. Better to get inside before any alarms sounded. He slotted the dog shaman's ID stick into the lock and punched in the code, hoping she had access.

Sure enough, the maglock solenoid clicked back the bolt and opened the doors. *Must be my lucky day,* he thought. And he found memories of Nadja coming back. And he recalled what Dunkelzahn had said about them being connected somehow. *Can't think about that,* he told himself. *Not now. Not until this is all over.*

Then they passed through, closing the doors behind them. Axler and Grind dragged the bodies of the guards inside. Now it was only a matter of minutes, at most, before the alarms went off and they were confronted with a huge number of those guards.

The corridor beyond the double doors was about twenty meters long, with two doors, presumably leading to the laboratories, on either side. The doors were metal with narrow windows of clear plexan. At the end, the hall widened into a small lounge area with vending machines and chairs. Huge windows looked down on the river.

Lethe led Ryan to the last door on the left. Once more, the dog shaman's card and code unlocked it, and Ryan was about to step through when McFaren put out his hand. "Wait," he said. "There's a ward on this whole room, and it's not like anything I've ever seen. It's loaded with spells, and all of them anchored. It looks like if anything triggered it, the ward would go off like a fragging mana bomb. And the damn thing would probably kill or wound any living thing that got too close to it. Very tricky."

It sounded tricky to Ryan. Not to mention dangerous. "Can you break it?" he asked.

McFaren turned to examine the ward. Ryan watched in the astral as the mage's aura detached from his physical body to circle around the glassy blue shine of the ward. After almost a minute, McFaren's astral form rejoined his meat body and he looked at Ryan in the physical world, shaking his head slowly back and forth. "This is very advanced magic," he said. "I might be able to punch a hole in the ward, but it'll probably explode and kill us all."

"Jane, any ideas?"

Jane's voice was curt, "What about Lethe?"

Ryan looked at the spirit. "Can you get us inside?"

"I think so," Lethe said. "But I can't be sure the ward won't explode."

"What if you help McFaren?"

"It's worth a try."

"Let's do it," McFaren said. "We don't have much time."

McFaren sat down with his back against the wall, then his body went lax as his astral form rose from it. Ryan watched as McFaren and Lethe constructed magic designed to weaken the reflective blue. He saw wisps of energy obscure the ward's shine, then bend the surface until slowly but surely the ward warped around the entrance to the lab.

This was pretty elaborate magical protection, he knew. The Dragon Heart must be extremely valuable to warrant it.

Two long minutes ticked away as they waited for Lethe and McFaren to finish. Finally, Jane's voice came over the radio in Ryan's ear. "Silent alarms are sounding," she said. "How close are you?"

"How much longer?" Ryan asked McFaren.

"We're almost done," McFaren said. "I can't believe it, but

we're almost through. Think of it as defusing a bomb. Can't rush it or . . . Kaboom!"

"Did you get that, Jane?"

"Yes," she said. "And you've got three minutes to abort. Repeat, three minutes to abort."

"Copy that. Three minutes."

Twenty seconds later, they were through. McFaren's meat body was still slumped on the floor, with Grind standing over him. Ryan passed through the door and into the room beyond. It was a large space with tables and benches adorned with carvings of arcane symbols. Tiny sculptures and feathers and bones lay strewn on every surface. Books and tomes, both ancient and new, jammed floor-to-ceiling shelves on all four walls.

A slow blinking red light showed that the internal security camera was on and watching. But Ryan didn't have time for stealth or to mask his heat signature. He scanned the room. "Where is it?" he said. "Where the frag is it?"

It was Lethe who answered. "I sense it, but it isn't out in the open. It's inside a small chamber under one of the benches."

"Small chamber? You mean a safe?"

"What is a safe?"

"A small chamber with thick metal walls, and—"

"Yes, that is it."

"Fragging great," Ryan said.

"This is a good thing?"

"No, I'm being sarcastic. You know what sarcasm is?"

"No."

"Never mind. I'll explain it later. If we make it out of here alive."

Ryan found the safe set into the far wall. It wasn't large, but it did have a complicated electronic lock. He hoped Jane could open it. Axler handed him the remote box again.

"Jane?" Ryan said. "You ready?"

"Jack me in," she said.

He snugged the datacord into the lock and waited.

"We've got company!" came Grind's voice from his position outside the room, where he was watching over McFaren's body. "Wait a minute. They're gone."

"What?"

"A whole drekload of fire elementals. They manifested and were about to fry me. Then they just disappeared."

"Thank Lethe," Ryan said. "He must've done it."

"I'm in," Jane said. "Open the door."

Ryan pulled down on the steel handle and found that the door opened easily. He looked inside and saw the Dragon Heart sitting on a bottom shelf surrounded by small items of talismana—bits of jewelry, gemstones, and small carvings. The item was larger than he'd expected, three or four times the size of a human heart and made of a dull gold metal that he recognized immediately. Orichalcum, a magical blend of all true elements. The heart shone like a small sun of white gold in the astral, and the experience of it moved Ryan deeply. It reached into his spirit and triggered something.

I must have it, he thought. *It's mine. I know that now. Dunkelzahn meant for me to have it all along.*

Ryan knew on some level that the safe was warded, but he couldn't stop his hand. He couldn't wait, but reached out to seize the Dragon Heart.

"No, Ryan—" Axler's cry was too late.

As Ryan's hand penetrated the plane of the circle inscribed by the talismana, he broke the ward. Fire raced up his arm like napalm as his fingers closed around the Dragon Heart. The flames spread up his arm and over his body, engulfing him in a white-hot fire that seared into his flesh.

Pain shot through Ryan as the flesh of his arm was flayed to the bone by the fire. His whole body crackled on the verge of explosion, his flesh on the brink of detonation, of being blown apart into tiny chunks of bone, blood, and sinew, each bit consumed by the magical fire.

This is it, he thought. *This is the end.*

Abruptly, Axler crashed into him, sending his body sprawling away from the safe and out onto the floor. For an absurd moment he stared at his blackened and withered arm, smelled the overpowering aroma of burned flesh, and he saw that the bones of his hand still clutched the Dragon Heart.

I've got it!

Ryan tried to channel away the pain, but it was too great. The damage too extensive.

A surge of power passed through him just then. Adrenaline? Magic? The pain gave way to the euphoria of the transcendence that he felt. Like he was dying. His spirit was rising from his body. He was growing wings. He was changing.

The Dragon Heart.

The power came simultaneously from within him and from the Heart; it healed him completely. His pain was gone. His fatigue was washed away, and his injury—his burns—regenerated in a flood of magic.

Ryan leaped to his feet and crossed the short distance to Axler. "Let's go," he said.

"Wha . . . What just happened?" she asked. "I thought you were dead."

Ryan shrugged. "The Dragon Heart," he said as if that was the best explanation he could come up with.

"Are you two done jacking around?" Grind called from the hall. "I told you we've got company."

"We're coming," Axler said. Then gave Ryan a questioning look.

Ryan felt a rush of energy from the Heart, and he reluctantly stashed it in the nylon web bag on his belt. Then he was behind Axler, who seemed to be moving slower now. There was a loud crash as they came into the hall.

The metal doors bowed out for a second before rattling back into place. "Jane scrambled the codes, locked them out," said Grind. "But it won't hold for long."

"Jane," Ryan subvocalized. "We've got the Dragon Heart. Let's get out of here."

"Copy," came Jane's synthesized voice. "Stand by for escape plan."

Another explosion rocked the building, and as Ryan spun toward the end of the hall, the big metal doors twisted off their hinges with an ear-splitting shriek. A roiling cloud of flame and smoke billowed through the mangled doors and into the hall.

"Jane," Axler said, "you got a scan of the opposition?"

"Not complete. Best guess is a cadre of Mystic Crusaders."

Grind picked up McFaren's limp meat body and rushed into the lounge area, followed closely by Ryan and Axler. Had to get out of any line of fire.

"A cadre?"

"Twenty. Well-armed. Well-trained."

As if on cue, five warriors in military-grade armor stepped through the smoke. They wore helmets with integrated gas masks and power-assisted strength. The first three carried shoulder-mounted gyros with attached miniguns floating in their hands like alien wasp stingers. The miniguns whirred and fired. A screaming hail of bullets ripped up the hallway, shredding the sheet rock, chewing up the floor, blowing fist-sized holes in the lounge windows.

"We're in serious drek, Jane!" Axler screamed. "Get us the frag out of here now!"

38

In her chamber of the San Marcos *teocalli,* Lucero stared at her naked body reflected in the full-length mirror. She used to be beautiful, before the scarring. Before her addiction to the blood, her slavery to the dark stain on her soul.

Her head was bald, dark brown skin shaved smooth. The shape of her skull was delicate and pretty, like an egg. Her face was unmarred as well. Large eyes the color of worn leather, faded from time but resilient and strong. Her narrow nose was delicate and her mouth full.

Below the neck, however, her brown skin was a tapestry of scars. Deep-etched runes, like embossed tattoos bled of their ink. They covered her arms and shoulders, her breasts and stomach, back and buttocks, thighs and legs. Such mutilation was a hideous and unnatural thing.

For the briefest of moments, she could see the woman she had been before Oscuro had found new uses for her. She could see the bright, intelligent eyes, the smooth, young skin stretched tight across her stomach. Unblemished and supple. She could feel what it had been like to sense the delicate touch of a man or a woman. To be desired.

The moment passed—a cloud across the sun.

A temple servant poked her head through the doorway. "Señor Oscuro is ready for you," she said.

Lucero turned. She would go to Oscuro, the dark man with the black soul, so dark that his aura was a confusion of blank patches. She would go to him and let him tempt her with the blood, and she would do this for one reason alone. She wanted to return to the place of light and beautiful song. He would send her there again, and perhaps she would get to stay this time.

She knew deep down that Oscuro wanted to destroy that place, or change it so fundamentally that its beauty was ruined, but she could not stop that. She could only obey and hope that the goddess of the song would prevail, that the music would wash away the taint of Lucero's blood.

She followed the servants into the sanctuary as before, and as before, Señor Oscuro waited at the altar for her to arrive. She said a silent prayer to Quetzalcóatl as she passed his sculpture, asking to be free of her addiction. To be beautiful again before she died. For she knew that she would be vulnerable to the blood that Oscuro would use. She would shudder with want for its taste, and without help, she would succumb.

Oscuro escorted her up onto the altar, and bade her lie down. Lucero heard the chant of the Gestalt then, and remembered that the blood mages were conducting a ritual at the apex of the temple. They were assembled to add to her power. After having been part of them for so long, it felt strange to have the group so close now, and yet not be able to join them.

She knew what they looked like, ten humans in ceremonial robes, sitting in a circle. Their skin, like hers, was marred with runic scars where they had cut themselves to power the blood magic. And as they sat and chanted, connected by physical tubing that allowed the blood to circulate from one to another through the whole Gestalt, the blood mages coalesced into one astral entity. One magical creature that held the sum of their combined power.

Part of Lucero still longed for the days when her blood became one with the Gestalt entity. Part of her still yearned for that power. But the Gestalt Blood Mages did not know of the song; they did not share in the beauty of the light. Perhaps they were too deeply scarred to see beauty anymore.

The chanting increased in volume as she lay on the stone altar. The rhythmic voices grew in volume as she entered the trance. As she fell into the dark embrace, the abyss of Oscuro's spell.

When she opened her eyes, she was assaulted by the beauty. Confronted by the wonderful brightness that radiated from the goddess. The song filled Lucero with its splendor, washing through every pore of her mangled skin to replenish her beauty. She felt young and clean.

But the light could not penetrate the blackened spot in her heart. She wanted it to fill the bottomless well of her taint, but it could not. And soon she felt the power of the Blood Mage ritual within her, and the additional mana of the huge obsidian stone. The Locus, not yet fully active.

The stain within her grew, spreading like an infection against the pure white. Like a pestilence over pristine land. Soon Lucero could see her feet on the hard, cracked stone. The light retreated a few meters around her as the blood strength coursed through her. She was strong again, a part of a greater whole.

She hadn't felt that way since she'd lost her power and was exiled from the Gestalt. Now she was one of them again—the focus of their power.

The darkness kept growing and growing until Lucero found that she could move inside the black circle. She heard the perverted cries and moans of the creatures who were frozen across the chasm by the song. They longed for Lucero to succeed; they wanted the goddess rent limb from torso. The dark part of Lucero understood their desires.

Suddenly, Señor Oscuro appeared in her circle, standing next to her with his hand over his eyes, shielding them from the light. The widening darkness allowed him the space to come across himself. Oscuro grimaced in pain from the sound of the exquisite music, even though it was muffled and weak at the center of the black circle.

He muttered something and an acolyte appeared—a boy of about thirteen. Oscuro drew a ceremonial sword of obsidian black—a *macauitl*. The acolyte stood stunned, hypnotized by magic. Oscuro swung the sword, making a clean cut through the boy's neck. The boy's head fell to the ground, and blood gushed from the severed neck, spraying the ground with its ichor as the body bent and doubled over.

Lucero watch in fascination as Oscuro dragged the boy by his feet, marking out a circle with his blood. The song dulled more as the circle of blood was reinforced with that of two other acolytes. Until Lucero could barely hear it from where she stood in the center of the dark stain.

She felt herself crying. She was destroying beauty, possibly the very essence of goodness. She was scarring the earth beneath her feet just as she had scarred her own flesh. Just as she had marred her own beauty. It was already too late for her, she knew that now. And soon, if Oscuro got his wish, it would be too late for the rest of the world.

39

Ryan crouched around the corner at the end of the hall as bullets ripped up the wall across the room and shattered the windows on his left. The sound was deafening, like a constant bludgeoning rain of stones. Smoke and debris filled the room, making it hard to see.

Ryan felt the overwhelming power of the Dragon Heart pulsing through him. It had healed his fire-withered arm and had made him stronger and faster. Enhancing his physical adept abilities. He wanted to take on the whole army. He felt invulnerable, though his mind knew that not to be true. The Silent Way taught that stealth was always the best option, but when it failed, Ryan turned to strategy and strength.

Escape was the best strategy right now. But the one exit was blocked by certain death at the hands of the Mystic Crusaders. What was taking Jane so fragging long? Suddenly, tear gas grenades hit the floor and bounced near Ryan and Axler.

An androgynous voice bellowed from amplified speakers. "Cast your weapons down and surrender," it said. "You have ten seconds to comply."

Jane came on the line. "Stay out of the hall!" she yelled through his earphone.

"No drek," Axler called. "They've got miniguns."

"Dhin is about to—"

Ryan saw it—out the window that overlooked the arboretum and the river, the helo in a steady hover, sinking down like an elevator from the floor above. Took some excellent flying to keep it that close to the wall without the blades hitting the concrete.

Ryan leaped out of the way as the circular barrel of the helo's autocannon swung toward them. Axler and Grind pulled McFaren's limp body into a near corner. In the astral, it seemed as though McFaren and Lethe were still working to close the hole they'd made in the ward that protected the research lab. Ryan didn't understand exactly what they were doing astrally, but he knew they needed to be delicate to prevent an explosion by the ward's powerful mana.

"I hope you're out of the way," came Dhin's voice, " 'cause here I go."

A deafening roar filled the room as a barrage of rounds from the rotary autocannon plowed through the window, blowing it to shards in seconds. The miniguns started to answer, but only one or two sputtered before there was no sound from the hall.

Ryan used his mirror to get a scan of the hallway, but all he could see was a haze of smoke and debris. Limp and fallen bodies, their black and crimson military armor pitted with bleeding holes. There was some movement, shadows in the haze, but nothing he could make out distinctly.

"They're either dead or retreating," Dhin said. "Get in! Now!"

Ryan pulled a smoke grenade and tossed it into the hall, adding to the already low visibility. At the same time, Axler moved to the decimated window, grappling hook in hand. She swung and tossed it through the helo's open door. It caught on the support for one of the seats.

"Perfect," she said. "Let's go. Grind, you first."

Dhin took the bird up and slightly away as Grind scrambled up the rope. No problems so far. Next was McFaren's limp body. Axler tied the rope around the mage's waist and chest in a makeshift harness to keep him balanced. Grind pulled him up.

Two down, two to go.

Jane came on-line, "I placed a smartframe in the Fire Department's host. They think the building's on fire. That means you'll have company soon. It should distract security."

Guns fired through the smoke as Axler climbed the rope. One round caught her thigh, the wound opening up like a red flower. Ryan watched her wince and flinch on the line, falling for a split-second before catching herself again. In obvious pain, she pulled herself toward the hovering helo.

Seeing Axler get hit slotted Ryan off. Energy rushed into

him as he turned toward the hallway. He couldn't see his attackers in the physical world, but he felt their astral presence. He drew from the power of the Dragon Heart as he sent a telekinetic strike out toward them, lifting their bodies into the air. Slamming them into the walls. He struck one, then another until there were six unconscious elves lying in the smoke.

Sirens sounded as if from a great distance. Ryan turned to see two rescue helicopters swooping down next to Dhin's craft. Wanting to see if they could help with the evacuation.

"—can you hear me, Ryan?"

"What?"

"I've been yelling at you." It was Axler's voice. "I'm up. You're the last one. Move! Now, before they get the helo targeted with a missile or something."

Ryan shook his head. He hadn't heard anything. He'd been focused on revenge. *The Dragon Heart must be affecting me.*

He turned and grabbed the rope.

Lethe appeared next to him in astral space. "Tell them to move the helo!"

"What?"

"The ward is going to blow."

Ryan subvocalized, "Dhin, go! Pull up and out. Now! The building's going to explode."

The insane scream of the helo's rotors increased in pitch as it lifted up and away. It pulled Ryan with it, a dangling spider on a narrow thread. He hung on and watched the hallway. He could see a few figures in astral space. More elves in combat armor.

A flash of blue light lit up the sky as the ward exploded. It was shaped in a perfect toroid—a donut of magical power. The front wave caught the unsuspecting elves and obliterated them. Their expanding bodies blew out their armor, their clothes, their skin and muscles. It ripped out walls, blew furniture out through the shattered windows.

Ryan watched the expanding wave in the astral, barreling toward him like a wall of roiling white silk. He ducked his head into his chest to protect his eyes from the hail of broken body armor, atomized flesh, and needles of mana. But the wave dissipated as it rolled outward so that by the time it swept past Ryan, its strength was only enough to cause a ripple of intense pain. He grit his teeth and held on, swinging beneath the rising helo, hoping Dhin was good enough to weave between the whirling blades of the rescue choppers.

When the rope had steadied, and the Hughes Airstar was clear in the splotchy charcoal sky, Ryan pulled himself up the rope and into the helo. He fell into a seat with a heavy sigh, and Axler closed the hatch. Then they were gone into the night.

Surprisingly, there were no missile attacks and no immediate pursuit. Probably due to the confusion with the fire emergency teams. Lethe monitored the astral while Dhin monitored the radar with Grind's help. Ryan helped Axler patch up her leg. He also tried using the Dragon Heart to heal her like it healed him, but he didn't really know the magic of healing others. That wasn't one of his abilities.

McFaren's meat body remained slumped. Lethe said the mage had died in the blast, his astral form tangled in the fabric of the ward when it had collapsed. Axler didn't want to believe it was true.

Lethe ought to know, Ryan thought. But even if McFaren's astral form had somehow survived, the mage would have to get back to his body soon. Otherwise, his spirit would wander forever.

Jane had been monitoring the Tir border near La Grande so that their crossing back into Salish-Shidhe territory would be perfectly timed and seamless. But the border had tightened all around, and she finally recommended setting the 'copter down in the ash beds just west of John Day. It was a sparsely populated section of the Tir, and they should be safe for a day or so until the border loosened a bit.

The flight to the ash canyon near John Day took several hours. The sun was just coming up as they descended, the helo's wind sending up a fine mist of the loose volcanic ash around them. Turning the sunlight a deep red and burned orange. Ryan felt the fatigue hit as the helicopter's runners touched the flat bottom of the narrow canyon where they would hide out.

He had succeeded. He had the Dragon Heart now. All he needed to do, according to Dunkelzahn, was find the mage Harlequin and deliver the Heart to Thayla at the metaplanar site of the Great Ghost Dance. His fatigue hung on him like wet clothes. He was too tired to think about the rest of the mission right now.

Besides, why the frag should he give up the Dragon Heart? He was much more powerful with it than without. Much stronger. If he just kept it, he could use it to combat Dunkelzahn's enemies. It didn't make any sense to give it away. It was a part of him now.

I'll keep it, he decided. *It was willed to me by Dunkelzahn, and it's mine.*

40

Lethe saw something in Ryan Mercury. The man's aura had changed, shifted somehow since he'd made contact with the Dragon Heart. He was stronger than before, faster and more capable of fulfilling the task of getting it to Thayla. Lethe tried to imagine the glorious music of Thayla's song. He tried to feel the penetrating warmth of her light.

He failed. His memory could not compare to his experience of her.

Lethe used the static nudge he'd used before to get the attention of Ryan, who was helping Axler throw camouflage netting over the helicopter. The human focused for a minute and said, "Lethe?"

"I'd like to talk about how you plan to get the Dragon Heart to Thayla," Lethe said.

Ryan's aura darkened momentarily. "Give it a rest," he said. "I've just been through major drek. I don't want to think about it right now."

Lethe paid no heed. "There's no time for that. Now that we have the Dragon Heart, we must deliver it."

"There's plenty of time for all that," Ryan said irritably. "I told you I don't want to talk about it right now."

The cloudiness Lethe saw in Ryan's aura was the same sign of deception he'd noticed before. It had raised his suspicions then too, but what else could he have done but hope his perception was flawed in some way and that Ryan Mercury was truly the right one for this task? After all, Dunkelzahn himself had chosen this human.

"Besides," Ryan said, "we don't even know how to get it to the metaplanes. That involves a powerful magical ritual known only to a few mages. We would need to find one of them, and I don't have any idea where to start."

Lethe saw that the darkness in Ryan's aura was growing. He was lying for some reason. "How long do you want to wait?"

The hint of a smile touched Ryan's physical mask, showing as a wash of dark red across his aura. "Just until things settle down."

At that moment it occurred to Lethe that Ryan meant to keep the Dragon Heart. He was addicted to its power.

Ryan was still talking. "I need to find a mage to look into the situation."

But Lethe wasn't listening. The realization that this short-sighted human would jeopardize the fate of the whole world for a brief taste of paltry power was maddening. "You can't keep the Dragon Heart," he said. "It was not meant for you."

Ryan took a step back, surprised. "I don't intend to keep it."

Lethe scrutinized Ryan's aura as he spoke. The human was not only lying, but actually stating the opposite of what he meant. There was no doubt now. Ryan was not planning to complete Dunkelzahn's mission.

"You don't understand what you are doing," Lethe said. "I won't allow it."

"I don't see how you can stop me," Ryan said. "The Heart is mine, and I don't think even you can hurt me now."

Lethe ignored the threat. "Personal power is meaningless. You must understand that your petty desires may help destroy the world."

"Slot off!" Ryan focused his power and pushed Lethe away. Perhaps his power *was* greater.

"I will not give up," Lethe said. And with that he was gone, blasting across the astral landscape. He went high, to the very rim of the manasphere, coming back down thousands of kilometers from Ryan in the physical world. His whole journey passed in the exercise of a thought.

It took longer to locate Nadja Daviar once he was in the Washington sprawl. But time was relative. It was still morning when he came across the elf in a highly secure mansion. He moved past the astral watchers and into her new office.

Three others were in the office with her—two ork security guards and a human of Asian background who was conversing with Nadja. The orks were guarding her, and as Lethe examined their astral bodies, he realized that none of them would have the ability to translate for him. Reluctantly, he decided to possess one of them. This time he would be more careful to exit the body before it died. But he had to speak with Nadja and saw no other way to do so.

He moved his spirit into the body of one of the orks, trying to be as gentle as possible with the spirit of the metahuman. The body jerked slightly as he took control quickly. "Excuse me, Nadja," he said, using the ork's voice. "It is Lethe, and I'm reluctantly using this guard's body because it is imperative that I speak with you now."

The other guard drew a weapon.

"Lethe?"

"Yes, it is urgent, and I don't have much time. I don't want to accidentally destroy this body as I did the last."

Abruptly, Nadja turned toward her guest. "I'm sorry for this interruption, Rai'kun-*sama*. It was not anticipated or expected. However, I must speak with this spirit. Will you excuse me for a few moments? We will continue the discussion of your claim at that time."

The man stood and bowed to her. She returned the bow precisely.

When he had stepped out and closed the door, Nadja turned to Lethe. "What do you want?"

"Ryan Mercury has failed," he said. "We succeeded in getting the Dragon Heart, but he has succumbed to a desire for its power. He has decided to keep the item and has given up on his mission."

Nadja sank into her chair at the words. Stunned.

"You are the only one who might be able to persuade him to carry out Dunkelzahn's instructions," Lethe went on. "To complete his mission."

"Me?"

"He loves you."

She nodded, but said nothing. She squeezed her eyes shut for a moment before pushing to her feet. "Okay, Lethe," she said. "I will intervene. Something happened to Ryan in Aztlan. I don't know what it was, but I'm sure it was Roxborough who did it to him. He's just not the same. He may never be the same. But the mission Dunkelzahn entrusted to him is crucial. I would be failing them both if I didn't try to help."

"Thank you," Lethe said, then exited the body of the security guard. The ork's spirit stayed, but the body fainted from the transition. After a minute, he was back to normal. Lethe was pleased.

Then Nadja was talking to her secretary, connecting through to Jane-in-the-box. Making emergency travel plans.

Lethe watched her for a few minutes. He felt a deep affection for Nadja. She had a pure spirit, one of the only such metahumans he'd encountered.

Lethe hoped that she was persuasive enough to influence Ryan Mercury. Which would be greater, he wondered, Ryan's love for Nadja or for his newfound power?

16 August 2057

41

Ryan had finally gotten to sleep when Jane came through with the news that the border patrols were thinning near LaGrande. It was time to move.

The late afternoon sun shone down hot and bright into the ash canyon where they'd been hiding out. The whitish gray walls had heated up over the course of the day, and the temperature was becoming almost unbearable. But Ryan was so exhausted that he'd slept a little despite the heat.

"Let's roll," came Axler's voice.

Ryan rubbed his eyes and sat up in the seat of the helicopter, snapping his vertebrae into line. "I'll help you get the camouflage netting off," he said.

"Already done."

Dhin powered up the rotors and they lifted off, headed back toward the compound above Hells Canyon. He vectored out and cranked up the jets to maximum velocity. Soon they were sailing across the border. Jane's plan had worked; they'd evaded the Tir border patrol through patience and proper intelligence.

A few minutes after they'd crossed into Salish-Shidhe territory, Ryan's wristphone beeped. It was Jane, and for a second he wondered why she wasn't using the communications relay in the helo.

"I needed to speak to you privately," she said. "It's about the Dragon Heart."

He brought the phone to his mouth. "What about it?"

"I hear you've decided not to carry out Dunkelzahn's mission."

"Has Lethe been talking to you? I—"

"Is it true?" Jane's tone was accusatory.

"Not exactly," Ryan said. "I just want to think about it first."

"What's to think about? You've always done the dragon's bidding. That's what you do. That's why he chose you."

"Maybe I need more now," said Ryan.

"Like what?"

"I need a reason."

"A reason for what?" Jane's tone was sarcastic and grating. "To save the world?"

"A reason to risk my life for someone else's plan. A plan, I might add, that I know nothing about."

"You have to trust Dunkelzahn."

"Well, I don't anymore," Ryan said. "I don't trust anyone."

"So you're committed to this new course?"

"I'm keeping the Dragon Heart, Jane," Ryan said. "It was willed to me, and I can use it effectively against whatever enemies Dunkelzahn had. I'm going to track down whoever killed him, and bring them to justice."

"I'm afraid," Jane said, "that I will have to intervene."

Ryan laughed aloud. "Am I supposed to be scared?" But the line was dead before the words were even out of his mouth.

Slitch! Ryan thought. *What can she do to me anyhow?* He wanted this whole run to be over, and he needed rest. Soon they'd be on the ground again. Maybe then he could find a proper bed and get some sleep.

42

Burnout stood with Slaver and La Sangre, hard mountain rock beneath their feet. From their vantage slightly upslope and a few hundred meters away, Burnout had a clear view of the whole compound. Assets, Inc. It was a small airstrip cut into the eastern cliff above Hells Canyon. The only buildings were a dilapidated hangar made of rusted sheet metal, an attached mobile home that looked like it dated back to before the turn of the century, and four smaller storage sheds.

Cyclone fencing surrounded the compound, but it was only necessary on the two flat sides. The other two were bounded by cliffs, one straight up and the other straight down, nearly two full kilometers to the bottom of the canyon.

They had been waiting for only thirty minutes since dropping down from the Aztechnology helicopter a few kilometers away. The 'copter's rigger had been instructed to stay out of sight until called upon.

"See anyone?" Slaver asked.

Burnout shook his head. He hadn't seen signs of anybody, and La Sangre's astral reconnaissance had come up dry as well. They were already gone. And Burnout couldn't help but think that all this wouldn't have been necessary if Slaver had only let him make his move back in Washington.

Ryan Mercury would be dead now. Mission accomplished.

He heard something then, in the distance, a low rhythmic harmonic. It grew louder and louder until he recognized it as a helicopter. "Someone is coming," he said.

" 'Bout fragging time," Slaver said. "Told you they'd come."

Burnout saw the helo at the same time as he felt the magic. Like a yearning force, like water to his parched throat.

Something on that helicopter was powerful, and Burnout
wanted it. He felt the strength of it grow as the helo crested
the cliff below the compound, rising up from the canyon,
pivoting and touching down on the tarmac.

It drew him in like a mana vortex, a gritty knife edge that
cut to his very heart. He knew he had to have it; no choice.
Whatever it was, he must get it for himself. Perhaps it could
restore his magic, perhaps not, but either way he would
remain incomplete without it.

"Where are you going?" Slaver asked. "Frag, I can't take
you anywhere."

Burnout turned, feeling the hatred tingling at his extremities. Hovering like a hidden beast just outside his awareness.
Waiting to pounce. He realized then that he'd already taken
several steps down the slope toward the compound.

"I'm going in for a closer look," he said.

"Not yet," Slaver said. "We wait until I get a positive ID.
Too many of them right now anyhow."

Burnout shrugged and continued his descent.

La Sangre straightened, its flayed nostrils flaring, causing
even more foul-smelling blood to drip from it. The spirit
seemed to sense something was amiss.

"Drek for brains," Slaver said to Burnout, "get back here.
Now."

The hatred hit, sending off little flares in Burnout's eyes.
Tiny fireworks as he pivoted. The world seemed to click into
slow motion around him. Recognition dawned on Slaver's
face, but it was too late. Burnout crossed the distance
between them in a fraction of a second, clicking his ankle
spurs into position.

A spell went off just as Burnout kicked—a sweeping strike
across the chest, diagonally up to one shoulder. A shock
wave shook through him as the discharging spell threw him
back. It felt as though a panzer had hit him. But the barb on
his cyberspur had caught on Slaver's collar bone, lifting the
mage's body into the air.

Blood spilled from the cut, pouring out like a river as
Slaver mumbled spells to try and save himself. Burnout
jerked his foot, trying to free the cyberspur, and as his foot
came away, it ripped the bone with it, causing Slaver's neck
to jerk with a sickening snap.

The drug tried to kick in just then, and Burnout knew it would hit. The chemical placator. In the seconds before he went placid, Burnout lifted the limp and mangled body of Slaver, then swung it in a wide, vicious arc. Slamming it against the unyielding surface of a large boulder.

There was blood everywhere, glistening red on the rocks. The satisfying crunch of bones inside Slaver's limp bag of skin came to Burnout's ears just as the drug hit. And with it came peace.

Next to him, La Sangre watched in fascination. He looked at Burnout. "Thank you for freeing me," he said. Then he disappeared.

Leaving Burnout alone. Content for the first time in as long as he could remember.

After a time, the yearning returned—his desire for the magic he felt in the compound below. And Burnout found himself on his feet, moving toward it, leaving the remains of his master behind for the scavengers.

43

Ryan jumped out of the helicopter, planting his feet squarely on the tarmac. He was tired, but it felt good to be done with a mission well accomplished. The Dragon Heart rested in the nylon web bag at his belt, a little uncomfortable. Too big, too heavy. He would have to get a safer place for it, but he didn't want it too far from him.

I'll carry it for now, he thought.

Axler and Grind came behind, carrying McFaren's body. The mage's spirit had never returned, and Axler had finally resigned herself to his loss. It was too bad. McFaren had been an excellent mage and a good runner.

The sun was setting now, painting the sky red and orange in the west. The mountain peaks above the compound turned the color of autumn leaves in the sunset as Ryan made his way to the hangar. As he walked, he tried to decide how to proceed. After his phone conversation with Jane in the helicopter, the other runners had grown distant and suspicious. The remainder of their trip back to Assets had been silent and tense.

Ryan didn't give a frag. After all, he *owned* them, didn't he? Assets was his now that Dunkelzahn was dead. They had no say.

It was all Lethe's fault for talking to Jane. Ryan distrusted the spirit now. Lethe wanted the Dragon Heart for himself. He didn't understand its power, didn't realize how Ryan could use it to build an army, use it to fight whatever enemies Dunkelzahn had. Ryan's father, in his Roxborough past, had taught him well; never subvert an opportunity because of sentiment. Ryan would never make that mistake again.

The hot wind blew the smell of pine and sage up the

canyon wall, and Ryan caught the sound of an aircraft approaching. Sounded like a jet, tilt wing. VTOL. *What the—*

The machine crested the rim of the cliff, flying past the compound with a subsonic roar. Ryan ducked inside the hangar door, watching from grease-smelling shadows as the jet slowed and hovered fifty meters out over the edge of the canyon. The jet slowly eased over the airstrip and dropped to its wheels.

The machine had no official logos or other identifying marks, but Ryan got the certain sense that this was a corporate visit. Axler and Grind appeared at Ryan's shoulder. They carried no weapons and didn't seemed concerned in the least. "Looks like you've got a visitor, Ryan," Axler said coldly. "Nadja Daviar."

Nadja? What is she doing here?

The answer occurred to him then. *She's here to try to persuade me to complete Dunkelzahn's mission. What else could it be? Transparent slitch! Did Lethe talk to her? Or Jane?*

Abruptly, Ryan decided to leave. Now, before she could talk to him, before he saw her beautiful face. Before he heard her mesmerizing voice. The power of the Dragon Heart coursed through him as he broke into a run, making for the helicopter. Dhin was still inside the vehicle, checking out the systems, cleaning out the interior.

Ryan moved fast, a dark blur across the concrete. The jet was between him and the helo, and as Ryan ran, security personnel in dark suits came down the short stairs, cutting off his path.

Ryan slowed when Nadja emerged from the jet. Her black hair shone in the last light of the setting sun, a crimson tint to its ebony. She wore it down, like dark rain to her waist. She smiled at him, mistaking his run for the helicopter as urgency to see her. Or else faking her delight extremely well.

Ryan drew himself up and walked to her. He would not let his emotions get in the way. Father had taught him that. Besides, this woman's love for him was no more than an ephemeral transience, a momentary sentiment that would soon fade like the sunlight. "Nadja," he said. "What brings you all the way out here?"

Nadja stood her ground, surrounded by seven security, at

246

least one of whom was a mage. "I heard that you've abandoned Dunkelzahn's mission," she said, and there was such sadness in her voice that his knees threatened to weaken.

Ryan centered himself, focusing on the situation. He could take four or five of the guards, he was sure. But not all of them. One was a troll and might take too long to put down. The others—four humans and two dwarfs who looked like twins in their secret service suits and shades—would go down easily if there weren't so many. "I've changed," he said. "Become stronger. I'm no longer Dunkelzahn's lackey."

"Master had an intricate and detailed plan," Nadja said. "I know a great deal about it, but not everything. He entrusted you with this mission, even told you it was the most important one of your life. You remember that, don't you?"

"Dunkelzahn is dead."

"Yes," Nadja said. "And we must honor his sacrifice by carrying out his wishes."

"I intend to keep fighting for him," Ryan said. "But on my own terms. I won't be his servant boy any longer."

"Ryan, please . . ."

"Step aside, Nadja," Ryan said. "Let me go. I just need to sort some things out."

"I can't do that," she said. "I can't let you leave with the Dragon Heart."

"My missions are my own to complete as I see fit," Ryan said, his voice rising. "And I can't allow you to interfere!" He was shouting at her now, all pretense of civility stripped away. "Wasn't that part of our arrangement all along? Wasn't that why you despised my relationship with Dunkelzahn? Because it was more important than my relationship with you!" He spat the words at her, vehemently.

"Ryan . . ." Nadja was shaken by his outburst, but he knew she was trying not to show it. "This is different. You endanger the entire world by disregarding your mission."

"Fuck you! You just want the Dragon Heart for yourself."

"You know that's not—"

"Get out of my way!" Ryan took a step, angling around the knot of security.

They shifted to block his path, drawing weapons. Seven pistols aimed at him.

"They won't let you go, Ryan," Nadja said. "Not until you give up the Dragon Heart."

Ryan's awareness grew hypersensitive. The helo sat only ten meters away, just behind Nadja and the security agents. The jet was on his right, but there were more sec guards there. Nadja herself was two steps away; he tried not to see the concern on her features. He tried to harden himself to that. She was the enemy now.

She must be circumvented. Unless. . .

Ryan moved, quickly and with a suddenness that caught the security guards unaware. Energy from the Dragon Heart shivered through him as he crossed the distance to Nadja. The hulking shapes of the black-suited sec guards bled into one dark wall as he moved, too fast for their chipped senses. He threw one body out of the way with a distance strike.

Shots rang out, but they passed through the empty space where he'd been a moment before. Reaction time too fragging slow, chummers.

Then he was behind Nadja, one strong arm across her chest, pinning her arms. His Walther PB120 pistol was in his other hand, its warm barrel pressed to the soft space under her sharp jaw. "Back off!" he yelled.

The security turned in unison, surprised that he'd closed in so fast. Hesitation and confusion in their response. Half of them brought their weapons to bear on Ryan, the other half unsure.

"Guns on the ground," Ryan said. "And step back. Nice and fragging slow or the elf slitch loses her pretty head."

44

Peace inside. Tranquillity in the last rays of sunshine.

Outside, war.

Burnout stared at the scene on the tarmac. The man he recognized as Ryan Mercury—his target—held a gun to the head of an elven woman, threatening to kill her if the black suits interfered with his plan to escape.

Burnout saw all that peripherally, however, paying only marginal attention to it. The thing that drew him, that pulled him in, was the item Ryan Mercury carried on his belt. The size of a child's head, the thing glinted golden through the holes in the mesh bag.

Powerful magic. So potent that even Burnout could smell its force like a palpable aroma. Made his eyes tear up.

I must have it.

He reached the cyclone fencing at the near side of the compound, next to the mountain side. This was no obstacle for him. He merely bent his cybernetic legs and jumped. Up and over, landing delicately without sound.

The peace inside gave way to the craving, the hole that must be filled. The last vestiges of the drug's influence washed out with the searing desire for that powerful magic. He would accomplish his mission after all—Ryan Mercury would die—and Burnout would take the item as payment.

45

"Ryan, think about what you're doing," Nadja said.

Up close, the smell of her was overpowering. The feel of her against him, bringing back memories. Images of times past—the deep blue shimmer of the waves on Maui, a kiss stolen during a sudden impulsive moment behind the doors of her office on Prince Edward Island. The endearing sound of her gasp when he surprised her from behind, running his hands up under her shirt to tickle her back.

"You haven't been yourself, lately," Nadja continued. "Roxborough changed you."

"Tell them to put the guns down," Ryan said. His voice was a grating whisper; he was trying to stay anchored in the present. The handle of the pistol in his hand felt slick, sweaty in his grip.

"Try to remember who you are, Ryan," Nadja said.

"Shut up, slitch!"

"You said you remembered in Washington."

And he had remembered. Had felt the loss of Dunkelzahn so poignantly that he had crumpled to the floor and sobbed. He could still see the Washington sky full of flying dragons, weaving their tapestry of fire and magic. He remembered Dunkelzahn, his massive, sinuous bulk crouched beside Ryan as he gave instruction in the theory behind dragon magic. The fact that, in reality, no separation existed between the various kinds of magic—physical or spell or conjuring magic. These distinctions were a product of the limited minds of today's magickers, and were artificial. Dunkelzahn reassured Ryan that, in time, he would be adept at each kind.

The tide of memories came flooding back. Dunkelzahn's telepathic thoughts resonating in Ryan's mind. The jovial humor of the dragon as he reprimanded Ryan for a misplaced step or an awkward strike. Dunkelzahn was the only parent Ryan had ever really known. He didn't remember much of his life before the dragon had swooped down to save him in El Infierno. Now Dunkelzahn was gone.

I have no room for these sentimental feelings, he told himself. *I must get on with the business at hand.*

"I did remember," Ryan told Nadja. "And it nearly destroyed me." He pulled her with him, edging back toward the open door of the helo. He kept his eyes on the security guards. There must be no outward doubt about whether he intended to carry out his threat to kill Nadja. Even if he was no longer sure of it himself.

"But it didn't destroy you," Nadja said. "You have survived just as Dunkelzahn knew you would. Like *I* knew you would. It's Roxborough—whatever he did to you has affected your mind."

The edge of the helicopter's open side door pressed into the back of Ryan's thighs. He remembered his childhood as young Thomas Roxborough. The boy without want; the child with the most toys, but the fewest friends. But that was all right, because what he'd learned from Father was that friendships—all relationships, in fact—were transitory and superficial at best. It was a valuable lesson if you didn't want to get hurt.

"I'm not Roxborough," Ryan said, pulling Nadja with him into the cargo hold of the helicopter. "But not the Ryan Mercury you knew either. I'm both and neither."

It hit Ryan then that he hadn't been with either of his "fathers" when they died. He'd never had the chance to say goodbye to Frederic Roxborough when his body could no longer struggle against the VITAS infection. He'd also been absent when the explosion vaporized Dunkelzahn.

The depths of his own loneliness, which had shaken through his bones when he'd nearly died from acute lupus, had struck him as poetic justice. But it had been Father's lessons that had saved him then. He'd never given in to the disease, never accepted the doctors' six-month death sentence. The UniOmni vat had kept him alive; it was still keeping the original Roxborough alive.

Alive and alone forever.

"Ryan Mercury is still inside you," Nadja said. "I can see him when I look at you. I felt him in Washington. I loved him . . ." She broke down then, losing all pretense of composure as the tears welled in her eyes. And once they started, they flowed freely. "I still do."

"You're just trying to confuse me," Ryan said, and he heard desperation in his voice.

"No, Ryan, I just want you to *think*. There's something inside you that's making you selfish and devious. You can overcome that if you just think about it. If you feel what's in your heart."

"Give up the sappy bulldrek, Nadja."

"Dunkelzahn had confidence that you would always remain true. Otherwise he'd never have chosen you."

"Dunkelzahn abandoned us, Nadja. It's about time you realized that." But Ryan said it without conviction. He didn't really believe it. He didn't know what he believed anymore.

His grip on his Walther loosened. His focus wavered for just a second. Maybe he could believe her; he did love her.

Then again, maybe he should just kill her, make the world black and white again. Clear cut. Simple.

There is an evil voice inside us all, Ryanthusar. Learn to hear it within yourself and come to understand it, for it is a crucial part of you.

Dunkelzahn's words came rushing back into Ryan's mind as he held the gun to Nadja's head. *But always remember that how much you act upon what that voice tells you defines who you are.*

Am I a murderer? Ryan thought.

No.

It was a simple answer, but it struck him hard, like a sucker punch in his gut, making him gasp for air. "Nadja," he said, choking out the words through the tight constriction of his throat. "I'm sorry." Ryan lowered his hand, pulling the barrel of the pistol from her jaw and holstering it. "Help me."

Nadja turned and wrapped her arms around his chest. Holding him close. The smell of her filled his nostrils, washing through him like warm tonic. Her dark hair softly tickled his face. Her lips murmuring under her breath, "It's all right, Ryan. I love you. I love you."

The world tilted under Ryan, the solidity of the ground

rocking and shifting and sliding away like his fleeting will.
He leaned on Nadja for support. With her help, he had won.
He had beaten Roxborough. He'd overcome his desire for
power at the expense of his friends.

46

Burnout's world narrowed to a pinpoint.

In the waning light of the sun, his eyesight zoomed down to take in the scene. Burnout's awareness focused in on Ryan Mercury and the item that hung from the human's belt. The human and his hostage were inside the helicopter now. Trying to escape.

Burnout would not allow that to happen. He moved up to the side of the hangar, a silent ghost of metal and flesh. Longing for the power he sensed Mercury carried. It was the pinpoint, the center of Burnout's existence. And he would have it at any cost.

As he moved carefully and silently in the lengthening shadow of the hangar, Burnout swung the minigun and held it in one metal hand, ready to fire. He adjusted the ammo-belt as he rounded the corner of the corrugated metal building, making sure there were no twists or kinks.

He flipped his grenade launcher into his other hand, and surveyed the scene. A cluster of people crowded the helicopter. Three inside, including Ryan Mercury, the elf biff hostage, and the pilot. Seven others stood slightly away as the helo's blades began the slow rotation to power up.

No more than five meters from the helo, Burnout saw the VTOL jet—a Lear-Cessna Platinum III—cooling on its wheels. He estimated that no more than five people could be left inside. Besides, all he had to do was target the fuel tanks. Easy, loud, and spectacular to watch.

There were people in the hangar, but he would worry about them after he'd taken out the rest. The rotor spun faster. The helo's rising whine creeping through Burnout's circuits like a software glitch. Like that drekking psychosomatic itch that he could never scratch.

I will not let the power escape.

His universe collapsed then, his entire existence focused down on his goal, drawing him out of the shadows. Moving across the tarmac, his weapons ready to start screaming, Burnout accelerated up to full speed. Anyone in his path would be blown to tiny shreds of bloody flesh. None would be spared. None deserved the effort.

47

Standing inside the helicopter, Ryan breathed in the night air, drinking up the odor of Nadja. She felt solid and real in his arms, but he needed to know that she was well; he needed to regain her confidence. He had beaten the evil inside himself; he was sure of that now. He wasn't going to become another Thomas Roxborough. He trusted himself again, but did *she* trust him?

"You okay?" he asked her.

She looked into his eyes, the last rays of sunlight catching the dark emerald of her irises. "Honestly," she said. "I've had better days."

"I'm sorry."

"I know," she said. "I'm sorry too."

"You were right all along," Ryan said. "I'm still Quicksilver. But not the same as before. Roxborough is inside me too—his memories, his personality. It's part of me now, and it's helped me learn that I can no longer blindly follow the instructions of anyone. Even Dunkelzahn."

"But, Ryan—"

Ryan held her tightly to him, whispering in her ear. "Nadja, I've decided who I want to be. I *do* want to complete my mission, and I will. But for my own reasons, not just because Dunkelzahn decreed it. I believe it was important; it *is* important. Crucial to the survival of the world and all its people. I'm going to complete Dunkelzahn's instructions, but not blindly like I used to. Along the way I'm going to look for my own answers. I want to know *why.*"

Nadja nodded as if she understood. "Our roles have changed since Dunkelzahn died," she said. "We carry on his grand plan, but he's not here to instruct us on every step so of course we'll have to improvise."

She did understand, as he suspected she would. *I love her.*
The realization struck Ryan like a sledgehammer. And he
knew that he'd nearly killed her *because* of his love for her.
Roxborough's twisted logic at work there. An icy shudder
passed through him at the thought.

At the edge of his awareness, Ryan caught movement
across the tarmac. A silhouette running quickly, a shape he
recognized from somewhere. Then he heard the whine of a
minigun as it spun in the seconds before the bullets fired.
Then the deep boom of a grenade launcher.

Ryan threw Nadja to the floor of the helicopter just as the
minigun opened up, a staccato roar followed by the metallic
ping of bullets ricocheting off steel. Holes appeared in the jet,
and fuel erupted from them, pouring to the ground in a gush.
A second later a grenade bounced into the growing pool.

Ryan ducked to cover Nadja, drawing his pistol as he fell.
The security guards reacted as though in slow motion, turning in exaggerated surprise just as the grenade exploded in a
spray of flame and shrapnel. The report deafened Ryan and
the explosion blinded him for a split second, making it hard
to find their assailant again.

"Dhin," Ryan yelled. "Get us out of here!"

Then the jet's fuel ignited. Flames engulfed the machine
as more bullets from the minigun ripped through the knot of
surprised security guards. Their body armor offered little
protection from such an onslaught. The barrage of slugs
hit like a wall of force, the impacts lifting them bodily into
the air.

As the helo rose, and began to back away, Ryan watched
the massacre, a sick feeling in his gut. Three guards were
thrown back and tossed to the pavement like rag dolls. The
troll caught one in the head, the exit wound opening up the
left side of his face like a bloody eruption of sinew and gore.

The jet exploded just as Dhin pulled the helo off the edge
of the canyon. The aircraft was still only fifty meters away.
Ryan saw sheets of fire roll out from the silver hull just
before the body vanished in a blast that sent a mushrooming
cloud of fire and smoke into the hot evening. A second sun
in the growing darkness.

The wave of heat hit them a second later, burning around
the helo. Throwing them off course. The machine rocked and

pitched, falling slightly before Dhin regained control. Hovering a few meters out over the abyss of Hells Canyon, eye-level with the inferno.

"You all right?" Ryan asked Nadja.

"I think so," she said. "What about the others?"

Ryan shook his head.

The black shape streaked toward them. A speck of moving shadow against the red-orange backdrop. *Who is that? What is that?* Its silhouette grew and grew as it approached, moving too fast for a human, too smoothly. Ryan had seen it before, and as it got close, he remembered it. He had seen that shape—the too-small skull sitting bald and symmetrical on oversized shoulders. The malproportioned legs, the calves elongated like some perverted gazelle.

Ryan shifted his perception into the astral to make sure. Yes, the man before him glowed like a constellation of quickened spells. A fireworks display of greens and reds surrounding a dark core, an aura that was out of phase with his body.

Burnout.

"Dhin!" Ryan yelled. "Pull us up."

"What?"

"Get us farther up. NOW!"

But it was too late. Burnout reached the periphery of the compound and jumped. He was moving fast, having dropped his weapons to gain speed, up to about eighty klicks per hour. His leap carried him up, higher and higher out over the abyss, the darkness stretching to infinity below.

Dhin lifted the helo and angled it away from the compound, and for a second it looked like the cyberzombie would miss. That he would plummet into the chasm.

At the last second, Burnout reached out with a cybernetic hand. The last joint of his fingers cocked back as Ryan watched, blood dripping from the torn skin at the edges as the telescoping fingers shot out. The chrome snakes extended from his hand and touched the helo's runner below Ryan. Three of the fingers wrapped around the metal bar and hung on.

The floor tilted abruptly as Burnout's weight came down. The helo sank slightly, then centered as Dhin compensated.

Ryan drew his gun and pushed Nadja to the back of the cargo
hold as Burnout tried to grab hold with his other hand. Then
Ryan focused his energy, drawing strength from the Dragon
Heart, and pummeled Burnout's secure hand with a distance
strike.

The extendible fingers bent under the impact, two of them
shearing off. A hairline crack appeared in the third, the
weight of the cyberzombie hanging by a metal thread. It
snapped a second later, and Burnout fell.

Then the cyberzombie's other hand swung around and
caught the metal runner. Burnout started to pull his huge
body up, and he was looking at Ryan, his eyes narrowing to
pinpoints. "You will die, Ryan Mercury," Burnout said. "I
beat you once. This time will be no different. And when
you're dead, I'll take your magic."

Ryan slapped in his clip of armor-piercing rounds and
fired. The first bullet penetrated Burnout's shoulder, burying
itself in the synthetic muscles and stripping away some vat-
grown skin to reveal shiny chrome beneath. The second
missed as Burnout moved, swinging to the side and up.

Standing on the runner now, close enough that Ryan could
smell the machine oil, Burnout reached behind his back for
an Ares Alpha Combatgun. Ryan pummeled the cyberzombie's hand as the weapon came around. The quickness of
the move took Burnout by surprise. Ryan's foot shot out and
connected with the fingers just as they were about to ratchet
into full grip. The gun went flying out of the cyberzombie's
hand, falling into the canyon below.

Ryan pulled his foot back. *I'm faster now. I can beat this
mockery of life.* Burnout leaped from the runner, intending to
land inside the cargo hold. A sick feeling of déjà vu slicked
through Ryan as the cyberzombie loomed in front of him.

The mountain cliff above the compound framed Burnout's
silhouette in burnished red rock as Ryan struck, going for the
leg sweep again. But he wasn't going to make the same mistake as last time. When the two had fought in Aztlan,
Burnout had simply grabbed Ryan's leg in his unyielding
grasp, then tranquilized Ryan with a long, sharp needle that
slid out from a compartment in his arm.

This time Ryan changed tactics. At the exact same
moment as his leg struck for Burnout's ankles, Ryan used his

telekinetic strike, focusing his energy to bludgeon Burnout in the chest. Trying to knock him backward. Trying to dislodge this unrelenting beast and send him plummeting into the depths of Hell where he belonged.

The cyberzombie lifted his feet to dodge the leg attack, but he wasn't expecting the third strike. For the briefest of moments, Burnout was airborne in mid-jump. Instead of holding on to the helo, his hands reached toward Ryan. It was in that moment that Ryan's invisible pummel landed. Like a ram in the center of Burnout's chest, the power of the Dragon Heart behind it.

The blow lifted the heavy metal body of the cyberzombie and sent him reeling back. He sailed out the open door and fell.

Ryan saw the expression on the cyberzombie's face as he realized he'd been beaten. It was a combination of surprise and admiration. That he had finally met an adversary he could respect. Then the expression changed to one of sheer hatred as a leer flashed across Burnout's features.

The chrome fingers shot out again. Broken off and flailing, the metal snakes flashed toward Ryan. They weren't aiming for the helo's runners. They came directly for Ryan.

He brought up his hands in defense, but realized Burnout's true goal too late. At their furthest extension, the fingers touched Ryan at the waist. They curled their sharp and mangled ends around the nylon net bag that held the Dragon Heart. And when they snapped taut, the whole weight of Burnout's body came down like an anchor.

Ryan jerked forward at the waist, pulled off this feet, flying for the door. He scrabbled for a hold, frantically grabbing for anything. He found nothing but grooved flooring. He fell out the side door, the hot air of Hell baking around him as he followed the cyberzombie down.

"No, Ryan! No!" came Nadja's scream.

The helicopter's runner caught Ryan in the gut, knocking the wind out of him. But it slowed him enough that his hands found purchase, wrapping around the hot metal. Then he slipped over and their combined weight pulled at his grasp.

His sweaty fingers slipped against the metal of the runner. White-hot needles jabbed the back of his hands and arms as he tried to focus, tried to hold on.

"I will have your magic, Ryan Mercury," said Burnout, his voice the grating of metal on metal.

Ryan looked down. Below him, Burnout hung suspended, his metal parts tinged with the pink of the dying sun. Framed by the impenetrable black of the abyss. Ryan felt his fingers giving way, slipping on the smooth round metal as his strength waned.

Then the nylon web bag tore, ripping away from his belt. And Burnout fell into the dark canyon below. He made no sound as he fell. He simply disappeared, a dark silhouette melting into the inky void. The Dragon Heart went with him, his chrome fingers still clutching it. Still gripping the one thing Dunkelzahn said could save the world.

How could this have happened? At the very moment Ryan had finally come to accept that it was his mission to deliver the Dragon Heart, he'd lost it for the second time.

48

Lethe watched Burnout fall, the creature of metal and flesh plummeting from the helicopter. Holding the Dragon Heart in his cybernetic grip. Taking it from Ryan Mercury, who hung from the runner of the flying machine.

In the astral, the cyberzombie glowed brightly against the dark wasteland of the narrowing cliffs as he fell. The center of his aura was a black emptiness, a void where his spirit should be. Instead, his spirit was diffuse, a dim edge of light along the periphery of his aura.

All around Burnout's aura were magics designed to seal the spirit inside. Those spells were all that kept him alive; there wasn't enough natural flesh left. It was like a boat riddled with holes that had been patched too often and refused to sink only because the pumps continued to work overtime.

Lethe followed Burnout's plunge, watching him bounce off the narrowing canyon wall. Hells Canyon was a giant, wedge-shaped slash in the earth, and at the bottom of the slash flowed the Snake River. It was the deepest gorge in the world—the longest fall. But the walls were angled, not perfectly vertical.

Burnout hit the rock wall again, smashing down on the Dragon Heart still clutched tightly in his mangled metal hand. He bounced off and continued falling. The cyberzombie would certainly die during the fall; he should be dead already. His continued existence was a perversion, a violent abuse of magic that would only lead to astral pollution.

But the Dragon Heart must not be allowed to be lost or damaged. Its magic seemed intact to Lethe as he moved close to Burnout. But when the huge cyborg hit the cliff again, what then? And if Burnout landed on top of it when he crashed with it on the bottom of the gorge, would the Dragon Heart survive intact?

Lethe could allow nothing to happen to it. He would not disappoint Thayla. The sanctity of her song must be protected from the spread of the dark stain. Only the Dragon Heart could help her.

This perversion of metal and flesh was the only thing Lethe had left. He could not let Burnout die. He must protect the Dragon Heart at any cost. There was only one way he could be certain that all of Burnout's effort, every last vestige of his energy, was devoted to preventing harm from coming to the Dragon Heart.

And if the cyberzombie survived somehow, Lethe could take control of his body and use it to deliver it to Thayla. It was evident that Ryan Mercury could no longer be trusted, despite Dunkelzahn's confidence in him. And despite Ryan's display at the very end, when he seemed to have overcome his internal struggle, Lethe did not trust him. Would never trust him.

Burnout was the obvious choice.

Lethe moved up close to the falling cyberzombie and entered his body. He possessed the mind and flesh of the man who had been Burnout. And by the time Lethe realized the magnitude of his mistake, it was too late.

It was way too late.

49

A midnight blue-tinted sky darkened to black in the east. A hot wind, stirred up by the helicopter blades, stung Ryan's skin as he climbed back inside the hovering Hughes Airstar. He was tired and in pain from the fight with Burnout, but he couldn't stop yet. He had to get the Dragon Heart back. Pain shot in bolts up his legs as he sat next to Nadja. He clenched his teeth against the pain, too fatigued to use magic to channel it away.

A calm sense of purpose filled Ryan. An almost surreal understanding of who he was and what he must do. His indecision gone. Dissipated into the night. "Dhin," Ryan said. "Take us down to the bottom."

"Now?"

"Now! And power up a search light so we can see."

"Jane?" came the ork's voice over the speakers, "do I trust him?"

It was Nadja who answered. "Yes," she said. "Do it."

Dhin complied a few seconds later, sending the 'copter into a plunge. "Got the spotlight on," he said, "but can't see him."

Ryan stood and looked out the side door. The Snake River was about ten meters across at the bottom, flowing slowly, a black-glass surface in the darkness. The canyon walls rose precipitously from the surface of the water, no ledges or outcroppings in sight. But the spotlight could illuminate only a tiny circle, and Burnout could have fallen anywhere. He could be under water; he could have been swept downstream.

Ryan shifted his focus into the astral. The river lit up with life, algae and fish and bottom plants. But he could see no sign of the cyberzombie. If he had come this way, Ryan should be able to see a slight shift in the astral, a trail of pollution like a bad odor left by Burnout's passing. He should also be able to sense the Dragon Heart if it was close. And where was the spirit, Lethe?

Ryan saw no astral trail. He felt no Heart, and Lethe was nowhere to be seen. Ryan sensed nothing.

After an hour of searching, Dhin called back, "We're running low on fuel."

"Thanks, Dhin," Ryan said. "Take us back up. We'll try again in the light."

As Dhin brought the machine up the canyon and over the rim to the compound, Jane's voice came over Ryan's wristphone. "Can I talk to you?" she said.

"Hoi, Jane. Sorry about whatever I said to you back there."

"It's blank memory," she said. "Forgotten."

"Thanks," Ryan said. "So what do you want to chat about?"

"I need a favor."

"Name it."

"It requires that you enter the Matrix and meet a friend of mine. Alice."

"Oh?"

"You can use the 'trode rig that Axler has," she said. "I'll explain everything after you're in."

Ryan wondered just what Jane was scheming, but decided not to question her now. "Will it take long?" he asked. "I'm beat."

"Not long," Jane said. "And I promise you'll like what Alice has planned." Then Jane's voice cut off.

Dhin set the helicopter down, giving wide berth to the ruined hull of Nadja's jet, which still burned on the end of the airstrip. Axler and Grind stood near it, checking the fallen security guards for signs of life. Ryan felt a wave of sadness as he watched. It was his fault that those people had died. *Because of my weakness,* he thought.

Because I lacked the strength to beat Roxborough, Burnout killed those people and took the Dragon Heart.

Ryan had failed, but not completely. He had beaten Burnout. He had overcome Roxborough. But all that seemed empty without the Dragon Heart. Until he got it back, he would feel like he was letting Dunkelzahn down. Like he was letting himself down.

That was why he wouldn't rest until his mission was complete.

50

Thomas Roxborough dreamed he was in a real body.

One minute he was sitting at his virtual desk, analyzing productivity numbers. The next minute, the walls of his mansion were dissolving, their planar uniformity splitting in constituent bits and floating away on an invisible current.

He floated in a void, his consciousness drifting. Then he felt his body around him, sensed every detail as though he were inside actual flesh. He felt the delicious rise and fall of his chest as he breathed, the gentle sensation of sprinkling rain on his face. The smell of cigarette smoke. So close, so real it could not be denied.

At first he thought that Meyer had performed the spirit-transfer without telling him. *Or perhaps I just forgot that the ritual had been scheduled,* Roxborough thought. But then he wondered where he was. Which body he was in. He opened his eyes.

Skyscrapers towered above him, their facades all blue glass and mirrors, reflecting the city's street lamps. There were no sounds of traffic, but he heard the whisper of the falling rain and the soothing rush of wind through the buildings.

Roxborough stood up and surveyed his body. It was a form he was used to even though it had been many years since he'd been inside it. A large belly protruded over his waist, his naked flesh a pasty white, covered only by a threadbare rug of black hair follicles. His feet and bones ached dully from the exertion of standing up. He was in his old body.

"Hello, Rox," came a voice he recognized. A voice that belonged to a woman who had plagued him on and off in the Matrix since the Crash of '29.

He turned to look at her—a medium-height human woman leaning her shoulder against the scratched plexiglass of an old-style phone booth. Her blonde hair was cropped at the shoulder. Her eyes were the blue color of oceans; Roxborough could almost see the sparkle of sun off the water when he looked at them. She wore black jeans and a white cotton halter, and a cigarette rested between the fingers of her right hand, smoke from its tip curling up along her arm.

"Taking up smoking, Alice?" Roxborough said.

"Yes," she said, taking an exaggerated drag from her cigarette. "After all, it can't kill me."

Roxborough laughed. "Very humorous," he said. "So where am I?"

"Welcome to Wonderland," Alice said. "But you can call it Hell."

"Whatever do you mean?"

"I mean that I've finally given you your wish," she said. "A real body."

"How did you—" Roxborough stopped as a man stepped up next to Alice, coming from behind the phone booth. The man was tall and well-muscled, but his movements were jerky and not quite natural, as though this was a simulacrum instead of a real person. It was Ryan Mercury.

"Hello, Tommy," Ryan said, calling Roxborough by the name Father had used. "I gave Alice the access codes to get into your system." Ryan tapped his forefinger against his temple. "Many of your memories are in here," he said.

Roxborough stared at Alice. "What have you done?"

"I've trapped your consciousness," she said. "Quite simple once Ryan gave me the codes I needed. I've also reconfigured your own system so that you'll never be able to get back inside. Escape is quite impossible, I'm afraid."

"But why?"

Alice took a final drag on her cigarette and flicked it into the street. "I want to torture you," she said simply. "I want you to know what I went through after the Crash. You know what it feels like to be a prisoner, but do you understand what it's like to be thrust into a world completely out of your control? Where you don't know the rules? Where the most innocuous things can kill you?"

"It wasn't my fault, Alice," Roxborough said. "It was

merely bad luck that you were in my system when the Crash
virus flatlined you."

"I'm still gathering evidence. Ryan can't remember the
specifics of your involvement with the Crash, but suffice it
to say that I think you're full of drek."

"I did not cause the Crash."

Alice shrugged and lit another cigarette. "Time and evidence will judge you," she said. "For now, I've created a
new home for you, a special little ultraviolet space. It's part
of Wonderland City, but the rules of the reality are very different. Consider it enforced poetic justice."

Roxborough turned to face Ryan. *How did this human
escape from both Meyer's ritual and Darke's hit team?*
"How can you participate in this?" he said. "You know my
past. Haven't I already suffered enough?"

Ryan shook his head. "I helped her because it's the only
way I can truly beat you. I almost became you, and that
scares me. Even now, your past is part of me, and I've
accepted what you did as part of my history. It's made me a
more complete person, but I've decided not to act like you.
I'm better than you."

Ryan said this last with his finger pointing directly at Roxborough's chest. "You showed me that I have choices," he
went on. "But ultimately, I made my own choice, and it
wasn't the one you would have made. I resisted the evil
voice."

In the following silence, Roxborough began to clap his
hands together, applauding. He forced a laugh. "Nice speech,
drekhead," he said. "Sentimental crap, but well stated."

"Alice's plan for you might just change your mind,"
Ryan said.

"Doubtful," Roxborough said.

Alice took another of her deep drags and exhaled smoke
with her words. "In a way," she said, a twisted smile on her
face, "this is your dream come true. You get what you've
always wanted—a 'real' body."

"I suppose you want me to say thank you."

"No."

"Then what?"

"You'll soon find out," she said.

Then Alice and Ryan were gone, and Roxborough was

standing on a lawn of brilliant green in an English garden. A quiet pond sparkled in the morning light in front of him, and as he turned to look around, a large white rabbit wearing a waistcoat ran by him saying, "Oh dear! I shall be too late!" The rabbit took an old-style watch from its waistcoat pocket and glanced at the time, then jumped under a hedge.

Oh no! Roxborough thought. *I don't think I'm going to like this at all.*

ABOUT THE AUTHOR

Stranger Souls, Book One of The Dragon Heart Trilogy, is Jak Koke's second Shadowrun® novel. His first, *Dead Air*, was published by Roc Books in mid-1996. His third novel, *Liferock*, will be published by FASA Corporation as part of its Earthdawn® series in October 1996.

Koke has also sold numerous short stories to AMAZING STORIES and PULPHOUSE: A FICTION MAGAZINE, and has contributed to several anthologies such as *Rat Tales* by Pulphouse, *Young Blood* by Zebra, and *Talisman*, an Earthdawn® anthology.

Koke invites you to visit his webpage at http://www.sapermedia.com/koke/. You can also send him comments about this and any of his Shadowrun® books care of FASA Corporation.

He and his wife Seana Davidson, a marine microbiologist, live in California with their four-year-old daughter, Michaela.

MEMO

FROM: JANE-IN-THE-BOX
TO: NADJA DAVIAR
DATE: 20 AUGUST 2057
RE: THE LEGEND OF THAYLA

Dunkelzahn's Institute of Magical Research just unearthed this document. Thought you'd be interested. Text follows:

Ages ago, before written memory began, lived a queen of great beauty and even greater heart. Thayla reigned over a rich green valley nestled between two mountain ranges that rose like spikes into the heavens. Under her rule, the land she loved prospered, and her people lived their days in joy.

Each morning Thayla greeted the rising sun with a Song. She sang in a voice as clear as the air and as bright as the great burning orb itself. Nothing foul or dark could prosper in her land, for her voice was too pure for such abominations to bear.

One night an army of dark creatures made to enter the valley, seeking to overrun the prosperous land and corrupt it with their vile presence. Thayla rose that morning as she always did, and upon seeing the black army, sang. Her voice filled the valley with power and hope.

The evil horde, shown the depravity of their existence by her voice, had no choice but to flee. And as they did—running and flying with wild abandon for refuge beyond the valley—one black soldier slowed and, for the briefest of moments, listened to Thayla's Song.

Days passed, and the terrible army remained beyond

the valley, fearful of the Song. Finally, driven by their dark masters, they surged forward again. And again Thayla sang.

As before the foul creatures fell back blindly, unable to stand even a few pure notes of her voice. But again the lone, tall warrior with hair and eyes of dark fire lingered and listened, if only for a few moments, before fleeing the valley.

The next time the creatures approached Thayla's domain, less of the army came. The rest were unable to marshal the will needed to enter the valley. But again, the lone dark soldier fell back last, so that he could hear her Song.

Finally, not one of the black army would come. Not even the terrible threats of their vile masters could push them forward. But still a single warrior in ebony and red armor would slip into the valley before each dawn and listen, and after a time, watch as well.

The black figure advanced to where he could see Thayla standing high upon the terraces of the great sprawling city that surrounded her palace. And he would watch her every morning as she rose and greeted the new day with the Song. And as he listened, blood flowed from his ears and his skin blistered from the powerful purity of her voice, but he would not turn aside. He would not flee from her Song. And so he stood, listened, and watched.

Then one night, the dark warrior slipped into the city as Thayla slept. He crept into her citadel, sat at the foot of her bed and watched her.

When she woke and found him there, she called for her guards, but none were strong enough to move the dark warrior. She called her sorcerers, but none were wise enough to banish him. She sang to drive him away, but though his body and spirit were wracked with pain, he stood strong and firm, enraptured by her beauty.

Unable to drive him away, the great Queen Thayla decided to ignore him. Though he stood at her side, she ate without speaking to him. Though he ran alongside as she took her horses out for exercise, she did not look at him. And though he stood silently nearby as she slept, she did not acknowledge his presence.

Each morning she would rise and greet the sun, singing loud and strong so that the dark army waiting beyond the valley could not enter. And each morning he stood beside her and cried tears of blood and fire at the pain and joy her voice gave him.

And so this went on for some time. Thayla slept, sang, and performed her royal duties. But the black warrior stayed at her side, and slowly the land began to darken from his presence. The animals of the field sickened, as did the people. The crops would not grow, and dark and terrible clouds filled the sky over the valley.

Thayla knew the black soldier was the cause of all these things, and so she asked him to leave. He did not even answer her. She tried to trick him into leaving, but he would not be fooled. Then she tried to force him away, but he could not be broken. Finally, she begged him to leave.

"But I do not wish to leave," he replied. These were the first words he had ever spoken to her, and his voice was like dried leaves blown on the autumn wind. "Your beauty is like none I have ever seen."

"But you cannot stay," she told him. "Your presence is destroying my land and my people."

"I care not for your land or its people," the warrior told her. "I care only for you."

Faced with his determination, Thayla wept. Slowly her people died. Finally, she called her greatest advisors together and told them what they must do.

"As you know, the presence of the dark warrior is destroying our land and our people," she said. "However, he will not leave my side. We cannot make him leave, and so *I* must leave the land and take him with me."

Her advisors wailed at her words. "But you cannot! It is only your voice that holds the black army at bay! If you leave, we will certainly die!"

Thayla nodded, for she knew this to be true, but said, "I will leave, but my voice will remain." And with that she charged her most powerful sorcerers with the task of placing her voice in a songbird that would great the rising sun each morning as she had.

They searched the land and found the finest songbird of all. And as the sun rose, they performed the ritual. When the first light appeared the next morn, the bird sang with Thayla's Voice, and the Song held the dark army at bay.

The sorcerers rejoiced at this, but when they turned to congratulate Thayla, she and her dark shadow had gone. They searched the land but could find neither of them.

But the Songbird rose each morning. And with a voice as pure as the clear air itself, it sang the Song, and the black army trembled in its tracks, unable to enter the valley.

Exciting excerpt
from Clockwork Asylum
Book 2 of the Dragon Heart Saga
by Jak Koke

20 August 2057

The air in Hells Canyon blew hot and dry even in first rays of the morning sun. The fiery ball crested the peaks behind him as Ryan Mercury walked along the edge of the cliff face. The sun battered down on him with its relentless scorching blaze.

Ryan looked over the edge of the cliff and down at the thin line of the river far below, taking a long drink from his water bottle and forcing himself to chew a soy protein bar. He wasn't hungry, and his stomach hurt so bad he wasn't sure if he was going to be able to hold anything down. Still, he knew he needed to keep up his strength.

The buzz of Dhin's drones came to his ears. The ork rigger was remote piloting the surveillance vehicles, scouring the canyon floor. *Burnout must be down there,* Ryan thought, *but where?*

The Assets Incorporated team had been searching for the cyberzombie's body for almost three days, with no progress. It was as if the metal man had simply disappeared, swallowed into astral space or disintegrated into his constituent atoms and blown away in the hot wind.

Ryan shook his head. The mood around the compound was starting to get ugly. Assets Incorporated was a front company Dunkelzahn had left Ryan in the old wyrm's will. The Assets compound consisted of an air strip cut into the eastern cliff face, complete with an old corrugated metal hangar and some ramshackle storage sheds. Ryan had commissioned the expansion of the underground facilities.

The personnel was Assets' real strength. A group of the most pro-level mercenaries it had been Ryan's pleasure to lead. They were shadowrunners, not a search and rescue team. They wanted action, not the numbing task of trying to find the proverbial needle in the fragging haystack.

They had found traces of vat grown skin on the rocks of the cliff face where Burnout had first impacted. Unfortunately, due to Burnout's metal make-up, the collision with the wall had literally bounced him outward far enough that he had landed somewhere near the center of the river, where the current was the strongest.

Ryan's wristphone beeped, pulling him from his angry self-recrimination. He looked at the small screen, which indicated that it was Jane-in-the-box on the line. Dunkelzahn's decker and a sometime member of his Assets, Inc. team. He took a breath and punched the connect.

Instantly, the tiny vid screen filled with a cartoon image—a tangle of lion-blonde locks, doe-innocent blue eyes, and a set of the largest breasts this side of a BTL porn chip, barely covered by a black leather halter, laced up the front with tiny silver chains. Her icon was a sharp contrast to the Jane-in-the-box Ryan knew from real life—a plain-looking human woman of about thirty-five with scraggy brown hair and a skinny body.

"Hello, Jane."

Jane's icon smiled at Ryan, flashing perfectly white teeth. "Ryan, it's good to see you eating something." Her full, gloss-black lips turned downward in a sneer, "even if it is that soy-supplement drek."

Ryan looked down at the remainder of his protein bar and absently pitched it over the side of the cliff, not bothering to watch its long fall. "What's biz, Jane?"

"Couple bits. First, I followed up on the magical support you requested. I'm sorry, the pickings are slim right now. All the top names on my A-list are otherwise occupied, as are most of the top names on my B-list. I finally managed to get a hold of the top name on my C-list. He's a man named Billows."

Ryan frowned. "What's wrong with him?"

Jane's icon shook its head, sending a shower of golden hair flying about her shoulders. "Nothing, really. It's just that he's very new to the game. Most of his study has been theoretical, seems he prefers his tomes to people. Still, he's a very accomplished mage, but you may have to kick his hoop into line once or twice. He has incredible potential, he just needs some experience."

"That the best you can do?"

Jane nodded. "I know this isn't a good time to be breaking in someone new, but you need a magical arm, and believe me, he's the best you're going to get right now."

Ryan nodded. "Thanks, Jane. Any news on Lethe?"

Lethe, named after the river of forgetfulness, was a powerful free spirit with a mysterious past. He had been instrumental in helping Ryan recover the Heart after it was stolen from Dunkelzahn's Lake Louise lair by members of the Atlantean Foundation. But the spirit had been missing for several days.

"Sorry, chummer," Jane said. "I haven't heard a fragging thing."

"Okay, what else?"

Jane's frown turned into a soft smile. "I have a message from Nadja."

Ryan winced as the pain in his gut doubled. "All right, give it to me."

Jane nodded, then vanished. In her place, the delicate oval of Nadja Daviar's face filled the screen. Her emerald eyes were set wide and beautiful, compelling and honest. Her long raven hair hung loose over her pointed ears. Her magenta-tinted lips curved into a delicious smile. "Ryan," she said, "I'm sorry this message had to be recorded. Things have gotten hectic, and it's the early morning hours here."

To Ryan, the sound of her voice was like the seductive sound of a slow moving stream, gentle and caressing. He couldn't take his eyes from her.

"Ryan, I know you're troubled about what happened a few days ago. I *know* you; you're not going to rest until this . . . problem is dealt with. So I think it would be best all the way around if you let the others continue the search, and you came to Washington."

Ryan shook his head and was about to say something when he remembered he was listening to a recording.

On the screen, Nadja's face smiled softly. "Ryan, I know you think this is a bad idea, but there's more. Not only do you need some closure on this issue, there are other needs we should talk about. Like *my* need to have you near. If you've seen the news, you know things have gotten out of hand here, and I need to talk to you, face to face."

Ryan's heart was breaking. Since Nadja had returned to Washington a few days ago, he hadn't been watching the news, had actually been trying to avoid any thought of Nadja at all. Ryan had been trying to convince himself that nothing mattered but the mission, nothing mattered except finding Burnout's body and recovering the Heart. Still, every moment his thoughts turned back to this beautiful woman and nearly killing her for the Dragon Heart. His thoughts were filled with shame and regret, but it seemed as if there was nothing he could do about it.

"Ryan, I know it would be hard for you to leave right now, but please consider my proposal. A break might just be the thing you need to put yourself in the right mind frame to find the Heart and accomplish your goal."

Ryan found himself listening not so much to her words, but to that soothing tone. Maybe she was right.

"I *am* right about this. Think about what Dunkelzahn would have advised if he were here." Nadja leaned in close, the screen filling up with just her eyes. "Please, for both of our sakes, come back for a few days."

The screen went dark, and Ryan found that he held his wristphone very close to his face. Instead of Nadja's face, he caught his own reflection in the black screen. Huge, bruise-colored crescents seemed to swallow his silver-flecked blue eyes, telling of days without sleep. His rugged face held the beginnings of a lush beard, but did nothing to hide the gaunt hollow of his cheeks and the tight grimace which chiseled lines into his cheeks and jaw.

Ryan's wiry, auburn hair was unkempt, and he ran thick, callused fingers through the tangle to smooth down some of the more errant strands. He looked like someone who needed a break.

Suddenly, Grind's raspy voice came over the commlink in his ear. "Quicksilver, it looks like we got company."

Ryan looked around, concentrating on his magically heightened sense of hearing. There, just over the rush of wind roaring through the canyon, he could make out the distinctive rhythmic thrum of helicopter rotors. "Number and distance?"

Grind was a dwarf, a combat and weapons expert who had served in a number of mercenary efforts before catching the attention of Dunkelzahn a few years ago. He was currently manning the compound's defenses. "Three bogeys just passed the southern radar. They're coming fast, attack formation, heading directly for us."

Ryan started running back to the entrance to the underground compound. "Have Dhin pull back his drones, get Axler out of the canyon. I don't know who these slots are, but I want to be ready for them."

"Copy," Grind said, with just a hint of excitement in his voice.

Ryan made it to the compound just as Axler swept up over the lip of the cliff in the Northrop Wasp single-man chopper. Axler landed the helo and climbed out. She walked to meet Ryan at the entrance.

Axler was a human woman of about twenty-five. Very attractive with shoulder cropped blonde hair and doe-brown eyes. Ryan knew she bore a great many cybernetic enhancements under her plycra bodysuit, but none were visible on the surface. All very discreet.

Axler's usually hard-set expression was slack from fatigue. "I got the buzz from Grind," she said, a hint of strain behind her words told Ryan just how hard she had been pushing herself. She was nearing the edge.

Grind appeared at the door next to Axler. The dwarf came up to her elbow, but was easily as wide. He was heavily muscled with obvious cyber arms painted the color of aircraft carriers. Grind's hair shagged on his head like a thick black rug. Grind smiled.

"You two ready to lock and load?"

"I was ready the day they cut me out of my momma's belly," said Grind, with a laugh.

"Axler?"

Her tone was cool. "Ready if you are."

Ryan didn't bother to respond to the subtle insult behind her words. She hadn't given him her complete trust since he'd tried to take sole possession of the Dragon Heart and had faced off with Nadja. "All right, then. This is a situation delta. We've got three unknown bogeys, in an offensive posture. If they attack from the air, we'll blow them out of the sky. Dhin?"

The ork rigger's voice sounded calm and steady over the commlink. "Ready to go drones-up at your signal."

"Copy. If they're hostile, Dhin's drones will take point, and we'll smoke them in a standard one by two, starting with the lead vehicle."

"Copy," said Grind and Axler in unison.

"If they land, we'll play it straight. Remember, Jane has registered us as an official weather observation station. So we'll take that angle."

Suddenly, the three helicopters broke the horizon, coming up over the rim of the canyon wall. And they weren't ordinary helos. Ryan recognized all three as Aztechnology Aguilar-Ex military choppers. Very high powered, lots of weapons and extremely expensive. They had ridden with sound suppression and had come in against the wind so that Ryan hadn't heard them until it was too late.

These people are professionals.

"Frag it!" Ryan keyed his wristphone. "Dhin, you got them?"

Dhin's rumbling growl wasn't quite as calm as it had been. "Yeah. What the frag are they doing here already?"

"I got a bad feeling about this, folks. Stay sharp. Especially you, Dhin. If things get ugly you need to put enough fire power in the air to stop that drek from getting anywhere near us."

"Making no promises, Bossman. The Azzies build one tough bird, but at the very least, I'll be able to slow them down."

Ryan watched as the three attack helicopters made their first pass. Like giant insects they buzzed past the cliff face, the red jaguars on their sides glittering in the sun. They broke from their attack formation. The lead helicopter made for the landing pad, while the other two took up defensive positions near the far wall of the canyon.

Dust from the landing pad twisted into a small cyclone as the big chopper settled its weight on the duracrete. The pilot cut the engines, and the flying dirt settled back to earth. The small hatch on the near side of the chopper popped upward, and a small man stepped out, followed by two other humans.

Ryan concentrated, and his vision shifted to the astral. *Chromed, almost beyond the pale,* he thought as he watched the dead parts of their aura. He relaxed and his vision shifted to normal.

"Smiles, everybody," he whispered. "We're playing it straight. If things get sticky, go to diversion plan beta."

With Axler and Grind at his back, Ryan stepped forward, forcing his lips into a wide grin.

The man in front was short, less than a meter and a half, but he was human, and was almost as wide as he was tall. He walked briskly, his spine straight, his shoulders back, and he wore a black jumpsuit which didn't quite cover the heavy body armor underneath. The red Jaguar looked like a spot of dried blood over his heart.

Everything about him screamed military, as did the bearing of the two warriors behind him. The shorter man stepped up to Ryan, his charcoal eyes sizing Ryan up in much the same way Ryan was doing to him.

His weather burned face was dark, swarthy, and his toothy grin was wide, even though there was no humor behind those black eyes. The man stretched out his hand. "I'm sorry for disturbing your work, sir," he said in a deep voice, heavy with a clipped accent. "This won't take long."

Ryan shook the man's hand, which was dry and warm, the grip relaxed and friendly. Ryan forced himself to match the man's grin. "We don't get too many visitors. It's a nice break from the routine. How can we help you?"

They both dropped the handshake at the same time. Ryan looked over the man's head to the two guards, scanning the area like professionals. Their body posture held a high-tension stiffness. They were ready for battle at the slightest provocation.

Ryan just hoped Axler and Grind were pulling off the relaxed look better than their counterparts.

The man's smile dropped. "This is a very delicate situation, and I hope I can count on your discretion."

Ryan looked over at the Aztechnology attack copter, and nodded. "Seems like you've come quite a distance, maybe a bit *too* far, but I'm sure we can keep this visit quiet. As long as you're not here to . . . acquire any information regarding our weather satellites."

The short man laughed, a clipped, strangled sound, as if his throat was unused to the action. "I am General Voitra, and I can assure you, Mister . . ."

Ryan forced his grin again. "Deacon, Phillip Deacon."

The smaller man smiled, a slow secretive gesture which indicated that he saw through Ryan's facade. "I can assure you, Mister Deacon, that we have no interest in your satellites." He looked at Axler and Grind. "May I have a word with you . . . in private?"

Ryan nodded, and they both walked to the edge of the cliff.

"Mister Deacon, my country has lost a very valuable piece of hardware, and I'll be honest with you, our last trace of him was near this very site. I have no idea what he was doing here, or why, but we do know he was here."

Ryan shook his head. "I thought you said you lost a piece of hardware."

"I did."

"Then why are you referring to your hardware as a 'he'?"

Voitra's smile was tight and dangerous. "Once again, I'm going to be forced to rely on your discretion. Have you seen anyone out of the ordinary around here in the last couple of days? He would be hard to miss as he is quite large."

Ryan stopped walking. "I still don't get it. Did this guy *steal* some hardware from you?"

The smaller man's face took on a look of impatience. "Just answer the question, Mister Deacon."

Behind him, Ryan heard the rustle of clothing, and the distinctive sound of an automatic weapon's slide being pulled. Both he and the Azzie turned, the smaller man just a bit slower than Ryan.

The picture before Ryan was a still tableau of impending violence. Axler and one of the Aztechnology guards stood face to face, the muzzle of Axler's Predator dug a groove in the man's neck as the guard's pistol jammed into her sternum.

Grind had dropped to one knee, his Colt Manhunter dead set on the second guard's forehead. The second guard was trying to play it cool, but Ryan could tell he was jumpy.

"Nobody move!" yelled Ryan.

"At ease!" said General Voitra.

Ryan turned to the small man. "Have your men back off. We don't want any trouble."

The swarthy man looked up at him with a cocked eyebrow. "For a man who is so large, you seem to have a fear of direct confrontation. Tell me what I wish to know, or I will have all of you killed. It is as simple as that."

Ryan nodded. "All right, yeah, your guy was here. About three days ago. He stole a chopper and bugged out before we could catch him."

Voitra looked Ryan over, and for a second Ryan felt that his aura was being watched. Then Voitra nodded and turned to his men. "Rico, stand down."

The man who was face to face with Axler didn't take his eyes off her as he said, "But, General, this woman is—"

"I don't care, Captain. Stand down!"

The man slowly removed his pistol from Axler's belly.

"Axler," called Ryan. "Back off."

With a deadly smile, she lowered the Predator. "Go back home to mommy, chrome boy. This is a dangerous place, and it would be a shame if something happened to you."

Both Axler and Grind stepped back to a little more than five meters, but both still held their weapons at the ready.

General Voitra turned back to Ryan. "I appreciate your cooperation, and I apologize for the overzealousness of my officers. You should also count yourself lucky that you were not able to intercept the man in question, otherwise I would have been having this pleasant little discussion with a corpse."

Ryan shook his head. "You got what you came for, now get the frag out. If I see your ships on the radar again, I'll be on the horn to my government so fast they'll take you down before you hit the canyon."

General Voitra smiled. "I'd expect nothing less. By the way, I hope your . . . weather research goes well. Good day, Mister . . . Deckerd."

"Deacon."

"Of course. My apologies." With that, the short man walked to the chopper, followed closely by the two guards who walked backwards, weapons still drawn.

Within minutes, they were gone.

Ryan walked over to Axler and Grind, who were talking and laughing. "Nicely played, you two."

Grind turned. "Thanks, Quicksilver. I think we were about a half beat too late, but it was difficult to read your body language."

Ryan shook his head and smiled. "No, any sooner, and he would have known something was up. You were both right on."

Axler shook her head. "Those boys were good."

Ryan looked at her. "Explain."

Axler looked pensive. "Quicksilver, when we made our move, I would stake all the chrome I've got that they were just waiting for us to make a play."

Ryan nodded, and looked at the skyline where the choppers had disappeared. "I got the same feeling."

"They were looking for Burnout, weren't they?" asked Grind.

"Yeah, and they know we were lying about this being a weather station. But I think they bought our story about him hitting us and disappearing."

Axler shook her head again. "I got the distinct feeling we'll be seeing those boys again."

"Me too," said Grind.

Ryan turned his back on them, the familiar pain working at his gut. *Maybe Nadja's right. Maybe I do need a break from this place.*

He watched as the sun started to sink beyond the horizon, and wondered just what would happen if General Voitra found Burnout first. What would happen if Aztechnology got possession of the Dragon Heart?

The possibilities were just too ugly to think about.

ENTER THE SHADOWS **SHADOWRUN**®

YOUR OPINION CAN MAKE A DIFFERENCE!
LET US KNOW WHAT YOU THINK.

Send this completed survey to us and enter a weekly drawing to win a special prize!

1.) Do you play any of the following role-playing games?
   Shadowrun ———— Earthdawn ———— BattleTech ————

2.) Did you play any of the games before you read the novels?
   Yes ———————— No ————————

3.) How many novels have you read in each of the following series?
   Shadowrun ———— Earthdawn ———— BattleTech ————

4.) What other game novel lines do you read?
   TSR ———— White Wolf ———— Other (Specify) ————

5.) Who is your favorite FASA author?
_____

6.) Which book did you take this survey from?
_____

7.) Where did you buy this book?
   Bookstore ———— Game Store ———— Comic Store ————
   FASA Mail Order ———————— Other (Specify) ————

8.) Your opinion of the book (please print)
_____
_____
_____

Name ———————————— Age ———— Gender ————
Address ————————————————————————————
City ———————— State ———— Country ———— Zip ————

Send this page or a photocopy of it to:
FASA Corporation
Editorial/Novels
1100 W. Cermak Suite B-305
Chicago, IL 60608